For a Better Life

A Historical Novel of the Pacific Northwest

By

Dennis LeMaster

For a Better Life
A Historical Novel of the Pacific Northwest

by Dennis LeMaster

Published by SkillBites LLC

ISBN-10: 1-942489-57-9

ISBN-13: 978-1-942489-57-3

To my dear wife Kathy

to whom everything in my life

is dedicated,

and

To my beloved mother

who I now realize

was a much better parent to me

than I was a son to her.

Table of Contents

Foreword

This story is about the Hofmann and the Dubois families, who travel to the fictitious Suquamish Valley after the Great War for a better life in western Washington State. They are of different cultures, but alike in that both are from impoverished agricultural backgrounds. They overcome adversity by repeatedly coming together in the turmoil caused by two World Wars, the Great Depression, unprecedented and transformative technological change, and economic instability. The families are considered separately in the beginning, but are treated together later following the marriage of two of their children, namely Sonny Dubois and Lise Hofmann. Sonny and Lise also struggle, maybe a little more than their brothers and sisters, but finally gain a large measure of success through their own sustained efforts, a willingness to take risks, some remarkable help from family members, and plain good fortune.

Other similar family narratives exist, but the context of the Great Depression, war, transformative technological change, and sustained economic growth during the last half of the twentieth century make this one different, more so perhaps with its placement in space and time in western Washington during the logging of its magnificent old-growth forests. That space, its spectacular landscape, and the men and big equipment who exploited it are gone now and cannot be replicated. But what of the human spirit involved? It's still there, more or less. But wouldn't current and succeeding generations do well to examine, evaluate, and, in some cases, emulate the spirit of a successful earlier generation that they might learn and adapt and attain comparable achievements in their own quest for a better life, a better place, a better world?

Many of the stories are true. Some are not, at least not completely. A few are true only in spirit. The reader may decide which are which, for the writer is no longer able. Names of people and places have been changed so as neither to hurt nor offend.

Important Characters

(In Order of Appearance)

Name	Relationship	Notes
Chapter 1		
Henry Hofmann	Husband of Katie Hofmann	German immigrant from the Caucasus, Russia
Katie Hofmann	Wife of Henry Hofmann	German immigrant from the Caucasus, Russia
Joachim Hofmann	Son of Henry and Katie	Son of Henry and Katie Hofmann; born in Russia
Magdalene Diede	Friend of Henry and Katie Hofmann; wife of Phillip Diede	German immigrant from Russia; friend from North Dakota
Phillip Diede	Friend of Henry of Katie Hofmann, husband of Magdalene Diede	German immigrant from Russia; Friend from North Dakota
R. G. Lewis	Orchardist and employer of Henry Hofmann	Immigrant from England
Herbert Hofmann	Son of Henry and Katie Hofmann	Son of Henry and Katie Hofmann; born in North Dakota
Chapter 2		
Francis Claude "Tom" Dubois	Husband of Clara Dubois	Born in Idaho
Clara Dubois	Wife of Tom Dubois	Born in Idaho
Garrett Starker	Oldest brother of Clara Dubois	Born in Idaho
Liz Starker	Wife of Garrett Starker	
Leonard Carson	Clara Dubois's brother-in-law	Ranch owner near Horseshoe Bend,

		Idaho
Fred Starker	Clara Dubois's father	
Rebecca "Becky" Dubois	Oldest child of Tom and Clara Dubois	
Chapter 3		
Johann and Rudolph Hofmann	Brothers of Henry Hofmann who stayed in the Caucasus, Russia	Rudolph was Henry's youngest brother
Karl and Julius Hofmann	Brothers of Henry Hofmann who immigrated to the U.S.	Karl was Henry's oldest brother
Juliana Hofmann	Youngest daughter of Henry and Katie Hofmann	Born in Wallace
Nelda Hofmann	Oldest daughter of Henry and Katie Hofmann	Born in Russia
Martha Hofmann	Daughter of Henry and Katie Hofmann	Born in North Dakota
Clarence Clemmons	Boarder of Henry and Katie Hofmann	Teacher and principal, Wallace Elementary School
Chapter 4		
Joe Zach	Logging company owner	
Francis Claude "Sonny" Dubois	Son of Tom and Clara Dubois	
Eddie Dubois	Youngest child of Tom and Clara Dubois	
Clarence Pettigrew	Salkum banker	
Chapter 5		
Ida Mae Barton	Sister of Sonny Dubois	
Bill Barton	Brother-in-law of Sonny Dubois	
Frank Barton	Brother of Bill Barton	
Elmer Hofmann	Son of Henry and Katie Hofmann	
Mel Hofmann	Son of Henry and Katie Hofmann	
Madeline Dubois	Sister of Sonny Dubois	
Doc Nelson	Salkum physician	

Marcus "Mark" Dubois	Son of Sonny and Lise Dubois	
	Chapter 6	
Eric Haggen	Owner of Haggen Truck Lines	
John Dubois	Son of Sonny and Lise Dubois	Becomes civil engineer
Adele Zach	Wife of Joe Zach	
	Chapter 7	
Sergeant Corson	Armored car commander	
Lieutenant Parker	Reconnaissance platoon leader	
Phelps	Armored car gunner	
Hermann	Armored car radio operator	
Sergeant Sack	Platoon sergeant	
	Chapter 8	
Clarence	Clara's second husband	
Jack Dwyer	Friend and later business partner	
Janice Dwyer	Wife of Jack Dwyer	
Dan Dwyer	Father of Jack Dwyer	
	Chapter 9	
Randall	Bookkeeper	
	Chapter 10	
Michael "Mike" Dubois	Youngest son of Sonny and Lise Dubois	
Rick Contini	Economics researcher and colleague of Mark Dubois'	
	Chapter 11	
Larry	Bank loan officer	
	Chapter 12	

Family of Henry and Katie Hofmann

Name	Birth Order
Henry Hofmann	Father
Katie Hofmann	Mother
Joachim "Joe" Hofmann	Son
Nelda "Nellie" Hofmann	Daughter
Martha Hofmann	Daughter
Herbert Hofmann	Son
Elmer Hofmann	Son
Melvin "Mel" Hofmann	Son
Annalise "Lise" Hofmann	Daughter
Juliana Hofmann	Daughter and youngest child

Family of Tom and Clara Dubois

Name	Birth Order
Francis Claude "Tom" Dubois	Father
Clara Dubois	Mother
Rebecca "Becky" Dubois	Daughter
Susan "Suzie" Dubois	Daughter
Ida Mae "Ida" Dubois	Daughter
Francis Claude "Sonny" Dubois	Son
Madeline Dubois	Daughter
Edward "Eddie" Dubois	Son and youngest child

Family of Sonny and Lise Dubois

Name	Birth Order
Francis Claude "Sonny" Dubois	Father
Annalise "Lise" Dubois	Mother
Marcus "Mark" Dubois	Son
John Dubois	Son
Michael "Mike" Dubois	Son

1. Train West to Wallace

The Hofmanns, 1920–1929

Henry Hofmann watched the locomotive attach itself to the cars with a heavy metallic crunch and lurch. Silence. A whistle blew. Then a creak, a chug, and the train began to move; another chug, and another. The train was rolling and almost immediately at the outskirts of the small village surrounded by the Cascade Mountains jaggedly etched in the clear night sky. Henry walked back to his seat where Katie, his wife, was with the smaller children, most of them asleep.

"We will be in Wallace in about a half hour," he said to Katie. "It is nearly another hour before sunrise."

"I will be glad when we get there, even in the dark," she responded. "We have traveled enough. I want to walk on the ground, have some space. I am tired of sitting."

Henry and Katie were Germans from the Caucasus region of Russia, from the village of Romanovka near the mouth of the Terek River. They immigrated to the United States in 1911 with their two small children, Joachim and Nelda, for a better life. Arriving in Philadelphia, they took a train to McClusky, North Dakota, where Henry's two older brothers, Julius and Karl, and their wives had settled earlier. Henry and Katie had decided to use English versions of their German names, Heinrich and Katerina, but McClusky had a large Russian-German community where German was routinely spoken, so their use of English and their new names had not taken a strong hold by 1920.

A few minutes passed. Henry had seated himself and was looking out the window.

Katie said, "It is still dark out. But you can see the snowy mountains outlined in the night sky. And you can make out some of the trees. They are so, ah, *riesig!*"

"I was told there is a lot of rain here, and it is always cloudy, but the sky is clear tonight," Henry responded.

He watched the river surging beside the tracks, water cascading over and around huge rocks; deep, black, irregularly shaped pools; then lighter grays, white riffles, and rapids. The river ducked below them as the train crossed a bridge.

The train moved on through several small villages, each with a siding of flat railroad cars, many loaded with snow-covered logs. The train slowed, and the conductor came to Henry.

"Wallace is next, in about five minutes."

Henry turned to Katie, "We are here. You get the children off the train with the hand baggage. I will get the trunks from the baggage car." A moment later, the train stopped. The children, all six of them now awake, looked at Henry. He rose and said, "We get off the train now. It is still a little dark. Mind your mother. No fooling, no running. Joachim, come with me."

The cold early morning air greeted them as they disembarked. Each but the littlest had something to carry: a basket, a bag, a blanket. They took a few steps away from the train to make way for those behind them; when they turned, their breath was visible in the cold. There were piles of snow to the side of the small depot, and frozen mud everywhere. Steam curled from the locomotive before it drifted back beneath and to the side of the cars.

Henry and thirteen-year-old Joachim walked back to the baggage car. The door slid open, and a voice within shouted, "Four trunks for Henry Hofmann."

"*Ja,* this is me," said Henry. The baggage man slipped one end of the first trunk over the edge of the car, and Henry caught the handle, lowering it to the ground as Joachim caught the higher end. The process was repeated three more times, and the four trunks were moved away from the train.

A signal was given, and the train's whistle blew. A chug; the train moved. Another chug, and slowly the train rolled off, leaving Henry and Katie Hofmann with their four boys and two girls in its wake, alone together in the small village. Henry had an offer for a job with Mr. R. G. Lewis, grubbing and clearing land for a large pear orchard, which he had been informed of in a letter from Phillip and Magdalene Diede, friends who had left McClusky several years prior and who now lived in Wallace.

An enormous quiet followed as the train moved from sight. Henry and Katie had heard it before; in Russia, in North Dakota.

"It is six o'clock. I will go find Herr und Frau Diede. You stay here by the trunks," Henry finally said. As he turned to go, Frau Diede came around the corner of a nearby building, waving and shouting.

"Phillip will be here in a moment with a wagon." She extended her hand to Henry, then she turned and warmly embraced Katie.

"Guten Morgen! Willkommen, Katerina."

"Guten Morgen, Magdalene! Such a journey we have had." Katie's mouth began to tremble with emotion. She was an unusually sensitive woman for whom human bonds were very important. Her mother had died when Katie was seven; when she was twelve, she had been placed as a maid servant with another family who lived hundreds of miles away. She never saw her father, sisters, or brother again. Seeing family members or old friends after long periods of separation, let alone saying "good-byes" to them, was very emotional for her and would always be.

Phillip came rattling up driving a horse and wagon. He whoa'd the horse, a modest old gelding that was uncomfortable in his harness, like he had not worn it for a while. Phillip got off the wagon and extended his hand to Henry.

"Guten Morgen, Henry!

"Guten Morgen, Phillip!"

Henry and Phillip vigorously shook each other's hands while looking intently into each other's eyes, Phillip wanting to express assurance and Henry wanting to show trust.

"Are these your children? They are more in number than when we left North Dakota."

"*Ja.* Katie had two children in Russia, four in North Dakota. You have many children when you have a healthy frau," Henry replied and gestured to Katie. "She could have some more yet."

"We only have four, three girls and a boy. Andreas is six now, and Viola, our youngest, was born after we left North Dakota. Let's put your trunks and bags in the wagon and take them to my house," said Phillip, as he reached for the tail gate and dropped it down.

Henry picked up the largest of the trunks and lifted it up into the wagon.

"Always the strong bull, eh Henry," said Phillip, smiling.

"Two men should not do what one man is able. Waste of time and effort," Henry answered as he lifted the second trunk.

Joachim grabbed a trunk and attempted to lift it. He faltered at its weight.

"Like a *Mensch,* Joachim!" Henry said disgustedly. "You are a *Mensch* now, not *ein Junge.*"

"Here, I will help you, Joachim," said Phillip, grabbing one end of the trunk. He and Joachim placed it in the wagon. Henry loaded the fourth trunk, while Phillip and Joachim carefully put on the hand baggage. "We are loaded already. Come up with me on the wagon, Henry, and we will go to my house. It is a short distance. Magdalene and Frau Hofmann, you walk behind with the children." He clucked to the gelding, and the wagon lurched forward, past the side of the store, north across the main road, then down a side road a hundred yards or so.

Ten minutes later, they were behind Phillip Diede's house with the trunks and hand baggage unloaded and put into a shed.

Phillip turned to Henry and pointed, "There is a bench north of here. It will become clear in a few minutes when it is lighter. Below it, less than a mile away is where you will be working for R. G. Lewis. He wants two hundred acres cleared and a pear orchard planted. You will meet him at noon."

Henry nodded. "What kind of horses does he have?"

"He has a team for clearing, dark-brown crossbreds about seventeen hands high. He bought them last fall. There must be some Percheron in them. Where he got them, I don't know. But you will see them today." Henry was only partly listening for his eyes were on the mountains beyond, on three sides of him.

He asked, as his eyes cast about in the early winter morning, "Has he worked the horses this winter?"

"Not much that I know of. I don't know how good he is with a team. He must know a lot about fruit trees, because the orchard he intends to plant will be the largest in the state.

Katie, Frau Diede, and the children came toward them, picking their way along the road through the uneven frozen mud. Henry continued to look about. He saw that Wallace was located in a river valley that opened to the west. Mountains towered on three sides. It was a small village, twenty or thirty years old, with at least a score of wood-frame houses. While the village obviously had been platted, all the roads were dirt, including the main road, which ran east and west. They had ridden past the only store on their way to Phillip's house. He knew the town also had a schoolhouse and two churches, one Baptist and one Adventist, from earlier correspondence. He also knew that a sawmill on the east side of town had burned down four years earlier. Not much else was there. Wallace was about the same size as McClusky, larger than Romanovka.

Frau Diede said, "We have breakfast now, some oatmeal and bread. Herr Lewis comes for you after."

Henry nodded, "I know. Noon."

Phillip turned to the women and laughingly said, "We are standing here out in the cold like *Dummkopfs*. Go on into the house. Henry, Joachim, and I will join you in a few minutes." When they turned toward the house, two children in the window of the front room disappeared behind lace curtains. Phillip, Henry, and Joachim walked to the back to unhitch the horse.

"Cold, yes, but a lot warmer than North Dakota, eh Henry?" Phillip said as they walked. Henry nodded.

"So, how are your brothers in North Dakota?"

"Karl is struggling, too many dry years. I think he is looking to move. Julius is doing much better. He is farming four sections now, and raising beef cattle."

They had oatmeal and bread for breakfast, with warm milk for the children and coffee for the adults. It was delightful. Phillip and Magdalene reveled in being able to extend their hospitality. Henry and Katie were grateful that their journey was over, and to be with kind and generous people, people with whom they were familiar. The table conversation was entirely in German.

R. G. Lewis was on time, and he was driving his automobile, a 1920 Model T Ford sedan. Henry and Phillip went outside to meet him. Lewis got out of the car and introduced himself to Henry, shaking his hand. He acknowledged Phillip and shook his hand.

"I brought my automobile. Maybe it will take a couple of trips to get all of you and your trunks and hand baggage, but it is only a long mile to the farm, shorter as the crow flies."

Henry responded: "*Ich hohle meine Frau und Kinder*" (I get my wife and children)

"Let me help. I can follow with the wagon and trunks," Phillip offered.

"That would be kind of you," said Lewis. "We will help you hitch the horse and load the trunks."

R. G. Lewis spoke little as he negotiated the half-frozen ruts and mud in the road. Cut-over forest land was on both sides. Soon Henry could see the farm, for it appeared to be the only one, consisting of a small house, a barn, and some outbuildings, one of them probably a chicken coop. The rest of Lewis's land was covered with stumps of various sizes, many uprooted and strewn about, and brush—lots of brush. Lewis turned into the driveway, and they bounced up toward the farmstead.

After he stopped in the yard and everyone got off the automobile, Lewis said, "Mrs. Hofmann, you take the children into the house out of the cold. I built a fire for you. Henry and I must talk together while we wait for Diede." Katie nodded, and she and the children disappeared into the small farmhouse.

"Here is what I want, Henry. This land was cutover before the Great War, and I want to clear the stumps and brush for a pear tree orchard and some pasture. The big stumps were blasted and many were burned last year. Many smaller stumps were pulled. I want you to grub and clear as much as you can throughout the remainder of the winter and early spring because I want to plant pear trees this spring on the cleared land. After we have finished planting, I want you to grub and clear the remaining land so it can be planted with pear trees the following spring. Ultimately I want all the land grubbed and cleared and put into pear trees and pasture, 190 acres of pear orchard and ten acres of pasture. I will pay you $5.00 a day and you can live here at this house with your family. You can use part of the barn for a milk cow or two. What do you think? Can you do it?"

"Do you have tools and a strong root plow?" Henry asked.

"Would I be hiring you if I didn't? I am told you are a hard worker, know what you are doing in clearing land, and know how to work a team of horses," answered Lewis.

"May I look at them?" asked Henry.

"Sure. Most of the tools are in the barn, in the stall to the left as you go in." Lewis opened the barn door. "Look around while I wait for Deide."

Henry walked into the barn, a simple structure with two large stalls on both sides of a front-to-back alley and a hay loft on top. The stalls on one side were for draft horses. One of the stalls on the opposite side of the alley had been made into a tool and feed storage room. Shovels, mattocks, axes, peaveys, and crosscut saws of various kinds and lengths were on one side leaning against or hanging from the wall. Sacks of feed were stacked along the other. A doorway led to a shelter attached to the barn, used to store farm implements such as plows, disks, and harrows. The remaining stall had been modified with four stanchions for feeding and milking cows, obviously unused in recent months.

By the time Henry had walked through the barn, Phillip, Joachim, and Herbert, Henry's second oldest son, had arrived in the wagon with the trunks and baggage, which were unloaded and taken into the house. Phillip said he had to get the horse and wagon back, and with that he gave Katie a large basket containing a roasted chicken, bread, and kuchen. Katie thanked him profusely and continued to thank him even as he was heading out the gate.

Lewis and Henry went back to the barn, and Lewis brought his team of draft horses into the alley one by one. Henry approached each of them from the front so they could see him. When he had their attention, he steadily moved toward them and rubbed their shoulders and noses, talking to them in German.

"Have you had the horses long?" Henry asked.

Lewis responded, "I bought them about six months back. You seem to know what you are doing with them."

"I have worked horses in the fields since I was ten, nothing special, the way it is in Russia.

"Do you like them?"

"Some better than others. Strong, calm, and willing horses I like. These are good animals, and they seem comfortable with each other. How do they work in the field?"

"Good, but you will soon find out, Henry." After tethering the horses on rings on the side of the alley, Lewis showed Henry the tack and harnesses. Breeches, girths, pads, hames, and collars were on harness mounts. Their quality was the best Henry had ever seen or worked with.

"Again, $5.00 a day, and you and your family can live in the house."

Henry paused: "I should see the house."

"Sure, look it over. My wife and I lived in it for several months while we built our house in town. I will put the horses back in their stalls."

Henry walked back to the house and entered the kitchen and eating area, which was one big room. He could see the back of the house from where he had entered.

"Can you make a house here?" he asked Katie.

"*Ja,* there is a kitchen woodstove and a small woodstove in the bedroom in the back. The bedroom can be divided for a sleeping place for the two little ones. There is a loft over the bedroom for the others. The well is not far from the house, and the water is sweet. The outhouse is…is so-so. Everything needs to be scrubbed for sure. As you can see, Lewis has an old table and four chairs for us, and there is a wooden bed in back."

Henry paused; "We are here, Katie. We must do with what we have and work for more." He turned and walked outside. He told Lewis: "Okay, I start tomorrow."

"Good. Then I'll leave now."

"I don't work on Saturday. My wife and I are Adventists."

"Suit yourself. I want six days of work a week; so work Sundays."

"Uh, when do I get paid?"

"The last working day of each month, and I pay by check."

"May I use the team and wagon to get some things from town?

"Go ahead. If you are going to work for me, you must get settled quickly. And you and your family are going to have to eat. Do what you need to do to get settled. *Auf Wiedersehen,*" he laughed. "That is all the German I have." They shook hands.

"*Wiedersehen,*" said Henry as he watched the Model T leave through the gate

****

Later, Henry hitched the horses to the wagon and then went to town to buy food. Katie had brought some basics, such as flour, oil, salt, pepper, and sugar, but Henry wanted some meat and potatoes. He stopped at Phillip Diede's house on the way back.

"Hello, Henry. How did it go?" Phillip asked.

"Who is this Lewis, Phillip?"

"He's an Englishman—some say a Welshman—who was given his inheritance so he would leave England because he drank too much *schnapps*. He came to the States and settled here. He intends to become an orchardist and grow pears, and his orchard, if it ever gets completed, will be the largest in the state, like I told you earlier. He lives in town and drives out to his farm."

"He is rich?"

"By Wallace standards, I suppose he is. But don't worry, Henry, he has hired other people before you to work on his farm. He has always paid them on time. By the way, did you notice he keeps peacocks on his place?"

"*Nein*. I have not seen peacocks since I left the Caucasus."

"Peacocks are the males, aren't they? I suppose I should have called them peafowl. He has both cocks and hens."

"They come from Persia, don't they?" asked Henry.

"I think India."

***

Henry took Katie and the children to church on the following day. He didn't go in, said he would be back after church, that he wanted to look around and get a fix on this place. So he rode east of town, looking about. He was surprised by the extent of the cutover land he saw to the north, beyond anything he had ever experienced or expected. Further east on the south side of the river, he spotted, well up on a mountain slope, a lone, upright tree with its top and limbs removed and cables attached. From below, logs were being dragged up the mountainside, leaving black trails in the snow. They stopped on a landing, where they were heaped on top of each other. Another similarly rigged tree some distance apart, with a huge boom perpendicularly attached, was being used to load logs onto open railcars with steel stakes on their sides. Engines mounted on log skids were powering the activity, belching steam as they did so, winding cables in and out on huge drums. On the far side of the slope, Henry saw men standing on boards notched into individual trees, dragging long saws to and fro, felling the timber. The devastation was unsettling, like the mountainside was being blasted away by an unimaginable surface explosion of some kind. He told Katie about it when he returned home. He was too late to pick her and the children up after church. They walked home. Katie didn't mind the walk. What bothered her were the perceptions of the church members. They were new to Wallace and not off to a good start. What was Henry thinking?

***

Henry and Lewis normally worked apart. Henry grubbed and cleared while Lewis did his self-imposed assignments. They didn't talk much initially, except when Henry wanted a large stump re-blasted.

Henry's first paycheck was $115.00, and he and Katie felt rich.

The work for Lewis went faster than expected, in part because Henry had Joachim to help, mainly tending the fires, while Henry grubbed roots and stumps and cleared slash and brush with the team. Paying Joachim for his work had never entered Henry's mind. He had worked in the fields for his father for years without ever being paid. Lewis saw pay for Joachim as Henry's problem, if it were a problem at all.

Henry was preoccupied in his efforts to make a place for him and his family. He was forty years old, and by that age, Henry's father had successively owned three farms in Russia: in the Ukraine, the Crimea, and the Caucasus. Henry had worked harder than anyone else he knew, but he had yet to put a farm together. He had always provided for his family, but by working someone else's land. Katie had told him several times that he would do better if he would work a little less hard and little more smart, a comment which irritated Henry. What did she mean? What did she know? She was an orphan girl, a maidservant.

Henry and R. G. Lewis began planting pear trees in early May. Lewis clearly knew how he wanted the trees planted and where, and he made an effort to explain to Henry what he was doing and why. Henry was impressed with his knowledge, and they began having discussions about plants of all kinds, their parts, and how they grew. Their common interest in plants served as the basis for an enduring friendship. It also was the beginning of Henry's interest in growing flowers.

***

Katie frequently complained about Joachim's not going to school. All the other boys his age in their town were enrolled and attending. "He should be going," she said.

"So what would he be learning?" Henry asked. "Tell me. At least working with me he is learning something useful."

"He is not being paid for his work. You pay him or he goes to school in the fall."

"I will pay him when his work is worth something."

"Henry, he doesn't work like you, and he never will. You pay him for his work or he goes to school."

Joachim went to school in the fall, finishing the eighth grade at the end of the school year. He found work on local dairy and berry farms in the early summer, knowing he was expected to support himself. Then he went north to Alberta, Canada to work the wheat harvest on farms of distant relatives who had settled there. He returned to Wallace in the fall after the beginning of school and was able to immediately get a job at Stretch's, the local grocery and dry goods store, while living at home.

Joachim was obviously short of money, which surprised Henry since he knew Joachim was paid a fair wage in Alberta. On one Sabbath morning after Katie had gone to church, Henry asked Joachim what he had done with the money he had earned from the wheat harvest.

"It is none of your business, Poppa," Joachim stammered. "I can spend the money I earn how and where I see fit. This is America." He knew immediately he had gone too far.

"And I decide whether you can live in my house and for how long," Henry roared.

Henry was imposing to most men, with his powerful physique and gruffness. To Joachim, at fifteen years of age, Henry could be terrifying.

"I made a mistake, Poppa," he gulped, searching for even a hint of understanding and forgiveness from his father.

"So what is that?" Henry asked, his countenance indicating there was not the remotest chance of either.

"I spent my money in a whorehouse in Calgary," Joachim stammered. "I wanted to know what a woman was like."

"So you go to a whorehouse?!? You will never amount to anything, spending your money on whores, you fool!" He struck him as he raged.

"I know that now," Joachim sobbed. Finally, shaking his bowed head, he asked, "May I live here until I get enough money to rent a room someplace?"

"Yes. But your mother is never to know this. It would destroy her. Go now. Find something to do."

***

A fortuitous opportunity for Henry and Katie to buy a house presented itself in the spring of 1924. It was a two-story, wood-frame building on Second Street in Wallace, a few hundred yards from Phillip and Magdalene. It had a kitchen, living room, and bedroom downstairs, and an unfinished upstairs—an attic basically—all for $800. Henry and Katie made the down payment and got a mortgage loan from Citizens Bank in Salkum, a meandering six miles to the west.

The Wallace Lumber Company sawmill was located just outside of Salkum. It was among the largest in the valley, and Henry was concerned about his employment because he knew his work for R. G. Lewis was coming to an end. He stopped by the mill office on the way back to Wallace, at the encouragement of the bank, and asked whether there was any work. The man at the desk said there was, pulling lumber off the green chain. Henry took the job, working out an arrangement where he could take part of his wages in lumber.

Henry and Katie moved into their new house in June. She went about cleaning it with a vengeance. Everything was swept, mopped, and scrubbed with soap and water. The kitchen, of course, was the focal point. The stove was cleaned, pots and pans and dishes and glasses were put in cupboards, and flatware and cutlery were put in drawers. Containers of various sizes were arranged for flour, oil, sugar, coffee, salt, and pepper.

The second Sunday after moving, Henry installed a door to the stairs off the kitchen that led to the attic and nailed down 1" by 8" and 1" by 10" boards throughout the upstairs as flooring. Henry also built partitions separating the space: boys from girls, younger children from older. The following Sunday, he nailed 1" by 8" tongue-and-groove beadboard to the partitions, and

Katie suspended heavy cloth on rods for doors. Their children had places to sleep, and everyone was very tired.

After falling into bed, Katie said: "If you fix the chicken coop next Sunday, I can get more chickens.

"*Ja*, I will do it," said Henry as he began to drift off to sleep.

"And the root cellar needs to be made larger and vented."

"*Ja*, in July, I do this." With that, Henry was asleep, and Katie was left thinking about how they would feed the children in the winter. She also worried about the brick chimney behind the stove, which went up through the second floor by the new partitions, up through the roof.

Everything is made of wood here, she thought. *I cannot go through another fire. We would have lost Martha and Herbert in North Dakota if it weren't for Frau Wagner, our neighbor. As it was, we lost virtually everything in the house, everything we brought from Russia. Eight years later, we are still recovering. I don't like all this wood. The children would never get out if there were a fire.* These terrible thoughts bounded through her mind, until she finally and fitfully fell asleep.

Henry and Katie rose at 4:30 a.m. each morning. She prepared him breakfast, usually oatmeal and coffee, sometimes with a boiled egg, and packed him a lunch; he dressed, ate, and walked to Stretch's store where he was picked up at 5:30 for the six-mile drive to the mill. Henry had bought a used Model T by this time, but he preferred riding with someone else to work and paying for his share of the cost.

Working in a sawmill on a production line, sorting and stacking green lumber, was different from anything Henry had ever done. The work wasn't unusually hard, but it was repetitious and required constant attention. A foul-up of any kind could potentially cause a pileup of green lumber and shut the steel belts down, something that wasn't tolerated. The pay was good, however—45 cents an hour—and Henry could buy lumber for the house at mill prices.

By the fall, the chickens were laying eggs; the garden was yielding potatoes, beets, carrots, and cabbages; and the cellar had been expanded and properly vented. Sidewall partitions were built in the upstairs of the house from the floor to the rafters, with beadboard nailed to them like the ceiling and the other interior partitions, giving the upstairs a more finished appearance. There were no closets, so Henry built three traditional *schranks* for the children. The boys, Joachim and Herbert, dug a pit for a new outhouse and built a new, bigger, and ventilated structure: a "two-holer," one for the boys and the other for the girls. It was painted white, inside and out.

The Hofmann family underwent a transformation in Wallace during the 1920s. They accumulated some things: a house, a used Model T Ford, and several furnishings, including a large table and six chairs, bed frames and mattresses, and a chest of drawers for the bedroom. The family grew. The older children did not begin to leave home until 1926, when Joachim moved out of the house to work in Suquamish. Katie had three more pregnancies, all girls, of whom one died shortly after childbirth. The cause was later determined to be an unfortunate birth defect. The infant would nurse, but could not keep the milk down. She effectively starved to death.

The relationship between Henry and Katie, however, underwent the biggest transformation. Henry was usually away from the house, working in the pear orchard at first and later in the sawmill in Salkum. When he was paid, he gave his check to Katie, who made virtually all purchases for the home. She was good at it, able to stretch the purchasing power of the dollars they had available, and to save a little, too. So Katie became the day-to-day family decision-maker. Since she was more accessible to the children and more patient, she became the parent to whom they turned with their problems. She also was the family arbiter.

Katie was the more outgoing of the two, developing fast friendships with other women of the local Adventist Church, all of whom were German immigrants from Russia. Henry's best friend in Wallace—Phillip Diede—was killed in late 1924, struck by a log rolling down a mountain slope. Friendships for Henry developed even more slowly after that.

Katie attended church every Sabbath. Henry's attendance was less frequent, usually because he wanted to complete self-imposed tasks around the house and garden. Katie wanted them to become members of the church as man and wife. But their membership was denied, and when the pastor came to explain—the concern being Henry's less than full application of the practices of the faith in matters of daily life, as well as his occasionally imbibing in blackberry wine and *schnapps* he made from pears—Henry replied, "*Genug*! You leave now!" Katie was mortified. After the pastor left, Henry was unyielding.

"What does he know about my beliefs? *Nichts*! I have obeyed God's law and worked hard. To what end? We have little. Why have we been treated so unfairly, when we have worked so hard?"

Katie only wept in response. She understood Henry's outburst and how destructive his chronic melancholia could be. He could not comprehend the massive breakdown of everything he had thought was normal in Russia, and the murderous hostility to all the people he knew. His father and mother died in 1919 from starvation and exposure after being forced to leave their farm. His brother Rudolf and his family suffered terribly during the Russian Famine of 1920–21; Rudolf's wife and three daughters died one after the other. Later, Rudolf and his second wife and family were forced off their stead to a collective farm, where Rudolf raised poultry, but still feared lack of food. He had written letters begging for money—money that Henry and Katie simply did not have to give.

Henry also could not come to terms with the disaster North Dakota had been. The promise had been great, and he had thrown himself into achieving it. But crop failures from drought, hail, and locusts, and then their terrible fire in 1914, had left them with less than they'd had when they arrived in the United States in 1911. All that the nine years in North Dakota had yielded were four more mouths to feed. His older brother Karl had had a similar experience, and he and his family had moved to northern Idaho in 1920. Julius, Henry's third brother in North Dakota, was still scrabbling there with his wife and four children. God only knew how he was doing.

Katie understood Henry's frustration with the pastor. Yet for all her strengths, her compassion, her loving kindnesses, she, too, was fearful. She read the bible daily. Knew it well, and she was fixated upon Moses' interpretation of Pharaoh's dream, seven fat years and seven lean years. Despite the turmoil they had experienced while getting established in Wallace, by the summer of 1929, she was convinced that their time there was a period of relative prosperity—their "fat years"—and that they were about to end.

It can't go on this way, she thought.

2. Stump Ranch on the Hill

The Duboises, 1920–1929

"Let's get going. All the boxes and bags are in the car. We will be in Salkum this evening," Tom Dubois said to his wife, Clara, with his usual optimism.

"You sure you know the way there? she asked. You sure you can find where Garrett and Liz live?" Tom herded their three girls and son toward the idling 1918 Hudson Super Six. Clara carried their infant daughter behind him.

"Sure. I got a map from a fellow at the warehouse, who was on the west side of the mountains last week. We take the Sunset Highway over Blewett and Snoqualmie Passes down to the first town on the other side, then north to Martinsburg, like Garrett said. Salkum is east of Martinsburg."

"Well, tonight I will find out what $1,200 will buy. All I really know at this point is we have a small house and a couple of sheds on forty acres on a hill," Clara said.

"It will be okay, Clara. Give it a chance," said Tom, as he engaged the clutch and slipped the car into gear on the spring morning in 1921.

This was Tom and Clara's fourth move in eight years. It pretty much had to be good. They had owned a 320-acre homestead south of Horseshoe Bend, high up on a hillside that sloped down toward the Payette River, which they sold in 1916 for $2,500. The country's involvement in the Great War was coming for sure, and Tom was fearful he would be drafted. He didn't want to leave his nineteen-year-old wife and three little girls on a remote ranch ten miles from the nearest town. They moved to a two-bedroom house on ten acres in Emmett, which was a bust because Tom was unable to get steady work.

So they sold the Emmett house, bought a Hudson Super Six, and drove northwest toward Wenatchee, Washington, with the intent of getting a job in one its fruit packing warehouses. On the way, for some extra money, Tom worked the wheat harvest near Lind in the Big Bend Country of eastern Washington State, while staying at the wheat ranch of Clara's brother, Garrett Starker, and his wife, Liz. Garrett was a full-time locomotive engineer and a part-time wheat rancher.

Tom got work in Wenatchee with a fruit packing company soon after their arrival, but it was seasonal, and work was sporadic in the winter. He thrashed around Wenatchee for almost three years, him getting nowhere in terms of securing a good, steady job, and Clara getting pregnant and delivering their fourth child, a son, in 1918, five days before Armistice Day.

Then Tom and Clara got a letter from Garrett in the fall of 1920, telling them that he and Liz had moved to Salkum, Washington where he was working for Salkum Railway and Timber Company as a locomotive engineer. He also wrote that there were jobs working in the woods, including opportunities to tend and operate the heavy equipment used in logging. The prospect excited Tom. He had some mechanical knowledge and abilities he wanted to develop. He had really liked working on the threshing machine in eastern Washington, and the steam-powered tractor that drove it was a mechanical marvel. Being a heavy equipment operator had a future, a much brighter one than being a wrangler, or fruit picker, or some kind of farm laborer.

The letter had also made it clear why Garrett and Liz had sold their wheat ranch and moved to western Washington. Their son, Willis, had drowned after falling into a cistern for watering livestock. Garrett was away too much in his work for the railroad, and Liz was doing more work than two people could handle, with keeping house, raising children, and working the ranch. Accidents happen when people are stretched in different directions.

Several weeks after the first letter, Garrett wrote that a neighbor up the road was selling his house, some sheds, and forty acres. Tom and Clara, given the descriptions by Garrett, believed the ranch was their "dream come true." They had Garrett negotiate the transaction, which he did successfully—unsurprising to Tom and Clara, for they both admired and trusted him. Garrett was four years older than Tom and thirteen years older than Clara. He was known as a go-getter, a doer, and for being smart, too. Tom and Clara were elated at the prospect of having family nearby, for neither of them had had much of that. They were somewhat disturbed by the grief and obvious strain on the marriage caused by Willis's death. But that pain would pass, they thought. Garrett and Liz would come around. They were no strangers to death.

The graveled highway turned south toward Blewett Pass, and the grade quickly steepened from the Wenatchee River canyon floor.

"Did you see the road forking off to the west?" Tom asked. "It will be another way we could go in a few years. They are building a road over Stevens Pass, pretty much alongside the Great Northern Railroad. It's going to be a major route over the mountains, just like Snoqualmie Pass. And it is going to run right through Salkum on the other side, all the way to Gardiner and Seattle."

"That will be good for Salkum, won't it?" asked Clara.

"Sure. Anytime a railway runs through a town or a highway, it is good for the town's economy," Tom replied.

The road steepened again as they neared the top of Blewett Pass, and the views became more dramatic. There was evidence of gold mining; some mines could be seen from the road. Very few appeared to be operating, however.

Tom shuddered as he thought about working in a mine.

"That's not for me," he said aloud, "Too cramped, too dirty, and too dangerous. Finding and digging ore out of some mountainside is something I am not about."

"What?" Clara asked.

"Oh, I was just thinking aloud. I am sorry. I was thinking how it would be working as a gold miner."

"There was a lot of gold mining in the Boise Basin, which is what brought my dad's family to Placerville. What my dad wanted though, was to be a cowboy, to raise horses. He loved horses," her voice drifted away. "So he and my mother settled in Garden Valley."

The Sunset Highway west of Cle Elum offered dramatic views of mountains and forests even to two people born and raised in Idaho. There were huge ponderosa pines going up much of the east side and magnificent Douglas-fir, western hemlock, and western red cedar trees coming down the west side. Tom and Clara expected to see towns off in the distance as they came down the Snoqualmie Pass summit, but as far as they could see, at every turn, was green forest.

On the west side, when there was a lull in the chatter and demands of the four children, Clara asked, "How soon do you think you are going to get a job?" Tom glanced over at her, and he understood his answer—one he had given her before in various ways—had to be thorough and reassuring. Clara was tough. She had lost her mother when she was eight, and she had bounced back and forth between older sisters and her father after he had remarried. She was used to temporary living arrangements, but never comfortable with them.

"I can't give you the number of days it'll take, but it will be soon. I'll be looking for work at one of the logging outfits near Salkum as soon as we unpack the car and put our things in the house. There are several of them around there, and they are all operating full tilt according to what I hear. These are pretty good economic times, Clara, and they need workers. I am looking for a job as a tender to some kind of heavy equipment, like a donkey or a locomotive. I want to develop skills so people will hire me in good times and in bad, and working with heavy equipment is my best opportunity. Look how successful Garrett has been. He taught me plenty while we were in Lind. That's where we are going. I am going to do my best, and I think we are on the right track. It'll happen. I think our ship is coming in."

Clara said nothing for a moment. "I hope it does, Tom. I've got all my eggs in your basket, and four chicks in the back and one at my breast." She laughed to herself at how they and everything they had were crammed into the car. She also noted how the sky had become overcast, and raindrops appeared on the windshield. "By the way, what is a donkey?"

Tom chuckled. "It's a steam-powered machine that turns a drum around which a cable is wound for dragging logs to a spot where they can be lifted and loaded onto railroad stake cars. It has another drum for pulling the cable back out to bring in more logs."

Tom was a small, wiry man with a ruddy complexion. People liked him for his easy laugh and agreeable nature. Unfortunately, Tom did not have much behind him. His father, a cobbler, was forty-five, and his mother seventeen, when they'd married, his third and her first. Tom's mother kicked his father out of the house when Tom was eleven because he was cruel to their four children. Tom did not see his father again until two years after his marriage to Clara in 1913. He received a letter from a daughter in Brownsville, Oregon, from an earlier marriage, saying she could no longer care for their father, that he would arrive in Boise on the afternoon train on a specified date and to please pick him up. Tom collected his father by wagon and took him back to the ranch. They didn't have much to say to each other on the way back, for his father was constantly wheezing and coughing. He died two months later, in July, at the ranch, from asthma and dropsy, and was buried at Morris Hill Cemetery in Boise without ceremony. Taking his father back to Boise to be buried was a bad trip for Tom. His father's diseased body had become so bloated with gas in the summer heat that he was impelled to stick him with a knife to relieve the pressure, as he might a bloated cow. He didn't know what else to do.

Tom's mother did about as well as any woman could under the circumstances of her life. She was a Quarles from Arkansas. Her father and mother and six children had driven four Missouri mules and a Schuttler wagon up to Boise in the 1880s, a grueling trip by any measure. They were farmers, and later moved to eastern Oregon in the Burnt River country.

Tom had left school after completing the sixth grade and subsequently picked up odd jobs around Boise to help support his fatherless family. He got a job rolling cigars for a while. At sixteen, he started working as a ranch hand at several large ranches north of Boise. He met Clara while he was a wrangler on one such ranch owned by Leonard Carson, the husband of Clara's oldest sister, Zelda.

Clara was surprised, somewhat amused, when she'd learned Tom's given name was "Francis Claude" during their marriage by a justice of the peace in Boise. He'd laughed and told her "Tom" was a nickname, that he was called Tom because of the physical resemblance he had to a neighbor whose name was Tom. It had started out as a family joke, but the nickname stuck. He told her he preferred his nickname.

"That's what I know you by, so that is what it will be," she'd declared.

Following the map, they turned off the highway at the first town and headed north on the east side of the river, picking their way from town to town on local roads. The rain was a steady drizzle.

After getting into Martinsburg a little after six, they refueled, then pushed on through Salkum and turned north onto the Basin Road. They arrived at Garrett and Liz's place a few minutes before seven. It was easy to find because it was almost by itself, in the middle of a huge thirty-year-old clear cut.

Tom turned off the engine and started to say: "You kids stay by the car with Mom, while I get keys and lanterns from Uncle Garrett and Aunt Liz," when the door of the house flew open and Garrett and Liz came running with their arms stretched out welcomingly. The families embraced. They hadn't seen one another for almost two years, since Garrett and Liz passed through Wenatchee on their way to Salkum.

Garrett said, "We made some soup for you. Come on in and have some. Then we can go to your place, look around, and you can settle in for the night."

Clara responded, "That's mighty fine hospitality, Garrett, and we will take you up on it. The kids and I are bone tired. I don't know about Tom."

After supper, Garrett, Liz, and their daughter, Lorraine, led in their car to Tom and Clara's new home less than a mile away. They got out by the side of the house, lit lanterns that cast flickering shadows about, and walked to the back porch. Tom unlocked the door, and the family beheld the kitchen of their "dream come true."

"Bigger than I thought it would be," Clara said matter-of-factly. "Wipe your muddy feet on those rags in the corner, kids." They went to the front room, where one of the lanterns was left in the middle of the floor. The other was used to explore the downstairs bedroom and each of the two bedrooms upstairs. Excitement spread among Tom and Clara and their children as their anxiousness about their new house evolved into varying levels of satisfaction.

Tom said, "By golly, this is going to work out just fine. Thank you, Garrett, for looking out for us and putting the deal together. I am really pleased. Aren't you, Clara?"

"I would like to see the whole thing in daylight before I let on how pleased I am, Tom. But thank you Garrett and Liz for helping us," she nodded in their direction. "I sure am happy to be here."

"Okay," Tom said, "Let's go back downstairs, and I will get the bags and boxes out of the car. All of us will sleep on the floor in the bedroom downstairs tonight."

"Well, we sure are happy everything has worked out, and that you are here," Garrett said. "You want to go to work with me in the morning, Tom, and see about a job?"

"Better not," Tom responded. "I think I would do better to stay here and help get settled. I will drive out to the camp toward the end of the day."

"Suit yourself. See you tomorrow."

In the light of the next day, everything was a little better and a little worse than it had appeared the night before. The forty acres were less sloped than they had appeared, but they also needed a lot more clearing of stumps and brush. The house was smaller, but in better condition than Clara had first thought.

She said aloud, but more to herself, "I guess it looks like $1,200 worth. It can be made to work."

Tom went down the hill into Salkum and found out where the Salkum Railway and Timber Company camp was located. It was a spine-jolting ride getting there, but it was worth it. He got a job as a tender on a donkey, a good start. Two years later, he would be its operator. Logging operations were going full tilt, and there were too many loggers who were "green," Tom among them. You had to keep your eyes not only on what you were doing, but on everyone else around you.

***

When Tom was not working in the woods, he and Clara were improving their ranch. They cleaned and improved the outhouse, enlarged the root cellar, repaired the well and made it much harder for children to fall into, and converted a small shed into a barn for two milk cows, including a hay loft. They also built a small chicken coop and a pigsty. None of the outbuildings looked like much, but they were functional. As a wrangler, Tom had learned how to improvise with the materials at hand and with minimal tools. Clara was good at it, too. They seldom bought new lumber, instead using what they had or could scrounge. They always had the Wallace Lumber Company sawmill down at the bottom of the hill, which usually had some off-grade or damaged lumber that could be bought cheaply.

By the time the children of the appropriate age began school in the fall, Tom and Clara had two milk cows, three young pigs, two dozen chickens, and shelter for all of them. The chickens ran free; the coop was for roosting and nesting, and it had doors that were fastened each night to keep out predators. They had also met all their neighbors, in addition to Garrett and Liz. One of them showed Tom how to blow and burn stumps. That was the big project for the fall, before the rain and snow became too great. He knew he wouldn't finish, but he would have a start.

Maybe Tom is right. Our ship might have come in, thought Clara.

***

Clara complained of feeling like she was coming down with the flu on one fall morning in 1925 as she was fixing Tom's lunch pail. Tom was concerned, but Clara urged him to get to work. A few hours, after the girls and Sonny had gone off to school, she started having a headache and running a fever. Her neck was stiff. It was all she could do to care for Madeline, their youngest. Clara was in bed when the kids came home from school. By the time Tom got home from work, her condition was grave. He rushed her down to Salkum to see Doc Nelson, who diagnosed her with meningitis and put her in the local hospital. It was a long, scary night, but Clara survived. Her fever finally abated after several days, though she was in the hospital for two weeks afterward.

Clara had a two-year convalescence following her meningitis. She stayed at home and was in bed most of the time, with Liz helping out in a big way. As Clara became stronger, she got the kids off to school, and their oldest daughter, Becky, prepared the evening meal, usually under Clara's direction. Gradually, Clara was able to do more and more chores around the house. In the end, however, her recovery was less than complete. She lost all her hearing in one ear and some in the other.

She also lost her brother during her convalescence. Garrett and Liz became estranged, not able to move beyond the loss of Willis. In the end, Garrett just left one day after dropping off the Starker family bible with Clara, who was taking a nap at the time. He moved to Seattle and got work as an operating engineer for a construction company. He and Liz subsequently divorced, but it was a legal formality. The marriage had expired years before. Lorraine stayed with her mother.

Tom worked throughout Clara's illness and recovery, never missing a day of work. He and the children fed the animals, milked the cows, and secured them at night. All of them pitched in to keep the house clean and in reasonable order, and Tom and Becky did most of the food preparation. There was no more any of them could do.

Once, Clara came into the kitchen in her house coat and ranted, "This house is a damned pigsty, an utter mess. You are living like a bunch of hogs."

Tom, seated at the kitchen table with dishes and utensils all around him, responded quietly: "Clara, the kids and I are doing as well as we are able. And we will continue to do what we are able, when we are able to do it. Now let us be."

Clara burst into tears. So did the children.

Clara tended to assess men in terms of her father—her father when she was growing up—even though she knew the measure was flawed. Fred Starker was an impressive man in appearance: handsome with dark hair, penetrating eyes, a strong jaw and a square chin. He usually wore a bold moustache. He was stocky and muscular with huge, powerful hands that befit the wrangler, blacksmith, and rancher he was. After his wife, Clara's mother, died in 1905, he sold his ranch, parceled out the children living at home among relatives—Isabelle, Clara, and Johnny, the baby—and moved to Boise, where he opened a blacksmith shop, which was modestly successful at best. He remarried, but even Clara as a young girl could see it was more of an arrangement made from expediency and convenience. They were soon divorced. Clara never saw her father after her marriage in 1913, but the images and memories she had of him were those of a young girl for a father who was a handsome, larger-than-life figure, who somehow incongruously—two decades later—seemed to have provided all the love and security a small girl could ever want.

Tom was sensitive to Clara's comparisons with her father, knowing he did not measure up. The circumstance of their marriage was also a problem. He was nine years older than her—a man—and she was barely sixteen when they married—a girl. He should have known better, was her view, and looked out for her. But he was only thinking of himself, like men too often do.

Her brother Garrett was no better after his divorce from Liz, at least to Clara's way of thinking. It was not Liz's fault their son had drowned. Tom urged Clara not to take sides.

"I wasn't, but Garrett shouldn't be divorcing Liz," she snapped. "It's not right."

Tom's reputation as a "donkey puncher"—or more accurately, a yarder operator—grew in the valley after Clara's illness. He was known for conscientiously maintaining the equipment for which he was responsible, and therefore major breakdowns resulting in downtime were few and far between. He was very conscious of crew members' locations while they were working, and no serious accidents had occurred while he was operating the donkey. Yet he was still yarding almost 70,000 feet of timber day in and day out, which was right on the button in terms of production. A side boss for one of the biggest logging outfits in the Suquamish Valley offered him a job right after Garrett's departure to Seattle, but Tom turned it down. He liked working for Salkum Timber Company, and he liked the big Willamette compound-geared Humboldt yarder he operated.

The yarder had three drums. The biggest was the main-line drum, spooled with a 1¼-inch cable, used for dragging logs to the landing. The high speed haul-back drum was spooled with ¾-inch cable, used for taking the cable out from the mainline drum to where the logs were located. The third drum was the straw-line drum, spooled with 3/8-inch cable, used for, among other things, pulling the haulback line out to the corner and tail blocks (pulleys). The three drums were compactly assembled and interconnected on a steel I-beam frame and arranged so they all rotated in the same direction, with the cable coils coming over the top.

With the boiler up and the yarding crew down the slope out in the brush with the bucked logs, two whistles signaled Tom to reel in the haulback line, which took out the mainline. The rigging slinger selected the logs for the chokermen to set the chokers (binding wire-rope nooses) and attach the butt rigging on the main line. With everyone clear, one whistle signaled Tom to reel in the mainline, and the of logs would be yanked up out of the brush toward the landing, across downed timber, logging debris, and stumps. The logs were dropped at the landing with clonks and thuds at the signal of the chaser, who unhooked the chokers and signaled Tom to reel in the haulback line, dragging out the mainline and butt rigging for another turn of logs.

The process was done over and over again, never routinely because of the tremendous strain that lifting and pulling the big timber placed on the cable lines, blocks (pulleys), and equipment. Something could go wrong very quickly, and with dramatic, sometimes catastrophic, consequences. Nothing was quite as frightful as a big log rolling down a mountainside uncontrolled, or rigging plummeting to the ground. Or a cable snapping, flying off in some unpredictable direction, scaring the "bejesus" out of everyone. Tom didn't force, jerk, yank, or jam equipment, or anything else on the landing. His style featured evenness. Throttles would be steadily increased or backed off; brakes were applied with steady pressure, not jerked or stomped on. Gears were engaged, not jammed. He didn't speak any louder than necessary to be heard over the equipment. He didn't panic, and he seldom became angry—such behavior in sharp contrast to most of the others, who tended to be loud, tough, and brash. Tom's evenness and concern over safety was a welcome relief to the other crew members. And they gave him his due. He was respected, a good guy, an integral part of the crew.

Tom also became part of a community for the first time in his life. He was invited to join the International Order of Odd Fellows (IOOF), one of the two main fraternal organizations in Salkum, late in Clara's convalescence. He was an enthusiastic member in his good-natured, low-key way. He regularly attended meetings, and he later got Clara to join the Daughters of Rebekah, the women's branch of the organization. It provided involvement with other women, something she had lacked up until that time of her life. The simple three-link chain of "Friendship, Love, and Truth" was especially appealing to her.

IOOF meetings were held in the Odd Fellows Hall, a two-story wood-frame structure with a false front, one of the largest buildings in the town. Its size and location had made the hall an important meeting place in the community. During one well-attended IOOF business meeting in 1928, several members, Tom among them, proposed holding monthly Saturday night dances in the large upstairs meeting room. These dances, the advocates offered, would provide much-needed entertainment for the community, and additional income for the local IOOF treasury.

While Tom's formal training in music was limited to what he had learned in grammar school, he could play several musical instruments passably, including the violin and clarinet. His capabilities with each were mainly because of keen interest and a fairly good ear. He enjoyed being a regular backup player in the band. He was a willing and enthusiastic performer, and so he became a mainstay in the group, whose number varied from month to month, but never saw more than five instrumentalists. Still, once a month at least, Tom and Clara would go down to the Odd Fellows Hall on Saturday night. Tom would play in the band, and Clara would sell tickets at the entrance at the top of the stairs. It was the most fun they ever had. And it didn't cost them a dime.

***

Becky looked up from her plate and asked: "Poppa, we have been learning about pioneers in school. Was your poppa a pioneer?"

Tom responded: "I am not sure what a pioneer is, but if you mean a person who came west in the early days, yeah, sure he was. He came out west to Oregon with his father before the Civil War, in 1852, when he was twelve, with his brothers and sisters. His mother died at Ash Hollow on the Oregon Trail in Nebraska, probably from cholera."

"Where did they come from?"

"I am not sure, probably Kentucky."

"Your father told me, Kentucky, Tom," responded Clara.

"Was your momma a pioneer?"

"I don't know. Her mother and father came to Idaho much later, in the 1880s. They were from Arkansas. Her father's family was from Tennessee. I know Grandpa Quarles was in the Civil War. They all live in eastern Oregon now. I don't know anything about Grandma Quarles. She didn't talk much.

"What about your parents, Momma?" asked Becky.

"Dad was born in Wisconsin, and he came west with his parents through Iowa and Nebraska in the 1870s. He married my mother in Laramie, Wyoming in 1881, and they moved to Idaho near his parents in Placerville. My mother was a schoolteacher. Her father was from England; he met his wife, my grandmother, after immigrating to the United States. They lived in Michigan for a while and later Illinois, where my mother was born. Then they moved to Nebraska, where she met my father. There is more information in the family bible, but that is enough for now. Finish your supper, and let's get the kitchen cleaned up for the night."

"Yes, Momma," said Becky.

Talking about family was not done much in Tom and Clara's home. Clara's family ties were loose, especially after Garrett left. Tom's ties were yet looser. He hadn't seen any of them since they left Idaho. What Tom and Clara had modestly accumulated was by their own efforts. Whenever there was a time when help was needed, responses of family members were meager if they came at all. It wasn't that they didn't care. Rather it was because everyone was struggling, and they were far away.

3. Struggle through the Depression

The Hofmanns, 1930–1936

The Stock Market Crash of 1929 did not attract much attention in the Suquamish Valley because few people living there owned stock. But as stock prices declined, the prices of other assets and commodities followed. Investors and consumers, feeling poorer, curtailed their buying, and inventories in stores accumulated. Suppliers cut back production, and workers were laid off in an insidious downward economic spiral that soon involved everyone.

The worst years of the Great Depression were 1932 and 1933, when one of every four workers in the United States was unemployed. Gross national product fell a record 13.4 percent in 1932. Logging camps in western Washington were operating at about 20 percent capacity, and wages of loggers declined from $5.80 a week in 1931 to $3.11 a week in 1932. Most sawmill workers were laid off, and those who kept their jobs had their wages cut. Companies went bankrupt. It is hard to overstate how devastating, pervasive, and demoralizing the Great Depression was in rural areas of the Pacific Northwest. There were no winners. Some people just lost more than others.

Henry Hofmann went to work at the Wallace Lumber Company sawmill in Salkum after the Christmas shutdown, and there was a sign that the mill would be closed for two more weeks. The workers went home puzzled—this was the first time there had been an unannounced extension of a shutdown. After the mill started up, lumber orders continued to fall off. Mill shutdowns became a regular experience in the valley, all the way down to Gardiner. The fear was that mills would close for good. And many did. Home construction had dropped by more than 80 percent by 1932, the year Henry lost his job with Wallace Lumber at the bottom of the Depression.

He was not alone. Hundreds of workers in the valley were out of work by then. Competition for what jobs were available was fierce. Workers who had jobs took pay cuts, often more than one. Skilled workers took the jobs of unskilled workers. Unskilled workers took whatever they could find. Men and woman went to local berry fields with their children to pick in the summer. They also went east of the mountains to pick tree fruit, hops, and vegetables, which Henry did repeatedly.

Henry's age put him at a significant disadvantage. He was in his early fifties, and as one logging boss put it to him, "Why in the hell should I hire a stubborn, old Dutchman when I could hire a young guy who is faster, stronger, and quicker, and whom I could teach everything he needs to know in a week?" Henry didn't answer. He knew he was old, that the farming skills he had were of little use in logging, and he hated asking for a job. The extent of his bargaining position was to be in the right place at the right time, when and where an employer wanted someone to do basic physical labor.

Katie was frightened by the lack of jobs for Henry, more so by the length of time for which jobs were unavailable. Her biggest concern, however, was her children. She would become frantic thinking about them. *What is the future for our children? What are they going to do? Joachim is married and has a job in Suquamish as a store clerk. Nelda and Martha are in Seattle working as maids and waitresses. What kind of places are they working in? Will they be able to keep their faith? Are they going to be able to find a good man? Herbert will be completing high school soon. What will he do? Will he be able to get a job working in the woods? Is he strong enough? Five children are at home. Are they going to be able to find part-time work and earn at least something to help? What are they going to do when they leave school?* She would fret and stew. It was useless to talk to Henry because he would get angry; at what, he knew not. So Katie would talk to the women in the church.

Afterward, she would wonder whether she had sinned. *Isn't it written that God will provide? Who am I to ask these things? Didn't the Apostle Paul write, "For I have learned, in whatever state I am, to be content?" I am content, O Lord, my God and Heavenly Father, I am content. Forgive me, but it is my children – children whom I have brought into this earth – about whom I am concerned. What will come of them?*

Katie was also fearful that Henry would become still more melancholy and withdrawn. He spoke to her sometimes of his mother and father dying in the North Caucasus after being forced off their farm during the Civil War following the Russian Revolution, dying from hunger and exposure in 1919 in a shed somewhere between the towns of Armawir and Wohldemfürst.

"Not even in a warm house, but outside in a shed," he would say. Henry's brother Johann died the same year. He had also fallen on hard times. And Rudolph and Maria, after returning from Iran to the North Caucasus, were faced first with the Civil War, then the Famine of 1921, then the long and cold winter of 1921–1922. Maria died in 1922, their two daughters shortly thereafter. *In what kind of crazy place did Henry and I live in Russia?* Katie thought to herself.

Henry was also deeply affected by the plight of his oldest brother, Karl, who emigrated from Crimea in 1900 with his wife and three children and settled near McClusky on a homestead. Karl was a very capable farmer and was able to assemble a 480-acre holding with a six-room farmhouse, barn, and several outbuildings after a few years. He grew flax, oats, and wheat, and did well during the Great War. But the winters became harder and took their toll. Karl sold his farm and moved to Coeur d'Alene, Idaho in the fall of 1920 with his wife and six children, and began farming anew on a 320-acre farm he had leased. Unfortunately, several promises by the lessor were not kept. Worse, prices of farm commodities declined during the 1920s. Wheat prices fell from $1.83 a bushel in 1920 to $0.67 a bushel by the end of the decade. There was no way Karl could keep up.

He left his Coeur d'Alene farm in 1929 and bought a wheat ranch near Farmington, Washington. While the land was fertile and crop yield ample, wheat prices still plummeted. Karl wrote a letter to Henry indicating that his wheat sold for $0.38 a bushel in 1932. Of course, falling wheat prices for such an extended period of time depressed the value of farmland and farm buildings, and much of what Karl and Maria had accumulated through farming during their twenty years in North Dakota had eroded away. Henry could not fathom how so many calamities could happen to such a capable, hard-working, and good man as his brother Karl.

Want of food was not among Katie's fears. The soil in the Suquamish Valley was fertile, and rainfall was abundant, so gardens and orchards were productive. Henry's bees yielded honey for a sweetener, and the chickens provided enough eggs for the family and a few more to sell. Raw milk from nearby dairy farmers was so inexpensive that Henry and Katie didn't own a milk cow.

"It would cost us more to keep a cow than to buy milk," said Henry. Surplus flour was distributed in the valley by the Red Cross at various times. And protein-rich lentils from eastern Washington were available from the church at very small cost. Meat, salt, oil, sugar, and coffee were the main food costs. Purchases of these were frugally made. Meat was eaten three times a week, sometimes two, not much different from when they were living in Russia.

Katie wanted to become a naturalized citizen, and she wanted Henry to become one, too. He declined.

"Why should we become citizens of a country about to collapse? Being a citizen of Russia was bad enough. They are all crazy over there, and the country has become hell on earth. If we had money enough to move, we would move to Canada."

"Henry, you talk so dumb. Six of our children are U.S. citizens. Are we going to move away from them?"

"If you want to become a citizen, do it alone. Have Magdalene take you. I have better things to do."

Joachim, who had stopped by to visit, interrupted them both: "Go with her, Pa. Help her out. You are not going to Canada or anywhere else. You are too damned old, and none of us will go with you. You have been in the States for twenty-one years. It is time you figured out whether you are going to be part of it.

"So are you a citizen now?" he asked.

"No." Joachim paused. Then he continued reflectively. "And I am wrong. I haven't taken the time to do it. I've isolated myself up here in the valley like you have, which is dumb."

Henry waved him off with his arm and walked outside into the yard. After the kitchen door closed, Joachim said: "Pa never listens. He is so stubborn."

"Yes he is. But he was not always like this. Hard times have crushed him, and I fear his spirit is nearly gone. Joachim, get naturalized. Take the time to do it. You must be a part of where you live. Do what you tell your father to do. You will have more opportunities."

Katie went with Magdalene on her regular trip to Gardiner and applied for U.S. citizenship. She took the oath of allegiance on December 8, 1932. Henry stayed in Wallace instead of attending the small, brief ceremony. He had gotten some temporary work for money, which he could not pass up. When she returned and told him, he just shrugged as if to say "suit yourself."

Henry got a job four months later as a laborer in a railroad section gang—gandy dancers—for Wallace Falls Logging Company, operating several miles northeast of Wallace. It promised to last only until the first major snow of the winter, but it was work, and wages would be coming in.

A letter came in the early fall of 1933 from Julius Hofmann, an older brother of Henry's. He and his wife, Katerina, had emigrated from Russia to the United States in 1893 to avoid military service. They had sold their farm near McClusky and moved to Castle Rock, Washington, where they were living on forest land bought by their daughter and son-in-law, a gyppo logging contractor. Julius had suffered large crop losses from hail for seven consecutive years, and then he lost his cattle herd. Unprecedented low rainfall and record high temperatures, combined with a massive grasshopper infestation, had devastated crops, hay meadows, and pastures. Many North Dakota ranchers were forced to either sell their cattle or let them starve. A government relief agency bought entire herds—ultimately more than a million animals—at $15 to $20 a head and then slaughtered the animals because the market for beef was already glutted. Julius and Katerina were financially ruined.

Henry wanted to see his brother and sister-in-law, who had helped them when they had come to North Dakota. Katie agreed.

"But," she asked, "How would we get there? Our auto is old."

"Ask Magdalene. Her auto is newer. It would make it."

Magdalene agreed to take them, but she insisted on driving. It was her car, and she was critical of Henry's driving skills.

"He drives a car like he drives a team of horses," she told Katie. Henry, of course, saw Magdalene's driving as wild and erratic. Two days later, four of them—Henry, Katie, Magdalene, and Henry and Katie's youngest daughter, Juliana—set out west to Gardiner, then south toward Portland, Oregon. By the time they got to Castle Rock and found the house—a one-room log cabin deep in the woods—it was dark.

The meeting of the brothers and their wives was very emotional. They had not seen each other in thirteen years. There was also the debilitating adversity each family had experienced. All of them wept.

After they had seated themselves at a small table, Henry looked at Julius and quietly and very seriously asked: "Are you a robber that you are living out here in the woods like this?"

Julius, nine years Henry's senior, a man who had once farmed four sections of land in North Dakota, replied, "No, Henry, these are just very hard times. Our Father in Heaven is testing me."

Henry quietly responded: "He is testing me, too. So what could you have done that He is testing you so severely? I don't understand."

"Where is it written you or I need understand? The requirement is that we fear God."

"I do, so help me," said Henry. "What else must we do? I am asking."

Julius, his eyes closed, shook his head from side to side. Tears again streamed down his cheeks.

"I only know scripture says we must have faith," he finally said.

Henry said almost nothing throughout the return trip to Wallace. Partway, finding his silence oppressive, Magdalene stopped the car and told him to move to the back so that Katie could come forward and sit with her so she would have someone to talk to. Henry went to the back seat without a word, like he had been struck dumb with despair.

***

Henry learned from a letter that Rudolph had remarried, and later, after his farm was seized, that he and his family were forced onto a collective farm, where he was made responsible for poultry production. The letter was written during the Russian Famine of 1932–1933, and Rudolph asked for money, food, and clothing. Henry put the letter down on the table after reading it. He sat quietly for a moment and then said: "We don't have anything to send."

"But can't we send Rudolph something?" responded Katie. "He is your brother, and I have five dollars we could send. We could also send him and his family some food like flour and lentils. I could collect some clothing from the people in church. It has had several clothing drives already this year for people in the old country."

"Enough, Ma. To be able only to send him so little is an insult to him and to me, and it wouldn't do any good anyway. I am not sure, if we sent money, whether it would arrive, even. Everyone is corrupt in Russia. Rudolph should have stayed in Iran. He was crazy to come back to Russia during the revolution."

"He came back to be with his parents, who are also your parents, and to make a farm for him and his family. You know that!"

"*Ja*, and he also came back because he thought he could stay out of the political mess and get some good farmland cheap. He was wrong, and I cannot make it right for him. No one can."

"Henry, it is wrong to not send him something because it would show how little we have. We should send him what we are able, regardless of what it indicates of our difficulties in America. He is your brother. It is only right."

"*Mein Gott, Frau,* understand what little we have. The only money we have is from the work I do. If I don't work, we have no money, and every day, every day is a struggle to find work. If we have five dollars today, if we have food today, we will keep it. Tomorrow we may have nothing, a real possibility. No money. No food. No future. And no one will care. Rudolph won't. He can't. This is all very sad, but it is the truth. And forgive me, I know you believe God will provide. I do not. With the mouths to feed that we have brought into the world, I don't have the right."

Katie saw no anger in Henry's eyes and heard none in his voice. What she saw and heard was frustration, and worse, resignation and loss of hope.

***

The Works Projects Administration, the WPA, came to the Suquamish Valley in 1935, allowing local communities like Salkum and Wallace to hire workers to implement local public works projects. Workers were paid less than prevailing wage rates, but more than they would receive if they were on relief. Henry was hired and paid $52.00 a month, later adjusted to $48.00 a month, to be part of a crew to improve streets and local bridges and to build school facilities and a small public park.

Henry was always looking for a better job, like the rest of the wage earners in the valley. They had an edge in one respect. Companies were distrustful in hiring new faces, fearing they could be labor organizers. Union organization efforts, stimulated by New Deal programs, including the National Labor Relations Act of 1935, were going on in the woods and sawmills at the behest of the Congress for Industrial Organization (CIO) and the American Federation of Labor (AFL). The Suquamish Valley, devoid of labor strife during the 1920s, was rife with it in the 1930s, not only between employers and workers, but between workers themselves in the CIO and AFL. In retaliation, at the first hint of union organization activity, logging outfits would decimate their work force and hire anew. Henry, like most Germans from Russia, was wary of labor and political organizations—as well as government in general—a result of experience, real and imagined, with nineteenth-century Russian tsars and twentieth-century Russian communists. He stayed away from labor meetings and rallies.

Henry finally got reasonably steady work as a gandy dancer with the Miller Logging Company. Based in Salkum, it was among the largest logging outfits in the valley, with good equipment and long-term cutting contracts to clear most of the timber on the south side of the Suquamish River. He worked with Miller Logging through 1939. Then he got on with Zach and Olson Logging. In 1941, he was back at Wallace Lumber Company, working in the sawmill. He had to. The work of a gandy dancer had become too strenuous for him.

***

Clarence Clemmons, a teacher and principal at the local school, was the first boarder in the Hofmann home in Wallace, taken in to provide some family income. The living arrangement was unique. He lived in the largest upstairs bedroom with the understanding that he could also have his own stuffed chair in the front room, his upright piano in the dining room, and that he would be able to teach piano lessons four afternoons a week. A short, thickset man, Clemmons was a marvel at playing piano arrangements of John Phillip Sousa marches. His short arms drove the keyboard like pistons, and having heard him, no listener ever doubted the piano was a percussion instrument.

The arrangement also provided that Mr. Clemmons would be provided two meals a day, six days a week. During breakfast one day, long after Henry had left for work, Katie said Elmer would be graduating from high school the following year, and that he would be their second child graduating from high school.

"Very good, Mrs. Hofmann. Soon every child will have a high school diploma."

"How so?" she asked.

"To get a job. Employers will want their workers to have a high school diploma because it shows they can read and write."

"My Joachim doesn't have a high school diploma. Nelda and Martha don't have one either."

"These are hard times, Mrs. Hofmann. Do they have employment?"

"Yes, Joachim and his wife run a hotel, and Nelda and Martha are waitresses. Herbert is logging, but he is very serious with a girl. They are talking about going to college. Her father has money."

"Good for them. Your other children should also get their high school diplomas. Encourage them."

She did. Ultimately, three boys and one daughter finished high school.

Henry and Katie's children defined her, made her life meaningful. Her reasons for bringing them into the world were complex, but included an evolving combination of ignorance, *Pflicht als Ehefrau* (the duties of a wife), and culture. She had ten children, several more than she ever wanted, and two died at or near birth. All were born into a world of adversity and incertitude, even, at times, despair. Yet she provided them with sustenance and security. She spoke with wisdom, taught kindness, and tended her household, never eating of "the bread of idleness." The surviving eight children grew, and as they each left home, they expressed their love for her.

Henry was more distant from his children. Work defined the man in his culture, and he was not able to successfully provide an adequate income for his family for extended periods. Lack of success in such an important cultural standard eroded his self-worth. The tough physical environment of North Dakota and the Great Depression virtually precluded any opportunities for accumulating property and wealth on a sustained basis. Regardless, Henry was never derelict in meeting his responsibilities. One way or another, job or no job, he eked out a living for his family. And as the surviving children left, the boys came to him, and he would shake their hand and nod his head, once. The girls would kiss him, and he again would nod his head, once.

For years afterward, the children would come back for Christmas and a holiday or two during the summer. The ritual was the same. Katie would talk with the girls in the kitchen as they prepared food for a family meal. Henry would sit in his chair in the living room and talk with the boys. An exception was in the summer, when softball games or contests of strength were arranged. Henry would pitch, and he never lost a strength contest with his sons.

He applied for and got his U.S. citizenship in 1936. It was done virtually devoid of passion. When Joachim heard about it from his Mother while visiting home, he shook his head and exclaimed, "About time!"

From the living room came a quiet but firm, "*Macht nichts.* It doesn't matter." Then, almost scornfully, Henry retorted "So, you are naturalized now, Joachim?

"Yes," he answered

"When?" Henry asked with obvious surprise.

"1933, a year after Ma."

4. Depression Despair

The Duboises, 1930–1936

The Zach and Olson Logging crew was unusually quiet during the early morning ride on the speedie to their logging site. When it stopped and they got off, they were met by Joe Zach, the logging boss and one of the company's owners. He told them to get their equipment and woods gear and to meet him over by the yarder; he wanted to talk to them. Ten minutes later, he began:

"We are going to shut 'er down for a while, men. Log markets have collapsed. We will pay you what we owe you tonight in town. So secure the equipment tonight, and take your personal gear home with you. I don't want it lying around. Check in at the office to see when we are going to start up again."

Tom DuBois liked Joe, and had only recently began working for him. Both were IOOF members, so Tom was comfortable in asking when they were by themselves: "You have any idea how long we will be shut down, Joe?"

He answered: "None, Tom. This economic depression has hit us hard, like every other logging outfit in the valley. All of you have jobs with us; you in particular. But we don't have a cutting contract or a timber sale, and I have no idea when that will change."

Damn it, Tom thought, *Clara is going to be pissed. We were just getting current on our monthly bills.*

When Tom broke the news to her after supper, her response was: "I knew it was going to happen. And so should've you, so we might have done something about it."

"Like what? The main thing going on in the valley is logging and sawmilling. Well, there is working for the railroad, but I can't get a job on the Great Northern without moving, and I like it here."

"I really don't care what you like or do. You took us here. Now it's up to you to make a damned living, Depression or not." And she turned away and took off her apron, folding it before putting it on the countertop. She turned back toward him and said with finality: "Tom, we are poor and always have been poor, and I am tired of it."

He stood there. Clara was quicker, louder, and more outspoken than he was. And she had a hard edge, made sharper by the hearing loss from her meningitis. Made him feel foolish at times, and generally ineffectual, like a loser—a term he hated because she often and pointedly used it. He hoped the day would never come when she used it in reference to him.

Zach and Olson Logging started up again three weeks later. It sputtered away in fits and starts, following lumber and shingle markets. Loggers worked when they could, and when they could not, they earned—or tried to earn—additional income by cutting shingle or shake bolts from cedar logs and stumps on cutover land. Those who had small farms raised livestock or cash crops like raspberries and strawberries. Some would go "east of the mountains" and work the harvests, which could be problematic if a crew member wasn't there when his crew was called up—he would lose his job. To supplement family diets, most loggers and sawmill workers fished and hunted, in season and out. It really didn't matter, it was a big country and everyone was hurting. Nobody would say anything.

***

Participation in political discussions after the IOOF meetings was new to Tom. Up to this point in his life, he had never been in a position where he could be engaged in political discussions. He was not even sure they were an appropriate activity for someone like him, an ordinary working man. But his interest was piqued one evening as he was leaving a meeting and overheard an IOOF member, whose name he could never remember, talking about Senator Borah of Idaho and his support for recognition of the Soviet Union by the United States.

The man went on to say: "Borah is chairman of the Foreign Relations Committee and was against ratification of the Treaty of Versailles, but now he goes on to support the communists in the Soviet Union. What kind of senator is he, anyway?" When the man saw Tom listening, he asked, "What do you think of this guy, Tom? Aren't you from Idaho?"

Tom was caught short, a little embarrassed. Finally, he chuckled and said, "Damned if I know. I left Idaho over ten years ago. He was a pretty popular politician there back then. He was the prosecuting attorney in the Big Bill Haywood trial."

The man shook his head in response, "I don't know. I wonder if people really know who they are sending back to Washington, D.C. They are a pretty weird bunch, it seems to me."

Tom went home later that night, and Becky was up, reading. She was always reading. Read too much for her own good, according to Clara. He asked her if she had heard of Senator Borah.

She replied, "Yes, a little. He is a senator from Idaho."

"Your school has a library, right?"

"Yes, a small one."

"Find out about him, what he stands for, and write a tablet page or two about him. The guys at the Odd Fellows were talking about him tonight."

"Okay, Poppa."

She wrote three tablet pages on Senator Borah, giving them to her father six days later. He was pretty sure he knew more about Senator Borah than anyone else at the IOOF Hall.

***

Tom and Clara's family was rapidly growing up. Because they both had only finished the eighth grade—a little less than that, actually—the education of their children was important since they were well aware of the opportunities closed to them because of their lack of formal schooling. They wanted their children to complete high school. Becky, Suzie, and Ida Mae, the three oldest, fulfilled these aspirations. The girls successively graduated from high school during the years 1930-1933, three high school graduates in the family in four years. The girls didn't have many choices after graduation, however. They could not stay at home because there were no beds or much food to spare. And what food there was wasn't very good, for Clara was never much of a cook. So the girls left home and got jobs, and when one was seriously courted by a young man with a job, she got married. The girls' choices were not difficult or uncommon. Their parents were struggling like everyone else.

The 1932 presidential election was about the collapse of the American economy and the failure of President Herbert Hoover to address it effectively. The challenger, Franklin Roosevelt, offered a "New Deal" for American workers, the evolving details of which he did not and probably could not specify. President Hoover had problems with the press, which became serious and contentious as the campaign wore on; Roosevelt, on the other hand, was an excellent communicator, who seemingly enjoyed dealing with the press. Hoover was from California, a mining engineer by education and training, and wealthy through his own efforts. Roosevelt was a New Yorker, a professional politician, and the scion of a wealthy family. Both were Protestants.

The choices, in Tom's mind, were not clear cut, and information about them was not readily available. Newspapers cost too much for the average woods worker. When he asked about his party affiliation, which was not often, Tom would normally answer "Republican." But that was because of his Idaho origins and his impressions of Senator Borah as a youth in Boise.

Conversations were lively after the IOOF lodge meeting in September 1932, all dealing with the Depression, lack of jobs, and the presidential election. The passion of the rhetoric was generally unfettered by lack of information.

"Something has got to be done by the government about this economy," a long-time member declared. "And Hoover isn't doing it. This fellow Roosevelt has some ideas. He says he's for the working man. One thing for sure, Hoover isn't."

"That's unfair. He tried," another member retorted.

"Trying ain't good enough! And restricting trade, raising taxes, and rousting thousands of veterans from their camp in Washington, D.C., some with their families, is all wrong. The veterans were just trying to get their bonuses for their military service. Two were shot and killed," a third member joined in.

"Shooting the veterans was bad. No question about it. Hoover got poor advice. But what has Roosevelt to offer the working stiff?"

"Roosevelt is one of them rich easterners. He doesn't know anything about the working man. He sure as hell doesn't know anything about working in the woods here in the West. He has been a politician all his life, jumped from one political job to another."

"I understand he's got polio and can't walk."

"He can walk. He uses crutches."

"Well, I got to ask, may not be entirely right, but how in the hell is a cripple going to get this damned economy turned around? Isn't the presidency a full-time job?"

"Sure it is. But it's a desk job, sitting around and listening to people. He can do that without walking. I want to vote for a candidate with some ideas, someone who is concerned about the little guy."

"Roosevelt has both ideas and the right concern: concern for the working man. He is the kind of candidate who will make some changes."

"Pretty thin soup. I want to know what a person running for president is going to do, a real plan for dealing with this depression. It is killing me, and it is destroying my family."

"I am not sure a presidential candidate can do that. If he announces his plan, everyone will rip it apart."

"Who do you like, Tom? You haven't said a thing so far."

Tom chuckled in his good-natured way. "Well, my politics tend toward the Republican side of things, as you know. But this depression is really bad, and nothing Hoover has proposed has seemed to work. So I am pretty much sitting on the fence right now."

"Do you know whether the 'Lion of Idaho' is endorsing Hoover?" a member asked sneeringly.

"I really don't," said Tom.

"Well, Senator Borah hasn't to date. And the speculation is he won't because he believes Hoover's policies are wrong and against the interests of the people of Idaho."

"Well, if that is true, I am on the other side of the fence then, ain't I?" answered Tom.

Tom and Clara voted for Roosevelt in the 1932 election. Clara's vote was pretty well determined once she learned

Eleanor Roosevelt was a Rebekah. FDR carried forty-two of the states and 58 percent of the popular vote. The vote was probably even more lopsided in the Suquamish Valley with the logging and mill closures. Many people didn't vote, though. They couldn't see that it would make any difference.

As troubling as 1932 was, the birth of their sixth child, Little Eddie, made it even more so. Their responsibilities were clear. How they would meet them was not. Everything was just a little more complicated.

***

The free fall of the economy slowed in 1933. It grew nearly 8 percent in 1934, but unemployment was still over 20 percent nationally. The following year, 1935, was similar. The economy grew a little over 8 percent. Unemployment was again over 20 percent. Logging and sawmills throughout the Pacific Northwest operated sporadically. Like Tom, workers might have jobs, but little or no work. A company would start logging, and then it would shut down. Fits and starts. Sawmills operated the same way. They would start up and fill their orders. When they were filled, the mill would close. Mill owners had no interest in accumulating lumber inventories. The future of homebuilding was unclear, so most of the lumber manufactured was to fill orders. This survival strategy of mill owners worked its way to the back end of the mills, where log inventories were minimized.

Clara was on a tear. "We are not making it, Tom. We can't even buy enough feed for the livestock."

"I'm doing everything I can, Clara," Tom responded.

"Dammit. So am I, and that isn't good enough, Tom. We need more money to pay off our monthly bills. We never get even. We have got to get out from under the continual debt we have or we are going to lose everything."

"Tell me how. How we are going to do that? How are we going to make more money?"

"I got a letter today from Leonard Carson, and he wants someone to help him at the store, while he works his ranch."

"How long has your sister Zelda been dead now, Clara?" asked Tom.

"Nine years," she replied.

"That old billy goat! I don't trust him. Never did. I wouldn't be surprised if he has eyes on your behind." Tom hesitated, then continued: "Getting my pay out of him when I was working on his ranch was a struggle every damned payday. He always had an excuse for not paying me and the other ranch hands. I hated it. Had to beg him for what he owed me every month."

"I know that. But what other choices do we have?"

"Where would you live?" asked Tom.

"Above the store or at the ranch."

"Clara. Clara," he shook his head, "Living at either place wouldn't look good. And I don't trust Leonard's motives. So what would happen when we get caught up on our monthly bills? Are you going to come back here?"

"I am not sure," she paused. "What I really would like to do is sell this place and move back to Idaho."

"Who is going to buy it, Clara, in the middle of this terrible economic depression? And what would we get for it? After everyone is paid off, would there be anything left?"

"Those are questions you should get answers for. You find out! I am tired of being poor. I want to go home, home to Idaho. If I am going to be poor, I'd rather be poor in Idaho. Western Washington has been nothing but rain and misery."

Sensing her frustration and determination, Tom asked: "Would you take Eddie with you? Someone has to care for him when I am working. You could do it while working at the store?"

"I think so."

"Write Leonard and find out what he has in mind. Try to pin him down on how much money you would be making at the store, where you and Eddie would live, and if there would be any rent involved."

"I will."

"I'm sorry things have turned out the way they have."

"I know, but sorry isn't good enough anymore. This has gone on for too long."

Leonard Carson's response was an offer of $40.00 a month, that she could live at the ranch, the upstairs of the store being too small if she were bringing Eddie, and that instead of rent, she could prepare his food and clean the ranch house.

"Those are going to be long days for you, Clara."

"I have long days now," she responded, "and I don't get $40.00 a month."

"Leonard also says the sawmill at Horseshoe Bend is starting up and is hiring workers. Sonny could go with me now that he has graduated from high school. He could work at the mill and help me at the store. There is no work around here I know of."

Two weeks later, in late June 1936, Clara, Sonny, and Eddie left the ranch in Salkum in a 1929 Ford pickup, loaded with suitcases, bedding, and furniture. Tom shook his head as he watched them go down the hill.

Clara is so damned determined to get her way, he thought, *even in the face of good sense and reason. Hope they get there safely, and everything works out.*

***

It didn't. The $40.00 a month pay for running the store was more of a goal that depended on the amount of business the store did each month. And times were at least as hard in Idaho as they were in Washington. Leonard Carson, 60 years of age, was a crotchety, lonely old man, impatient with young children and any mess they might make, and very demanding that supper be on time, which was 6:00 p.m.

After several months, Clara took a hard look around. She drove across the river one Sunday into Horseshoe Bend, where she had gone to school as a girl after her mother died, when she was living with Zelda and Leonard. It wasn't the town she remembered. She went east to Sweet, visiting her mother's grave in the small cemetery there, then south across the river to Montour, where she had lived as a small girl. Nothing looked the same. Everything was worse—more worn and poorer—than she remembered. When she got back to the ranch, she wrote Tom a letter and told him she was coming home. The next day, she told Leonard she was leaving at the end of the month, November. He asked her to stay on, but she said no, and with such finality, he said nothing further.

Sonny was stunned when his mother told him they were leaving.

"I have a good job, Mom. They got me working on the log boom now, and there is no word of a shutdown. I am making more money than you are." Clara's eyes snapped. She was at a loss for words, which was unusual. A long moment passed.

Finally, she stammered: "We are going home to Salkum at the end of the month. Pack your clothes and bedding. We will leave the furniture behind. It will lessen the load on the pickup."

"How are we going?"

"You figure out a way with as few mountain passes as possible so we keep out of the snow."

"Suppose that would be out to Fruitland and up to LaGrande and Pendleton, then north to Yakima and Ellensburg, over Blewett and Stevens Passes, and home."

"Okay, okay, Son; that is the way we came. I understand. But I want a safe trip and a sharp eye on the weather. I don't want any problems. We have enough as it is."

They arrived home in the afternoon of the third day, delayed because of a storm in the mountains northwest of LaGrande. It was raining when they drove into the yard, where Tom was under the hood of a 1930 Model A Ford coupe. He had rigged a tarpaulin over the hood, tied between two trees. He smiled and waved at them. Clara and Eddie got out as Sonny let the pickup idle a few minutes, cooling the four-cylinder engine before he shut it down.

"I was getting awfully worried about you. Don't get close until I get cleaned up. I got too much mud and grease on me. Norman here had some carburetor and ignition problems that needed fixing so he can go to Martinsburg tomorrow. He's got a new job. I will be through here in about a half hour. Right now, I am in a place where I got to see this through."

Clara smiled, nodded to Norman, and said: "Good to be home, Tom. Sonny and I will unload our bags."

"Nice to have you back, Clara. Like I said, I will be through here in about a half hour. Madeline's either out back or down at Kramer's."

An hour later, after fixing Norman's car, sending him on his way, and washing up, Tom came into the kitchen where Clara was rummaging about looking for something to prepare for supper. Tom kissed her, more of a peck than a kiss, for he knew his clothes smelled a little ripe, having not been washed in some time.

"Not much here to eat, Tom," she said with a note of frustration.

"Yeah, I know, I was going to go to the store today, but time got away from me. We have some bacon and eggs, and bread, milk, and flour, of course. We can make some pancakes and eggs."

"Any syrup?"

"A little. We can add some brown sugar if we've got any." Tom swallowed hard and cleared his throat. "The best I could do was to keep up, Clara. There was not much work in the woods these past few months. I made enough for us to keep up, but not enough for us to accumulate anything.

Clara's dark eyes turned fiery. "So I suppose right now, we are just about at the same place as when I left."

"That's right."

"Only with less food in the house."

"Yeah, I suppose. But the car is running well. I overhauled the engine while you were away." he said with a smile.

"God dammit, Tom. We got to get our bills current. We got to pay our property taxes. By the way, did you pay them for this year? Or did you forget? We could lose this ranch if we don't get control of things."

"I didn't forget, but I couldn't pay all of the bills. I just paid as much as I could on some of them. How much money do you have? How much did you bring home?"

Clara's face contorted with emotion and her eyes filled with tears as she sobbed: "$83.00. Everything you said about Leonard is true. He misled me. $83.00 is all I have left after driving here. We are a couple of losers, Tom. We know nothing about making money. And when we do make money, we don't know how to keep it. We are losers! Damned losers!" She wept openly, noisily and without control.

Finally he responded, "Maybe so, but the times are bad."

"Shit, Tom, the times are bad, the place is bad, but some people are making money. Read the damn newspapers. Buy one and read it. We don't know how to make money, and when we do make money, we don't know to keep it."

"I have got a good job, Clara. It pays pretty well."

"When you are working, Tom!" she raged. "And if you aren't working, good job or not, you are not making any money. Don't you understand that?"

"More than you know, but what can I do?" he said helplessly.

"Well, for one thing, quit giving away what you got. That is what I have done, and look at what it has got me," she responded. "Nothing; absolutely nothing."

"I don't understand."

"For chrissake, Tom. You are a nice guy, but you have limited capabilities and lots of time, just like me. And you and I are always 'helping out,' you fixing somebody's damned car because you have 'mechanical abilities' and me tending a damned grocery store. We don't charge the people employing us enough. We give it away. And when we spend time giving it away, we cannot spend time putting ourselves in a place and doing things where we can make enough money to live on."

"Clara, I am sorry I was helping out Norman when you arrived. I didn't know when you would be here."

"I don't give a shit about Norman," she yelled. "Get us in a place where you can make a damned living. Get us out from under this situation where month after month we get behind in paying our bills. Here is the $83.00. Get us right with everyone we owe. Take some of the money Sonny earned if you have to. But get us right with everyone. I hate owing people."

The house was quiet. Any children in it at the time had long disappeared to a bedroom upstairs or outside to the barn with Sonny.

Later, Tom went to Sonny and asked him for the money he'd earned at the sawmill in Horseshoe Bend, promising he would pay him back. He was a good kid. Sonny handed over $90.00 and said: "Forget about it, Pop."

Clara made bacon, eggs and pancakes for supper that night. There was almost enough syrup to go around. Apple butter was used for the remainder.

***

Clara, after thinking about it many times, after talking to some women she knew on nearby stump ranches, and after talking to some Rebekah friends, approached Tom as she was washing dishes after supper. He was having a second cup of coffee, and she knew he was tired because he had been cleaning out the barn all day.

"Tom, we paid $1,200 for this place in 1921. It's probably worth about $800 to $900 now, even with the improvements we have made. Other than the house, it has provided a garden, shelter for livestock, and pasture for the cows. I think it can provide more. It can provide us with additional income."

"How is that, Clara?" he asked absent-mindedly. He was thinking about how he had to put in and feed the livestock for the night and how miserably wet and cold it was outside.

"We got to get this ranch producing some income. Producing dairy milk requires too much time, and we cannot produce enough good quality hay on this place to get a herd of cows through the winter. Damned hogs stink and are too messy, and we were never good at raising them. Beef cattle take too long to yield anything, and we still would have the hay problem. I think we could produce eggs and make some money. All we would need is a chicken house."

"What are you talking about, Clara?"

"I am talking about building a chicken house so we could raise chickens to produce eggs to sell. I think we could make some money doing it."

"So have a lot of other people," Tom replied.

"What does that mean?" Clara asked, her voice rising.

"Means a lot of people have thought of doing it, and some have tried. Nobody I know has made any money at it."

"You're throwing water on my idea, and I haven't even got it all out," her voice rising still further.

"Well, get it on out then, and do it quickly, because I have livestock to take care of, and it is getting late, and I am tired," Tom replied with irritation. He knew she had a point, though, knew he should at least hear her out.

"Okay. I think we should raise chickens to produce eggs to sell. Everyone eats eggs. We can sell them to stores in towns up and down the valley. Three of our kids are gone now, and Sonny could be leaving any day. I have time on my hands. I could handle everything: the feeding and tending of the chickens and the collecting, cleaning, grading, and delivery of the eggs. You could keep working in the woods. The only thing I would need help on is building a chicken house."

"How big a chicken house you talking about? How fancy, and where are we going to get the money to build it?" Tom asked.

"I want a big chicken house, twenty by sixty feet, with windows and doors, nests and roosts, and a floor. Also there would have to be a space for chicks and another for pullets. We could borrow from the bank, and use the money to invest in growing out chickens and producing eggs. I think we could support a flock of 350 to 400 hens, and I expect we would make about $200 the first year and maybe double that every year after. What do you think?"

"I think I am going to take care of the livestock. While I do, I will think about your idea, and we will talk about it when I come back in," Tom replied.

It was miserable outside, but the livestock were cooperative. They wanted out of the weather and to be fed, which Tom did as he had a thousand times before. Now that he was out of the house, oddly, his mind was on Clara's proposal. She was right; they needed more money. If they did get a loan, and did get the chicken house built in the early spring, the chickens could be producing eggs in the late summer and fall. There would be money coming in. Maybe Clara's idea was not a particularly good or original one. But it was the only one either of them had. The Depression had wiped away all of his bright ideas, and most of his hopes with them.

When he was through, he walked to the back porch, took off his boots and barn clothes, and walked into the kitchen, where Clara was still working, finishing up for the night.

"I think you have a good idea," he said. "Better than anything I have. Raising chickens for eggs and selling them makes sense if you are up to it. I will help you. I'm not working tomorrow. Let's go down to the bank in the next day or two—after we get more information on raising chickens and proper chicken houses—and talk to Clarence Pettigrew about a loan. We will have to have one. We don't have enough money otherwise. That's the way it is."

Eight days later, Clarence Pettigrew got up from his desk and greeted Tom and Clara about as warmly as a small town banker might a logger and his wife. Both men were members of IOOF and had known each other for nearly ten years, but they had never socialized together outside of the IOOF hall. Tom was ready to make his pitch for the loan, having been thoroughly rehearsed by Clara that morning and on the way down the hill to town.

Clarence asked, "How can I help you, Tom?"

"Well, Clara and I have come to see about a loan. We intend to raise chickens for their eggs to sell and want to build a chicken house for commercial egg laying with all the equipment, and buy chicks to start a flock."

Clarence asked questions about the size of the proposed chicken house, the proposed size of the flock, estimated egg production after six months, after a year, equipment needs, whether Tom was going to quit working in the woods to run the operation.

Finally, he said: "I think we can help you, Tom. How much do you want to borrow?"

"$500.00."

"Hmm. You will have to put your ranch up for collateral, and we can go no longer than a year. Is that agreeable?

"Yes. How much interest would I be paying?"

"Eight percent. The monthly payments will be about $45.00."

"It'll be okay as long as we keep working in the woods," Tom laughed.

"That goes for most of us, Tom," responded Clarence. "We will draw up the loan, and you can come in tomorrow and sign, any time after one o'clock. Both of you will need to sign, of course."

"We will be here," and they shook hands.

Tom changed his clothes when he got home and quickly went to work, leveling the area where Clara wanted the chicken house. The next day, after they had signed the loan, Tom purchased the first six of many sacks of Portland cement. With the aid of a borrowed gas-powered cement mixer, Sonny, a few neighbors, as well as some mild weather, the pad was poured and troweled over by the weekend. The chicken house was framed, partitioned, and sided by the month's end, and the chick room, including a small woodstove to keep the chicks warm, was operational. Clara was amazed and proud of their progress. She received delivery of the chicks two weeks later.

Both Tom and Sonny were back in the woods, logging full-time. Tom was still working for Zach and Olson, and Sonny was slingin' riggin' for Miller Logging Company.

***

A virus hit Clara's chickens, Leghorns, in late June. They were effectively gone. The few that survived the virus looked bad. As Tom put it, "Don't know anyone who would want to eat one of those damned birds."

Clara was told by a County Extension agent to clean out the chicken house and let it sit to ensure the virus was gone. The idea was to buy more chicks in September. But there was no logging in August because of an extended fire season. Too dry to log. No work; no money. And they were behind in their monthly bills, except for the bank. Buying chicks was put off for a month.

Then Zach and Olson had no timber to cut and no logging contract, and the other logging companies in the valley weren't hiring. Tom and Clara were unable to pay the bank loan and their monthly bills. Sonny was a help, but he could only go so far. His mind was elsewhere.

It was raining when Clarence Pettigrew pulled into the yard of the ranch. The front yard was basically an infrequently mowed and somewhat leveled pasture. Cars and pickup trucks had routinely turned off the driveway and onto the grass, so the boundary between lawn and driveway was obscure. Attempts to plant shrubs and flowers alongside the house had long been abandoned. The driveway went along the east side of the house back toward the barn, the chicken house, and other outbuildings, the closest being a wood shed, and further out, a small pigsty with a board fence. Apple trees and a couple of pear trees were growing between the house, barn, chicken house, and sheds. Halfway between, on the west side of the house, was an outhouse. Clarence was not apprehensive. He knew Tom as a good fellow, well intended, but uneducated, who had been especially hard hit by the Depression.

Clarence knocked on the front door. Tom opened it, invited Clarence inside, and motioned him to a chair at the table in the kitchen. Tom seated himself at the table and asked Clara, who was washing dishes, to join them.

"So what is this about, Clarence? The loan, I suppose. I know we are a little behind."

"Yes. Tom, Clara, the bank has worked with you through several very difficult months, but it can't do it any longer. The economy is improving, people are going back to work, and the bank wants to be in a position to assist by making loans to new businesses, farmers, and home buyers. So, Tom, unless you can get your loan current in thirty days, and keep it that way, the bank is going to foreclose on its loan to you."

"You see evidence about an improving economy, which is unknown to me. You might as well foreclose on Monday, because we don't have the money. Thirty days won't do anything for us."

"I am sorry, Tom," responded Clarence.

Clara interrupted, "We don't have the money, Clarence. You can't get blood out of a turnip."

"I am sorry, Clara, but I have heard that hackneyed expression too many times. Please. I am here to tell you the bank is going to foreclose on your loan unless you get it current in thirty days and keep it that way."

"Where do we go? Where will we live?" Tom asked.

"The old Harrison place should be available to rent. It is less than a mile from here on the Basin Road. Herman Kessler bought the ranch, and no one is living in the house. Now unless you have any questions, I have another appointment. Good day to you both." Clarence rose and started to extend his hand to Tom, but it was clear Tom was stunned, speechless, and unable to comply with modest social conventions like shaking hands and walking visitors to the door.

"Good day, Clara." And he left.

Tom sat silent at an abyss of despair and emptiness. He heard Clara saying something like "I hate that goddamn bank," but she was saying it to no one, and it seemed she was far, far off.

Finally, Tom rose from the table, walked out to the back porch, and grabbed his coat from the nail on which it hung. He opened the outside door and started down the steps. Clara flew out of the house behind him.

"Where are you going?" she asked.

Tom looked at her silently for several seconds. Then he said, "I am going over to Herman Kessler's place to see how much he wants to rent the Harrison house."

"Shit! You have quit."

"I suppose I have, Clara. The ranch is gone, and there is nothing I can do about it. Now let's get us, the livestock, and all our things out of here before the end of the month. I don't want to pay the bank another damn dime."

"Is this it? Is this all we have after twenty-six years?" Then her face contorted, and a long, bitter wail came from deep inside her.

Tom walked away to the car. He was unable to provide her any comfort. Even if he could, she would be unable to receive it. They were virtually alone in their despair. Yet Eddie was still there, and he had to be taken care of. That he knew.

5. Meeting Lise

1936–1940

Sonny returned to Salkum about five months after going to Idaho, never really sure of the reason he had gone, other than that his mother had wanted him to. It was a good experience, however, working at the sawmill at Horseshoe Bend. He had worked on the log boom, sorting logs for the head rig, making $0.35 cents an hour. Most of the guys in his high school class had had to leave Salkum to find work. He was very lucky when he got back and got a job as a choker setter with Miller Logging Company the day after he returned.

It was pay day, and the night of the big winter dance in Salkum. The music was reverberating off the wood-frame walls as Sonny entered the IOOF building. By the time he got to the top of the stairs, his heart was pounding with excitement. Most of the people in town were there, at least everyone fifty and younger.

He saw his sister, Ida Mae, and her husband, Bill Barton. They had recently married after a fairly long courtship by local standards—almost seven months. Bill's brother, Frank, had apparently come with them to the dance. Both Bill and Frank had known a lot of instability in their lives, with their father being a logger, part-time farmer, and the unhappy participant in several failed marriages. He was now on his fourth wife. Bill had quit high school during his sophomore year when he got his first logging job after his mother divorced his father. He was still working for the same outfit three years later as a rigging slinger. Bill was good natured and had an easy laugh. He was steady and dependable, and usually said things that made sense. Frank was a year younger than Bill and also a logger, working as a choker setter. He was a lot like Bill in appearance, but bigger and louder. He liked a lot of attention and had a flair for singing. His favorite of the moment was "I'm an Old

Cowhand," which Sonny expected he would sing sometime during the night.

The music from the five-piece band was loud enough to make conversation difficult. Sonny walked over to Bill and Frank and asked: "How is it going, guys?"

"Swell, Sonny. How are you?" they responded almost in unison.

"I am just fine. Everything is going well. I got a job setting chokers with Wallace Falls Timber, and ole Joe Zach told me he would help me with learning how to climb and rig spar trees this winter."

"Listen to him, Sonny," said Bill. "He knows what he is talking about."

"Hey, isn't that Elmer Hofmann over there? His brother Mel, too?

"Sure is. I thought Elmer moved to Seattle early last spring. Wonder what he is up to."

"Let's ask him."

They sidled past Ida Mae and the group with whom she was talking, motioning to her where they were going. Ida Mae nodded.

"Hi, Elmer. What are you doing back in town?" They shook hands all around.

"I just came up for the weekend for the dance."

"So how are you putting bread on the table?"

"Selling hardware in Seattle. I'll sell anything that is legal as long as I am in a place that is clean, warm, and dry."

"Is working in the woods too tough for you?" Sonny said teasingly.

"I hate it. Why be miserable all day logging when you can be comfortable doing something else and still make enough money to live on?" Elmer responded.

"I tried to get him to work in the CCCs," said Mel to the group. "It is steady, and you get your room and board and $30.00 a month, but he wouldn't have it."

"I'll take logging: the noise of the big equipment, the 'swoosh' and 'whump' of a big fir hitting the ground, the sounds of logs being yarded up to a landing," Sonny extolled. "It's exciting, almost like an athletic contest. The money is good, too. Better'n anything else around here."

"Okay, Sonny, enough of the bullshit," Bill observed. "Logging is something we do for a living. I am in it for the pay for the work I do and the risks I have to take. Not enough pay and I am off at the first chance doing something else."

"Let's dance with some of the gals. I am sure tough enough for that," interjected Mel, laughing.

"I'll go get Ida," said Bill. "Looks like brother Frank is going to sing 'I'm an Old Cowhand.'"

"You bring anyone special, Elmer?"

"No, just Mel and my younger sister, Lise."

"Isn't she a little young? How did you get her out of the house?" asked Sonny.

"She's fourteen. As for how I got her out of the house, well, Dad was asleep in his chair and Mom was at church."

"Hey, there's Nancy Carmichael over there. Doesn't she look good?" whispered Sonny. "Look at those cans."

"I'm first for asking her for the next dance. I traveled here the longest distance," said Elmer as he stepped in front of Sonny and toward Nancy. Sonny pivoted and made a beeline to another group of girls, knowing he would get his chance to dance with Nancy later.

The dance was the best in months, if not years. Eighty-five or so people were in attendance: men, women, children, couples, singles; people of all ages. Babies were put asleep in the back on top of coats spread across folding wooden chairs faced together.

The 1935 Salkum High School football team, which included Sonny and Elmer and Mel Hofmann, assembled and disassembled several times during the evening, like a flock of crows. They were notable as a team because they'd had a winning season, not usually the case for Salkum. One of the reasons was that their tailback, Stan Borseth, could pass accurately, which he had done several times a game, normally to Mel Hofmann. Their running game, also led by Borseth, had been slow but effective. Borseth complained the backs were slower than the linemen, which was true and the reason why the team made limited use of the sweep. When they had, Borseth usually had reached the sideline before he'd reached the line of scrimmage. When he'd attempted to cut back, more often than not, he would run into one of the other members of the backfield, usually Elmer Hofmann, the fullback, known for getting two yards—unfortunately, no more—every time he plunged up the middle.

The strength of the 1935 team was its defense, led by Sonny, known for his fast, penetrating line play. The line was also known for being "mudders," meaning its members played well on muddy fields. Indeed, six of the eight games the team played in 1935 were in the rain. Someone said it was a league record, but who kept track of such things?

Sonny, tired after dancing for at least an hour straight, including two splendid turns with Nancy Carmichael, looked for Elmer, but he was nowhere to be seen. He couldn't see Mel either. Then he spotted Lise with several friends.

He walked over and asked: "Where's Elmer?" She looked at him questioningly. Then he said: "I'm sorry. I am Sonny, a friend of Elmer's."

"Oh, he told me about you," she responded. "I am Lise."

"Nice to meet you, Lise. Hope Elmer said nice things."

"He did. But I don't know where he is at the moment. He can't be far, because he has to take me home tonight."

"He'll be back. But you are pretty enough you could get your own way back," Sonny laughed a little suggestively.

"That's not what I want," Lise responded. "Elmer is my ride home."

"I know he is. I was just trying to pay you a compliment. You are awfully pretty. How old are you?"

"I'm almost fifteen."

"In other words, you are fourteen. Hey, here comes Elmer and Mel."

"We have to go, Lise. It is good to see you, Sonny," said Elmer.

"Yeah, still the same old Sonny, chasing skirts and dancing up a storm," said Mel.

"Let's get together next time you guys are in town," said Sonny. "I'll walk out with you. It's getting late. Ida Mae and Bill have already left with Frank."

***

Everything was going Sonny's way by mid-1938. He was nineteen, had worked steadily in the woods for nearly two years—except for while they were shut down for snow in the winter or fire in the summer—and had gone from choker setter to rigging slinger. He was learning to be a high rigger, which was known around town, and he liked that, although some thought he was too cocky, too full of himself. There was no question, however, that Sonny was hardworking and knew what he was doing in the woods.

Sonny was also still living at home, paying room and board. It was a common practice, helping out at home if you were earning money, and God knows his father and mother needed some. Sonny had a room in the house with Eddie, now that his older sisters had moved out. Before, he had been sleeping in a small room he had made in a corner of one end of the barn.

Sonny attended Madeline's graduation ceremony that spring. She was the fifth high school graduate of Tom and Clara's children. Taking a seat for the ceremony, Sonny observed Lise Hofmann several rows over and was surprised at how pretty she was—how her figure had filled out since the dance last winter. No, actually, he was stunned.

After the ceremony, Sonny made swift work of getting over to where Lise was standing with some friends. He introduced himself, asking if she remembered him.

"Yes," she responded. "How are you, Sonny?

"Fine. I am here for my sister Madeline's graduation. Whose graduation are you here for?

"All of the girls from Wallace. Elsie and Alma came with me."

"Are they German, too?"

"Of course we are," Alma laughed. "Everyone from Wallace is German, Germans from Russia by way of North Dakota, which makes us all kind of like cousins."

"So what does a young guy from Salkum do? Either log or work at the sawmill, I suppose. Not much else, is there?" asked Alma.

"I am a logger, working for Wallace Falls Timber Company," Sonny responded, his eyes on Lise.

"Who are they?" asked Alma.

"A logging outfit working east of Galena across the river. I am learning to be a high rigger," Sonny said with obvious pride.

"What is that?" Elsie asked.

"Guys who climb big, tall trees and cut the tops off so blocks can be rigged and cable passed through them to drag in logs," Sonny answered.

"What is a block?" Lise asked.

"A big steel pulley. Some weigh several hundred pounds," Sonny responded.

"Aren't you awfully young to be doing that?" asked Alma.

"A little," responded Sonny, loving the attention. "How did you girls get over from Wallace?"

"We got a ride with Mr. Walker, Alma's father," said Lise.

"Well, if it is okay with him, I will give you a ride back when the ceremony is over. I will even buy each of you an ice cream cone."

"Great idea! I'll ask my dad," said Alma. "I'm sure it will be okay."

Lise was the last of the three girls to be dropped off in Wallace, even though it really didn't make sense doing it that way. Sonny told her he would like to see her. She said she would like that, but she was an Adventist and went to church on Saturdays and worked at the inn in Wallace on Sundays, that she couldn't go out after sundown on Fridays because it was the beginning of the Sabbath, and that she didn't think she could go out on Saturday nights because she had never gone out with a boy before.

Sonny hesitated: "Well, if you're willing, I'll try to find a way to see you."

She smiled and said, "I'd like that. I like to play tennis at the school on Saturday and Sunday evenings in the summer." When she got out of the car, she waved and said: "See you, Sonny."

Sonny borrowed a tennis racket and was at the Wallace School tennis courts the following Saturday at 6:00 p.m.

***

"Alright, hot shot. This is gonna be our spar tree," the logging boss said as the rigging crew began its day. "You know what you are supposed to do, but one more time: climb the tree, taking off the limbs as you go up. When you get to the point where the tree is two feet in diameter, top it. On your way down, knock off the bark for block straps and guy lines. Get your gear on, and let's get to work."

"Sure," Sonny responded, sounding much more confident than he really was. He could do that well, which was good because most of the rigging crew was standing around within earshot. He was young to be a high rigger. But he looked like one, at five feet, nine inches and 170 pounds. He was strong, coordinated, quick, and fit.

Sonny already had his belt and spurs on. He tethered the short-handled axe to his leather climbing belt, then the one-man crosscut saw. He circled twenty-four feet of climber's rope—four strands of hemp over a soft wire core—around the tree and secured it to his belt. He looked up at the tree, took a breath, and pitched the rope upward, pulling himself up and toward the trunk, jabbing his long spurs into the thick bark as he went. The ascent was a coordinated, rhythmic pitch—pull, jab, jab, jab, jab; pitch, pull, jab, jab, jab, jab. He was thirty feet up into the tree before he got to the first branch, a thick, heavy one. He secured the rope and sawed off the branch, which swooshed as it hit the ground. Sonny moved up about six more feet and around the tree and cut off another branch with his axe. Up and around the tree he went, cutting off as many branches above the rope as he could reach. It was physically exhausting. He knew, however, doing anything less than finishing the job would make him the subject of ridicule.

Sonny looked down about seventy-five feet, sensing he was about halfway and had used up less than an hour. The foreman and the rest of the rigging crew were watching.

"Keep moving. You've just begun," he said to himself aloud. Up and around the tree, higher and higher he went; climbing, securing the climbing rope, chopping. He checked the diameter with the marks on his axe handle.

"A little further. There, I got it. Now check the wind," he said to himself. Sonny shifted so he was sideways to the wind, and he secured the rope to begin working on an undercut with his axe. He shifted to the other side of the tree for the back cut. For it, he used the crosscut saw, which did a neater job than the axe.

The top started over and away, as it was supposed to. Sonny dropped his saw to its tether, slipped down, and held on to what remained of the tree, which, relieved of its load, arced back and forth. He was exhilarated and frightened at the same time. He reoriented himself as the tree slowed its arc, and he saw fallers down and away on springboards, chopping and sawing at standing trees. Two man bucking crews were cutting limbs from downed trees and sawing or "bucking" them into logs. About a half mile away, using a spar tree that had been rigged a week earlier, saw logs were being yarded up to the next landing and stacked in a big, sloped, jumbled pile. Further behind, logs were being lifted from an earlier pile of logs, or "cold deck," and placed on flat cars with stakes. The coherence and complexity of the operation forced itself into Sonny's awareness. For the first time, he saw his work as part of an organized whole. He was part of something big and was even more impressed with himself and what he was doing.

"Hey hotshot, get a goddamn move on up there," Sonny heard from below. He waved to the foreman, pulled up his axe, and began removing the bark for the straps and guy lines.

"It is a helluva lot easier going down than going up," he said to himself and laughed aloud.

On the ground, Sonny started to take off his climbing belt.

"Hold it, hotshot, we have to rig the spar, and this one is all yours," the foreman laughed. "You want to be a high rigger. So get your bony ass back up there with the rig-up block. Phil will show you what to do. Rigging 160 feet in the air is a little different than rigging on the ground, a little less room for your feet," the foreman said loudly so every one of the rigging crew could hear. Sonny started up the tree with the rig-up block. Phil was behind him on the other side of the tree with the straw line. They climbed and climbed back up to the top.

When they got there, at least 160 feet in the air, Phil talked Sonny through hanging the rig-up block on a wire rope strap just below the top of the spar. *Wasn't too hard,* he thought. The pass line was put through it, and hoisting of the guy lines began. Tree irons were put in place to prevent the guys from gouging out the wood of the spar. Soon all six guy lines were fastened to the spar and anchored to stumps in a rough circle around the spar about 60 degrees apart. The main lead block—nearly a half-ton of steel—came up next, and it was hung on a heavy cable strap a few feet below the guys. The mainline was hoisted and put through the block. The haulback lead block was hoisted next and hung on a cable strap about six feet below the main lead block. In turn, the haulback line was hoisted and run through the haulback lead block. Finally, four buckle guys were hoisted and fastened one by one to the spar about one-third of the height of the spar from the bottom.

Sonny was totally spent by the time they came down off the spar tree, and he stumbled from fatigue when he took off his climbing gear, which embarrassed him. He didn't want to make a spectacle of himself. These were tough, capable guys whom he wanted to impress—he wanted to be one of them.

The foremen walked by and yelled over his shoulder, "It's your first, Sonny, at least for this outfit. Looks good, but you need to be faster. Too many people were standing around waiting on you"

Sonny gave Phil, who was standing next to him, a puzzled look. "What the hell you expect, Sonny? A compliment? We are out here to make money. Get your gear together. We are done for the day."

Several minutes later, walking down to the speedie, Phil cleared his throat: "A word of advice, Sonny. You're the youngest guy on the crew and making more than maybe half of them. Don't talk so much. No one really cares what you have to say about anything. It's only what you do that counts."

***

Sonny found a way to see Lise on weekends throughout the summer, which was difficult. He was working six days a week for ten hours a day. Her working at the inn on Sundays was another complication. There were also the Adventist religious restrictions—a strange and endless number, it seemed to Sonny—that precluded their participation in activities in which their friends regularly engaged, like dancing on Saturday night at the IOOF hall and going to movies together at the small theater in Salkum. But Sonny's passion for Lise was unrestrained, all consuming, and she was virtually overwhelmed by his fervor. She was normally a modest, obedient fifteen-year-old girl, the seventh of eight living children, and she had never experienced such attention before from anyone.

So they worked around the barriers to their seeing one another. They played tennis, picnicked, fished, and went for rides in Sonny's car. They also slipped into an occasional Saturday night dance without anyone but their closest friends knowing. Their relationship grew in mutual trust, caring, passion, and intimacy. The four-year difference in their ages became trivial.

Their relationships at home frayed, however. Lise didn't invite Sonny into her house. She was embarrassed by her parents; they were too much of the "old country." So Sonny usually picked her up at the tennis courts or on the way home from her working at the inn, and he left her off around the corner from her house if he were bringing her home during the day. Even if she had invited him into her house, she knew he would find an excuse not to meet her parents. He told her that Germans in the logging crews made him uncomfortable, particularly when they talked to one another in German. Sonny actually knew of Henry, Lise's father, even though he was usually on the railroad end of a logging operation, working as a gandy dancer. He was regarded as a tough, old *Kraut*, not friendly with anyone except old German guys.

Sonny's relationships with his mother and father, on the other hand, were complicated by their nagging financial difficulties. He understood times were hard, jobs were few, and pay was low. But his parents seemed to be having a harder time than most. They had difficulty making ends meet, which frustrated him. He was paying them room and board, and he always had a job or quickly found one, like when he went to Idaho with his mother and Eddie. His mother was a particular source of irritation. She complained about his spending money on his car and always being gone—to wherever he was going—when he was not working. His father said very little in a serious way. He liked to make light, little jokes about Sonny's obvious interest in girls.

Sonny brought Lise to his home one late Saturday afternoon, which he quickly regretted. His mother was not welcoming; she was even hostile in the way she ignored Lise.

She told him the next day: "That girl is too young for you, way too young. You're going to get yourself in trouble with her. She is not your kind, and you know it. She's one of those damned Germans, who came over here and took land and jobs from the people who actually settled the West, like my folks."

Sonny walked toward the open back door and snapped, "Shit, you don't know what the hell you are talking about." He left with screen door banging behind him. Out of the corner of his eye, he saw his dad, seated at the kitchen table, look up from his coffee and smile ever so slightly.

***

Sometime after school started, Lise missed the bus because she was vomiting. Katie insisted she stay home and rest. She almost missed the bus the following day for the same reason. Several days of vomiting followed. When she came home from school in the afternoon a week later, Katie looked at Lise observantly and said: "Put on some field clothes, I need help in the garden."

When Lise came into the garden, Katie was already stooped over and cutting and trimming heads of cabbage. She rose when she saw Lise.

As their eyes met, Katie asked in a firm, steady voice, frightening in its plainness: *"Warst du mit einem Mann zusammen*? (Were you together with a man?)"

"What do you mean, Mama?"

"I think you know what I mean, Lise. *Hast du mit einem Mann geschlafen?* (Have you slept with a man?)"

"I think so, maybe."

"Dann haben wir ein Problem? (We have a problem then?)"

"I think so, yes." Lise began to cry.

Katie bent over and put the cabbages she had trimmed into a wooden crate used for collecting vegetables. She stood up again—she actually loomed over Lise because she was a bigger woman—and put her hand on Lise's shoulder.

"I should have told you more. I thought you would learn from your sisters. Enough with the tears now. They serve no purpose. Much pain and heartache are involved in having children. Love and joy, too, but more pain and heartache than you might think. And mothers bear most of that burden. You have precious little time to come to terms with being a woman and to prepare for the arrival of an innocent child. *Verstehst du?* Do you understand what I am saying?"

"Yes, I think so," sobbed Lise.

"Weiß der Mann, dass du ein Kind bekommst? (Does your man know you are with a child?)"

"No."

"Is he that fellow with the noisy car who picks you up on the way home from the inn on Sunday and who drops you off around the corner?"

"Yes. How did you know?"

"This is a small village, and a small village has many eyes, almost as many wagging tongues. Does he have a job? Is he working? Can he provide for you and a baby?" her voice slightly rising with each question.

"I think so."

"Can you get him here to our house next Sabbath for coffee and *kuchen*?"

"I think so. I can ask him. Why?"

"He must ask your father for permission to marry you. Now bring him here next Sabbath afternoon for coffee and kuchen after dinner."

"Mamma," Lise begin to sob again, "I have sinned, and I am so sorry."

"Lise, listen to me carefully again. What has been done is done, and there is no undoing it. If there is a sin, it is between you and God. Repent and get on with living your life. You must learn quickly to be a woman and to prepare for having a baby."

Sonny came for coffee and kuchen the following Saturday. Henry scarcely took notice of him and left the table, which was when Katie talked to Sonny after sending Lise to the kitchen to begin cleaning up. Lise never knew what was said between them.

He came to dinner the Saturday after that. Six places were set, including one for Elmer, who had driven up from Seattle. A plump roasted chicken was prepared along with carrots, mashed potatoes, gravy, and lots of homemade bread and butter. After everyone was invited to the table and they were about to sit, Henry appeared from out of nowhere—at least, it seemed that way to Sonny—and sat down. The others followed. He said the blessing in German, which was incomprehensible to Sonny.

Noiselessly, the food was passed first to Henry, which he distributed on his plate and passed to his right. When his plate was full, he looked up and then began eating, a knife and fork in his hands. The others followed with little conversation except for some idle chatter between Elmer and Sonny, and to a lesser extent, between Lise and her younger sister, Juliana.

About halfway through the meal, Henry stopped chewing, looked around the table, and asked: "*Warum ist er wieder hier*? (Why is he here again?)"

Lise's stomach clenched. Katie stopped her chewing and responded: "Sonny is Elmer's friend. Lise's, too. He is our dinner guest today."

Henry's voice rose, "*Ich weiss wer er ist. Ich wusste nicht das jemand zum Abendessen kommt, und warum haben wir beide, ihn und Elmer aus Seattle? Warum?* (I know who he is. I didn't know anyone was coming for dinner, and we have both him and Elmer up from Seattle. Why?)"

"*Heinrich, muessen wir denn einen Grund haben, um Besuch zum Abendessen zu haben? Geniesse dein Essen and freue dich ueber unsere Gesellschaft.* (So Henry, must there be a reason to have a guest for dinner? Enjoy your food and enjoy the company)," Katie responded, smiling.

Elmer laughed uneasily, "What are you building in the garage, Pa?"

"Nothing. I was just sharpening my tools. I am building a chest of drawers, and everything needs a keen edge for the dovetailing, as you should know."

After the kuchen and coffee, everyone seemed to disappear—at least it seemed so to Sonny—and he was left with Henry, saucering his coffee with a sugar cube clenched between his teeth.

After a long, noisy slurp, Henry asked, "So why are you here? What do you want?"

"I want to marry Lise, Mr. Hofmann," he blurted.

"She is too young. She is a girl only," Henry responded dismissively.

"But I must marry her," Sonny pleaded. A very long pause followed while Henry examined what remained of the coffee in his saucer.

"You must, you say?" he asked, looking directly at Sonny.

"Yes."

"You must?"

"Yes, Mr. Hofmann."

"Then...so be it. Marry her." Henry rose from his chair and went to the kitchen, shaking his head with obvious disgust.

Katie came into the dining room a moment later and sat down.

"When do you marry Lise now?"

"I don't know. I must talk to my folks."

"You must do it soon."

"I know. I know, Mrs. Hofmann."

"A civil ceremony. We have no money for anything larger. I will sign for Lise.

"Okay."

"So go now," said Katie. "Say good-bye to Lise and Elmer. Then you should leave. We have had enough for one day. The Sabbath is a day for worship and rest."

Sonny drove the back way home. It was a clear and crisp October day, and the mountains to the north and east were cloaked in their coniferous greenery. Yellow splashes of turning big-leaf maples and red dapples of the vine maples were shaking from the light currents of air moving from lower to higher elevations. The natural beauty was moving, even on the verge of being overwhelming to Sonny at this particular, critical moment of his life. He was familiar with the fluid transience of the natural beauty of the landscape he knew and loved, shifting from one phase to another, as he was about to—leaving something and gaining something else—and it eroded his confidence in telling his mother and father about marrying Lise. Twice he stopped and pulled to the side of the graveled road, his engine idling. Once he started to cry, which embarrassed him. He was nineteen, a logger for chrissake! He tried to organize what he was going to say to them in five sequential, logical sentences. They would not stay in place, however, and became jumbled in his mind.

His mother would be the challenge, his father consumed by his financial problems. She would probably overreact, be very vocal, and use harsh words. He would have to expect that. She would be immensely disappointed as well, because she had very high aspirations for him. She said as much at least a hundred times, and she routinely likened him to her father.

"Sonny is built stocky and strong like my dad. Has the same square jaw. He's a Starker through and through. And he is going to amount to something." She would sometimes add: "Not like the damned Duboises."

His dad would then say: "Now, Clara, don't judge the whole family by my father. He was a black sheep in the family, I am sure. Every family has at least one."

Sonny pulled into the yard. Chickens scattered, and the dog got up from where he lay by the back porch, stretched, and ambled toward Sonny, his tail wagging. Sonny patted the dog's head, and walked through the back door into the kitchen. His mother was at the stove, reheating what appeared to be either a thick soup or stew.

"Hi, Mom."

"What are you doing home so early on a Saturday night? Wonders never cease. Thought you would be over in Wallace chasing skirts."

"Where's Pop?"

"I'm in here," a voice answered from the front room.

"Would you come into the kitchen, Pop? I need to talk to both of you." Clara stopped her stirring and moved whatever she was cooking to the side of the stove. Tom came into the kitchen.

"What's going on?" he asked. They just stood around the table, holding the backs of chairs.

Sonny told them of Lise and his intentions of marrying her. He didn't do it well. His words were awkward and his manner clumsy.

When he was through, Tom said quietly, "I am disappointed. This is not what I had hoped for you."

Clara looked at first to Tom and then to Sonny. Her face contorted as she ripped into him, bawling: "I'm not disappointed. I'm goddamned outraged! What in the hell were you thinking?!? I thought you were different, that you would amount to something. But you are just like every other goddamned man who can think only of himself!" She stopped, got her breath, and then she raged again. "Who the hell is this girl anyway? Not that ridiculous skinny thing you brought by a couple of months ago. God, what have you done? You're only nineteen. You are a kid, a kid wanting to marry a child. You need our consent, and I won't give it. I won't sign a damned thing."

The words continued in torrents. She ranted, she raged. Finally, her words slowed, and Sonny, like a prize fighter waiting for his opponent to tire, saw his opening.

"In a few days, I will be old enough that I won't need your consent. I am going to marry Lise. I won't be living here anymore."

"You can stay here if you want, son," Tom offered.

"Thanks, Pop, but you seem to have enough problems right now. As soon as I find a place for Lise and me to live, I will be leaving. Now I'm going into town for a while." He turned and walked out the back door. Clara was stunned. Tom shook his head and walked back into the front room.

Sonny searched to find a suitable place to live in the time he had available, but could find nothing. Frustrated, he told Lise of the problem. She suggested he go to her father and ask for help, which he did the following day.

Henry poured his coffee into a saucer, put a cube of sugar between his teeth, and took a noisy, thoughtful slurp.

"It wouldn't be good for you to live here for very long. I bought a lot across the street for a second garden and to use the little garden house on it as a tool shed." He went on, musing, thinking to himself aloud: "It's small, about twelve by twenty feet, but it could be used as a kitchen and living room combined. It already has a small kitchen woodstove. Another room could be added, a bedroom ten by twelve feet. It's the wrong time of year to start building outside, but if everything waited for the right time to start, not much would be done, would it?" Then he pronounced, "Assuming you would help, it wouldn't take long to build. You pay me rent when it is done."

"I can help, Mr. Hofmann. When should we start?"

"Now. We go look at it."

It was dark by the time Henry and Sonny finished cleaning out the garden tools in the house, staking out for the addition, and locating the door and windows.

On their way back across, Henry pointed to the outhouse; "I will leave it to you to clean the shithouse. I have done it enough already."

***

Sonny and Lise drove to Gardiner in early December on a very grey, very wet Tuesday morning to get their marriage license. Katie was with them to sign for Lise. Mixed rain and snow fell all the way down the valley and all the way back. The

Suquamish River was swollen and roiling. They returned Friday morning—there was a three-day waiting period—to be married by a justice of the peace. Friday morning, the weather was just as grey, just as wet, and the river was more swollen, nearing flood stage.

The ceremony was brief and efficient. By its end, Sonny and Lise knew they were married and had a document to show for it. They had their photograph taken at a local photography shop at 10:30 a.m. before lunch at the Carlton Public Market, which had a bakery, dairy goods store, butcher shop, delicatessen, and a small cafe all under one roof. Afterward, perhaps in celebration, they purchased a Stewart Warner table radio at a nearby appliance store.

Lise was stunned by the all the stores and goods and business activity in Gardiner. Automobiles were everywhere. When she remarked about it to Sonny, he gave a flippant response intended to make him appear knowledgeable of worldly ways and things, but she knew he was impressed, too. Katie was silent and walked behind them the whole time.

Sonny drove back to Wallace with more caution because the roads were wet and slippery, and it had become colder. He didn't want an accident. The gravity of what had occurred that morning was settling in.

Between Martinsburg and Salkum, Katie spoke, for the first time since she ordered her lunch: "Sonny, Lise and I have made up a bedroom upstairs at our house for you and her. You can stay there tonight if you like, if you have no other place."

Sonny hesitated. "I'd like that Mrs. Hofmann. I just haven't had time to make arrangements for a place, with fixing up the little house across the street. I am sorry, Lise.

"It's okay, Sonny. We will be in our house in a week or so, before Christmas, which is what really matters."

***

Working with Henry was an unusual experience for Sonny. It was structured and orderly. But what was to be done was communicated with only a few words of broken English and a large number of grunts and gestures. Sonny had grown comfortable enough with the old man to call him Henry, whom he truly wanted to please. But he found himself talking more than necessary, more than he would under normal circumstances. He also knew he was "dancing around," taking two or three steps when only one was necessary. Sometimes Henry would stop what he was doing and just look at him, then shake his head. Once in a while, he would smile. When Sonny would forget something, Henry would say: *"Was Mann nicht im Kopf hat, hat Mann in den Beinen,"* which, as Sonny learned from Lise, meant, "When a man doesn't use his head, he has to use his legs." She told him it wasn't a compliment.

Sonny began to earn the old man's grudging respect. Though a little smaller, he was as strong as Henry, and he had the edge on endurance because of his youth. Sonny was also quick mentally and could compute numbers in his head faster than Henry could on paper. A difficult moment occurred when Sonny knew Henry had computed a measurement for a saw cut erroneously. Should he tell him? How?

Finally, as Henry reached for the saw to cut the joist, Sonny said: "Henry, you might want to figure that length again. I may be wrong, but it looks a little short." A similar situation arose when Henry had reversed the angle in marking a saw cut for a rafter. Although Henry responded in each case with a grunt, the old man was taking Sonny seriously. He liked Sonny maybe a little more each day.

Meal time at the Hofmann's was a pleasant experience, better than Sonny was used to. The food was less greasy. Beef and chicken were served several times a week, never pork, which was against Adventist dietary restrictions. Soup was often served with lots of bread or rolls and butter. Katie made bread and rolls twice a week. Lise and her sister made the butter. Dinner table conversation was quiet, but informal, and Sonny, with his outgoing personality, was the major contributor.

"Henry, tell me about the old country and the Russians," Sonny asked Henry at dinner one Sunday afternoon.

"They are rough people, not to be fooled with," said Henry sternly, abruptly, scarcely slowing the chewing of his food.

"So how did the Germans measure up to the Russians where you were?" Sonny asked easily, casually, unaware of the emotions he was calling up in Henry.

"What do you mean 'measure up'?" Henry stopped and swallowed. "Why the hell should Germans 'measure up' to Russians?"

"Well, who was the toughest? If the Germans were to go to war with the Russians today, who would win?"

"You show your ignorance. War isn't a game. It is brutal and destructive. People are wounded, maimed, and killed."

"Were you in a war?" Sonny asked, his tone almost challenging, which made Katie very uneasy and Lise to look back and forth at Sonny and her father in apprehension, even fear.

"I was in the army during the Russo-Japanese War in Manchuria. The Japanese army won. What does it matter?" responded Henry. "Three of my four brothers were also in the Russian Army at different times."

"The Russians lost? The Russians can't be too tough, if they lost to the Japs," smiled Sonny. "How can a giant European country loose to a little bitty Asian country?" Lise half expected her father to ask Sonny to leave the table, and she wanted to crawl under it.

"If men want to fight, and they are organized and disciplined, they can beat a larger opponent," said Henry quietly, his eyes looking straight ahead.

"Why do you think the Russians would beat the Germans?" Sonny asked blindly, plunging ahead.

"Russia is too big, and it has too many people."

"But you said an organized, disciplined small army like the Germans would defeat a larger army," argued Sonny.

"I said they *can* defeat a larger army. That does not mean they *will* defeat a larger army. Why are you going on so about wars, armies, and fighting, and in such a way? These are not the kind of things people should be talking about around a dinner table. *Krieg sollte man nicht verherrlichen. Krieg zeigt den Menschen von seiner schlimmsten Seite. Das ganze Gerede ist nur Bloedsinn.* (Wars are not to be glorified. They bring out the worst in people. This is all foolish talk.)" He looked at Katie with an expression that pleaded, "is it really necessary that I be nice to this fool?" Katie nodded.

Not understanding German or recognizing Henry's expression, Sonny irrepressibly pushed ahead.

"What were the Russians like where you were?"

"Like you and me," responded Henry with irritation. "But most of the people in the Caucasus were not Russian or German. They were Circassian, Dagestani, Georgian, Azerbajani, and Kalmyk. Others, too. Many others."

"Never heard of them."

"No reason to think you would. But they are there and have been for centuries. Russia fought some of them for nearly fifty years during the Caucasus War."

"So they must have been pretty good fighters?" asked Sonny.

"Yes. But what they really were, were people who wanted to be left alone, to raise their animals, grow crops, and live in peace, to be free from Russia and its tsars. The Circassians surrendered only after the Russian army demolished their villages, destroyed their livestock and fields, and burned the forests around their villages. You could still see some of the destruction when we were living there. The survivors, mostly Muslims, fled to the Ottoman Empire or were resettled in the plains to the north of the Caucasus. Russians and Germans came to the Caucasus after the war. The remnant tribesmen in both the lowlands and highlands hated us settlers, and they often raided us at night."

"If the Russians are so rough and tough, why did they quit fighting during the Great War?" asked Sonny.

"There was no good reason for Russian soldiers to defend their county. It was in turmoil. The peasants and the workers were rebelling. There was continual political unrest after Bloody Sunday and with the Revolution of 1905. Tsar Nicholas II was inept. Everyone was tired of war. Enough talk about Russia."

"Did you ever want to go back?" Sonny heedlessly continued.

Henry hesitated, and Katie said, "You did for a while, Papa."

"*Genug*," he responded, looking at her sharply. Then, "Not after Stalin proved himself to be crazy and cruel," he said to Sonny. "He was worse than Nicholas II, who was bad enough. So are we going to have more coffee?"

"I will get it, Poppa," said Lise, and she was out of her chair, into the kitchen, and back with the coffee pot in a matter of seconds. Henry saucered his coffee with a series of long slurps. When he was through, he got up and motioned to Sonny to go across the street with him and begin working on the house. It was cold, wet, and generally miserable, so they built a fire in the stove in the little house and worked inside.

Henry did not talk. Instead, he spoke in short commands as to what Sonny should be doing, where he should be working. Later, Henry became silent, consumed by his thoughts, so Sonny put away his tools and left. He wasn't sure whether Henry even noticed.

Sonny and Lise moved across the street into the little house a week before Christmas. Its furnishings, all very used, were few: in the kitchen, a table and two chairs; in the tiny living room, a thread-bare armchair, an old rocker that needed repair, a fern stand, and the Stewart-Warner table radio; in the bedroom, a bed, chest of drawers, and a night stand.

"We sure have enough room for a Christmas tree," Sonny remarked. Lise laughed, which Sonny enjoyed seeing. He couldn't remember her laughing since early October.

***

Lise delivered a boy at home in late April after a very long and difficult labor. Katie and the midwife called in Doc Nelson, the local physician, but even with his presence, a half hour later, the birth grew more complicated. Lise was hemorrhaging. The midwife had the infant and was attempting to get it to breathe; Doc Nelson was feverishly trying to staunch the bleeding with Katie assisting him, trying to follow his directions. Lise was unconscious and frightfully white. Sonny stood helplessly in the doorway of the small bedroom, frightened, tears streaming down his face. He had never seen so much blood, even when butchering hogs in the fall. *What the hell have I done,* he thought.

Then Doc Nelson said in rapid succession, "I think we've got it. Give me a towel to wipe my hands. Here. Quickly! Where's the baby? Give it to me." And with his mouth on its mouth and nose, he blew three little breaths into its lungs, raised the baby up by its ankles with his right hand, and smacked its buttocks with his left. The baby gasped and began to cry. Doc Nelson clamped the umbilical cord, severed it between the clamps, and passed the baby to the midwife.

"Keep him breathing and clean him up as you are able; I am going back to Lise. Sonny, it's a boy, but we are not out of the woods yet with Lise. Get more towels and hot water. We need to pick up this place so we can move around more easily. Move!" As he was speaking, Katie was picking up the bloody towels from the bed, the top of the chest of drawers, and the floor. Henry appeared at the door with a pile of fresh, folded towels and said, "Here." Sonny walked out the front door and wretched. He cleaned his mouth with his fingers, spit, went back into the house, and heated more water. It was raining, and mud was being tracked indoors. Lise wouldn't like that.

Doc Nelson stayed for some time, repeatedly checking Lise's pulse and breathing, making sure the bleeding had stopped. He heated blankets and put them on her, wanting to keep her as warm as possible. He checked the baby over carefully and listened to its lungs and heartbeat. They seemed normal, even after the trauma of a hard delivery.

He wrapped the baby in a warmed blanket and gave it to Katie: "Hold it close and warm. You know what to do."

He left with instructions to call him if there were any changes in Lise's breathing or pulse, or if she started to hemorrhage again, and said that he would come back in the evening. And he did, and the next day, and the next. He told Sonny and Katie that Lise had lost a lot of blood because of internal injuries she had suffered during the delivery, and that she would need time to recover with lots of bed rest. He also told them the baby was normal despite the trauma of its birth. Sonny had not even thought it could be otherwise.

Sonny asked Doc Nelson how much he owed him, telling him at the same time that he didn't have any money and that the best he could do was pay $5.00 a month until the bill was paid off.

Doc Nelson said, "I will send you bill. Pay me when you can." He would never send Sonny and Lise a bill, and they never asked him why.

***

Katie stayed with Lise and the baby, who had been named Marcus, while Sonny worked. There was no particular reason for the name. Lise just liked its sound, and it was different. She was up and about and caring for the baby by the end of May. Still Katie came by twice a day, a short walk across the street, to check in on Lise, once in the morning and again in the afternoon. Katie also washed the baby's diapers three times a week.

Henry was working again, this time with Wallace Falls Timber Company, the outfit Sonny was working for, logging out of Index. When Sonny had heard there were plans for putting in another side, Sonny told Henry the same night.

He went to work with Sonny the next morning on the speedie and talked to the woods boss, Burt Larson, who said in a burst of broken English: "Well, I will be goddamned, old Henry. It's been a long time. So you want a job? You are getting awfully damned old, aren't you? Well, if you are up to it, I can always hire another tough, old *Kraut,* at least for a while. Don't get ornery on me now, or your ass is out of here. Start Monday, when I get the full crew together. You can take the next log train back to camp." Henry was elated.

***

Sonny had not seen his folks since December, when he had gone over and got some clothes and a few other personal things. Their attitude toward Lise and his marriage angered him. They could have come over and seen them at least once before Lise had the baby, with their living only six miles away. And they didn't even come over to see the baby after it was born, or Lise while she was recovering. Doesn't look good when a family behaves like that.

Sonny had heard rumors his folks were losing the ranch, but he didn't believe them at first because his folks seemed to be always having financial problems and yet got by somehow. Then it all went to hell, faster than Sonny could keep up with.

Sonny and Lise, their new baby with them, drove over to see Tom and Clara on a June Sunday. Sonny drove into the yard of the house they had rented and saw the usual chickens scattering, the same dog getting up from the back steps, stretching, and ambling toward the car, wagging its tail. He could also see his father working out in back. He told Lise to wait in the car, got out, and walked toward his father.

"Hi, Pop. Been a while. How you like your new place?"

"Sure has, Sonny, and I've missed you." He ignored Sonny's question and went on, "Things haven't gone well for your mother and me. I suppose you heard the bank foreclosed on us. We moved here for the time being."

"I heard."

"Yep. That your wife in the car?"

"Yep. Her name is Lise, remember? Baby is in there, too. His name is Mark."

"Sorry we haven't come over to see you," Tom said. "Your mother and I have just been tied in knots over losing the ranch. Heard Lise had some problems delivering the baby. Is she okay now?"

"Seems to be. Is Mom inside?" asked Sonny.

"So far as I know."

"Is it all right if Lise and me go inside and show her the baby?"

"Sure. I am sure she would like to see you. I'll go tell your mother you're here." Tom started toward the house, and then he stopped and turned. "Sonny, I am sorry about the way your mother and me have behaved these past several months. We were just plain wrong."

"Yeah, you were, Pop. But you and Mom are the only parents I have, so we are going to have to work our way through this. Thanks for the apology anyway. I'll get Lise and the baby."

Clara was in the kitchen when Sonny and Lise came through the door, Sonny carrying the baby.

"Sonny," she cried. "I have missed you. May I see the baby?"

Sonny started to extend the baby to his mother, but drew it back awkwardly. "Mom, you remember Lise."

"I do. How are you, Lise? How are you feeling?"

"I am fine. And how are you, Mrs. Dubois?"

Clara's eyes darted to Lise's and held as she said softly, "Since we are family now, I suppose you can call me Mom."

"It will take me some time," Lise responded evenly and without emotion.

"May I hold the baby?"

"Yes. Give her the baby, Sonny. His name is Mark," said Lise, her eyes showing a ferocity Sonny had never seen before. It made him uneasy.

They went into the front room, which was a mess, worse than in the kitchen. Boxes were everywhere. Tom and Clara's bedroom door was ajar, and it was also a clutter. Lise was looking around uneasily, and Sonny was embarrassed.

"Pop tells me you're slowly getting settled after the move."

"We are one sorry outfit for now, Sonny. But we are going to get back on our feet, aren't we, Tom? We have done it before; we'll do it again." She handed the baby back to Lise. "He is a nice, healthy baby. You must be proud."

"I am," Lise responded. "We should be going, Sonny. Mark has to eat soon."

***

The loss of the ranch stripped Tom of his dignity. He moved about mechanically at work and at home, and spoke as few words as he could. His characteristic, easy chuckle was gone. Clara's vitality was crushed. Eddie was the only child remaining at home. Madeline had married Helmut Bauman, a sawyer at Wallace Lumber Company, the previous fall, and they lived up the road. He was from North Dakota, and his father, a German from Russia, lived nearby.

All through the summer and the early fall, they went through the motions of living. The weather turned in November, and the old Harrison place was cold, damp, and drafty. Tom went out to the woodshed after supper to cut some wood for the woodstove in the front room. The woodshed was a mess. Large, irregular pieces of split wood were just tossed in, helter-skelter. Tom had never gotten round to stacking them since they had moved there: too many other things to do. Eddie was too young to do it right. The light from the kitchen offered a little illumination as he gathered pieces of split wood to be chopped into smaller pieces to fit into the heater. It was raining, and the wind was blowing. There were lots of shadows.

Tom used a double-bitted cruiser's axe for chopping smaller wood. It was lighter than a felling axe, so he could steady the larger piece with his left hand and easily swing the cruiser's axe with his right. The work went rapidly even though the light was poor and constantly flickered from the wind.

Tom swung the axe down on a larger piece of wood, and it split unexpectedly all the way to the chopping block, the axe head following. He felt a massive numbing pain from his left hand. Tom released his grip on the axe, grabbed his left hand, and felt a void where his thumb should have been. Raising his left hand into the light, he saw the open wound and the blood beginning to flow from it. The axe was sharp, and the thumb was gone. He dropped to his knees on the ground and felt about on the dirt floor littered with damp woody debris. He finally found it. In the light, it seemed like a small, broken off spike knot or a small gray stick. The pain was now severe and throbbing, making him nauseous.

Tom stumbled through the rain to the back door, holding his left hand in his right.

"Clara," he yelled, "Help me."

"Jesus, God, what have you done to yourself?" She knew before she had even finished her sentence and spun around, grabbed a clean dish towel, put the severed thumb into his left palm, and wrapped the towel tightly around his hand. She yelled to Eddie that Poppa had hurt himself, and they were going to town to Doc Nelson's house.

Tom was in shock, and the pain was the worst he had ever felt. When they arrived at Doc Nelson's house, he met them at the door as if he were expecting them. He quickly led them back to the examination room where he helped Tom lie down on the examination table and told Clara to sit in a chair. He unwrapped the towel from Tom's hand and put the severed thumb into a stainless steel bowl. Clara started to pass out. Tom stared blankly at his wound, while Doc Nelson staunched the bleeding with gauze squares as he examined the wound.

"You have a sharp axe, Tom," he paused, and then continued talking mostly to himself, "Very clean wound, pretty much to the joint. I can close it with sutures after I remove a little tissue. I'll have to deaden the hand first. You will need something for pain before I begin. Clara, hold this compress, and I will be right back. Oh," and he picked up the severed thumb and looked it over, "There is nothing that can be done with the thumb. It is gone." He pitched it back into the stainless steel bowl. He went into the next room and got some morphine. After injecting it with a syringe, he turned to Clara and said: "You should go into the waiting room and rest. You will be here a while. I need to close up the wound and stabilize Tom. He is in shock. He should rest. He will not be going to work for a week or so."

"All Tom and I seem to have is trouble. All poor people get these days is trouble, like flies to shit. I hate it."

"I know. Hard times, and for a long time."

"Tom and I don't have any money to pay you."

"I know. Pay me when you can. I have to work on Tom now."

***

Rumors abounded around logging camps in the Suquamish River Valley about how logging operations were increasing up in the Skagit River Valley, how plenty of jobs were available. Tom listened quietly and began asking fellows who seemed knowledgeable, whom he trusted, what they thought. All of them indicated the rumors were worth checking.

One said: "Hell, Tom, what have you got to lose? You're not going anywhere working here. The best you can get here is keeping the job you got." Tom winced at the words.

That changed the following Saturday when Joe Zach came by and told him he was going on his own—that he'd got a logging contract south of the Skagit River and well east of Mount Vernon in the foothills. Tom had worked for Joe, and they were friends, both members of IOOF. Joe liked Tom's easy-going nature, mechanical knowledge, and loyalty. Tom liked Joe because, although he was one of the toughest fellows he had ever met in the woods, he was also one of the fairest and most hardworking. Joe never asked his logging crews to do anything more than he could. And he never missed a pay day.

"I am putting together a crew, and I want you to be on it as a hook tender and yarder operator. I bought a gasoline-powered yarder up there, used, but fully operational if it is maintained right, which is why I want you. I am asking a few other guys from around here to go with me, like Ray Larsen as bullbuck and George Ashby as head loader. The rest of the crew I am hiring from up there."

Tom told Clara about the offer.

"How far from here is it?" she asked

"About sixty miles."

"That is a good distance. We would have to move."

"Yes. But Joe has given me an opportunity. I got to go someplace different. There is too much talk in town about us losing the ranch and me cutting off my thumb, like I am a damned hard-luck loser," Tom answered.

"But you have a job here."

"Yeah, and where is it going? I can do better. I know I can."

The conversation stopped, while each of them considered the moment and what they were about to do and how they felt about it. Clara spoke first. "Tell Joe you'll take the job. Take the car, go on up there on Saturday, and find us a place to rent. When you do, come back and get Eddie and me. I'll be ready. There is not much left to pack, really. Let's get the hell out of here."

Tom rented another Depression-beaten-down stump ranch, according to Clara, on a side hill near Clear Lake. It was the best

Tom could do in the time available. He repeatedly pointed out to Clara: "It's on the same side of the Skagit where I will be working."

When Clara saw the place for the first time, she observed: "It is pretty clear how we are going to get down to the road in winter, but how in the hell are we going to get back up?"

"I thought about that a bit, Clara," he chuckled. "I got on old block, a little three-eighth-inch cable, and a power winch, and I just thought I would yard our ass up there."

"You are crazy, Tom."

"The hell you say. Maybe our ship has come in. I start work tomorrow. Let's get unpacking. We've got a lot a work to do." He got back into his pickup truck, idling noisily, and started up the drive. Clara followed behind in their Hudson Six.

6. Move to Gardiner

1941–1944

Joachim Hofmann, who now insisted on being called "Joe," left Gardiner for Wallace at seven in the morning on Christmas Day. That he did not want to spend another holiday in his small apartment was the reason he gave for his coming home for Christmas. The real reason he wanted to drive up was because he knew if he stayed in Gardiner, he would find a poker game and drink all day and most of the night, like he had on Thanksgiving. It would cost him more than he could afford, and a hangover. He had been divorced for almost two years now, and holidays were tough, like they were for everyone who was split up. He might even drive over to see Lorna, his ex-wife, and the kids late on Christmas Day. He promised his mother he would. When his mother told him she would also have Lise and Sonny over for Christmas, he told her he would bring a turkey.

God, the weather is lousy, he thought as he drove across the trestle. It got worse as he moved up the valley on the other side of Tualco, where a steady rain fell, sometimes mixed with snow, not unusual for this time of year.

Joe had moved to Gardiner after his divorce and found a job as a driver for a local trucking company, Haggen Truck Lines. War preparations after the invasion of Poland by Nazi Germany were stimulating the US economy. The effects were evident even in western Washington State, which tended to lag behind the national economy, being out in the relatively remote Pacific Northwest. Logging operations and sawmills were operating near levels from prior to the 1929 stock market crash. Of course, many mills had closed during the Depression, so there were fewer of them—less competition.

Joe liked truck driving, liked going to the "dog house" at seven in the morning, having a cup of coffee from his thermos with the other drivers before getting his assignment from the dispatcher. He was a local driver, driving medium-sized trucks—pick up here, deliver there, usually in and around town. Sometimes he would have a longer run, down to Seattle, or up to various towns in the Skagit Valley. He would work off larger trucks as a "swamper" occasionally, when large loads were involved.

What made Haggen Truck Lines unique was that they had "a truck for every use"; they would haul virtually anything for a fee. So they had trucks of many kinds and makes, and the company would haul everything from canned goods to pulp bales to generators to heavy equipment, such as shovels, bulldozers, cranes, and donkeys. The company had remained profitable throughout most of the Depression and was in a good position to expand with the now growing economy. Eric Haggen, the owner, thought there were a lot of opportunities for hauling heavy equipment because of the rapid expansion in road building and logging operations. He needed another driver.

Joe thought Sonny, his brother-in-law, might be interested, and he told Eric Haggen about him. Sonny was a high rigger and loader for Greene Logging up in the Suquamish Valley who had experience with cable rigging and heavy logging equipment, which made him at least partially qualified for the job.

Haggen asked, "Okay, he knows rigging and equipment. Can he drive a truck?"

"Sure," Joe responded, not really knowing one way or the other, but from what he had heard, the kid seemed to be able to do just about anything in the woods. Haggen told Joe to invite Sonny down to Gardiner to apply for the job, which was his second reason for going up to Wallace for Christmas. He liked Sonny. He was a "goer," working for four different logging outfits in as many years. He always had work and each time he changed jobs, he got a better position.

Joe arrived a little after eight in the morning. He got the turkey out of the trunk and walked into the house.

"*Wie gehts,* Mama."

"*Gut, und du,* Joachim?"

He set down the turkey and hugged and kissed his mother. She turned to the turkey and began unwrapping it.

"Ahh, a nice fat bird! We will have a splendid Christmas feast. You know Lise and Sonny will be with us."

"*Ja,* and anybody else?"

"Julianna and your father, of course."

"Where is he?"

"*Hier,*" Henry's voice sounded from the front room.

"I will get a get a cup of coffee and be in there in a minute, Pa," Joe said, raising his voice so it would be heard in the other corner of the house.

"Go. Talk to him," said his mother in a low voice. Many wounds had been inflicted on Joe and Henry's relationship by each of them through the years, the last being Joe and Lorna's divorce, which Henry thought was stupid with two kids involved. An opportunity for a normal conversation between them might be healing.

Joe talked with his father a little longer than usual, which was difficult. Henry had become preoccupied with the war in Europe, which had been going on for over a year. He had voted for the first time in the 1940 presidential election—for Roosevelt—and unlike some, found coherence in the US military buildup, including the new draft and Roosevelt's assurance he would "not send American boys into any foreign wars." To Henry it was simple: Be prepared for war, even help allies in waging war against enemies, but don't become engaged until and unless national borders were violated. Henry hated the Nazis and loathed the Soviets. In his mind, they were of the same cloth, both beneath contempt. Hitler and Stalin were cruel, ruthless nutcakes. Their pact not to wage war against each other, signed the year before—which Henry had learned about on the radio—made them enemies after the invasion of Poland by Germany and the declaration of war against Germany by Great Britain. Henry would follow this argument with a recitation of how the Soviets had confiscated his parents' and his brothers'—Johann's and Rudolph's—farms in the Caucasus in the aftermath of the Revolution of 1917, how his parents and brother Johann had died from starvation during the Famine of 1921 and the terrible winter of 1921-1922, how his brother Rudolph was forced onto a collective farm, and how he was seized in the middle of the night in 1937 never to be seen or heard from again. Joe had heard the stories of his grandparents and uncles many times, and had known all of them as a small boy in Russia. All of them had been responsible, caring people and good farmers.

Henry had become aware of Rudolph's arrest in 1939 thanks to a tattered letter that obviously had been traveling in the USSR mail system for months, given the date on the letter, the postage date on the envelope, and the date of its arrival in Wallace. It had triggered a week of outrage in Henry, and then several weeks of moroseness to the point that Katie again became very concerned about him. He placed the letter in its envelope on top of a small fern table in the front room, where each subsequent observation would prompt an outburst: "Look. Damned communists can't even deliver a letter."

Joe left and went over to Lise and Sonny's house. He knocked on the door, which Sonny opened before the final rap of his knuckles, the house being that small, it could be crossed from one side to the other in seconds.

"Hi, Joe. Come in out of the rain."

"Hi, Sonny. Hi, Lise." He hugged Lise and shook hands with Sonny.

After many complimentary observations among the three of them, including how big baby Mark was getting, Joe began: "Sonny, Haggen Trucking does a lot of heavy hauling and wants to do more. They need another driver who knows rigging because they are often involved with hauling heavy logging equipment. It is a pretty good outfit, and I talked to the owner, Eric Haggen, about you. He would like you come down and talk to him. The pay is good, and the work is much steadier than what you have now. Safer, too. No guarantees, but I think you should see him."

"When?"

"What about Monday?"

"What do you think, Lise?"

"Sure. But not a word to Mom and Dad. They wouldn't like it."

"Okay."

"I told him you can drive a truck."

"Sure I can. And even if I couldn't," Sonny winked, "I sure as hell could learn by Monday."

Sonny drove to Gardiner the following Monday. Eric Haggen liked Sonny's confidence, his obvious willingness to take calculated risks, and his knowledge of cable rigging and logging equipment—the very knowledge the heavy hauling component of the company lacked. He never asked Sonny about whether he knew how to drive a truck. He figured Sonny would say "yes" anyway, and he clearly had much more than passing knowledge about automotive vehicles. Instead, Haggen called his head mechanic and asked him to check out Sonny on one of the big rigs. The mechanic selected the 1938 Kenworth with the Hall-Scott 177 gasoline truck engine. The "check-out ride" evolved into a demonstration of the mechanic's knowledge of Kenworth engineering and Hall-Scott engines, launched by Sonny's enthusiasm and numerous questions. Time got away from them both, and the ride itself was no more than a couple of blocks, with the mechanic doing most of the driving. They had to quit because the mechanic had to finish the repairs he was doing before the call from Haggen. Sonny passed and was offered the job, to begin the first Monday of the New Year.

Sonny asked about pay, and Haggen's response was "Teamster union scale."

"So what is that?" Sonny asked.

"It is the hourly wage rate negotiated with the local Teamsters union for the kind of work you would do, which is what I want to talk to you about. Sonny, I want you to understand what this company does and why we provide truck transportation services for companies, hauling whatever they want to wherever they want. It's pretty simple. We get paid for picking things up on time and delivering them on time, undamaged. Always undamaged, and I stress that to you. When we succeed, we make money. When shipments are late or damaged, we lose money. It is the same for heavy hauling. Labor problems are often the cause of late or damaged shipments, which I don't want because, again, they cost me money. The Teamsters, when the union is working well, helps us avoid labor problems. Perkins is the union steward here, and he will make arrangements with Local 38 for you to see about joining. It's up to you whether you join. This is not a closed shop. But I don't want any labor problems. So when you come to work here a week from now, I want you to have made a decision about the union, one way or the other. Is that clear?"

"How much does it cost?" Sonny asked.

"You go down to Local 38 and figure all that out. Okay?"

Sonny waited for Joe after work. At nearly 7:00, a truck rolled in and parked, and Sonny watched Joe stiffly get out and walk toward him, shifting his back like he was trying to get the kinks out.

"Hey, Joe, can I buy you a beer?"

"Sure. Let me punch out, and I'll be right with you."

When Joe returned, he climbed into the car and asked: "How did it go?"

"Good! Got the job and joined the union. I start Monday after New Year's Day."

"Swell. Are you going back up to Wallace tonight?" asked Joe.

"After I have a couple of beers and supper with you, I will," replied Sonny. "And I am buying."

Sonny told him of his plans during supper. He would come to Gardiner next Sunday and begin looking for a house to rent. He would bring Lise and Mark down from Wallace as soon as he got settled in his new job and located a suitable place to live. Joe told Sonny that he could stay with him until he had found a place to live. He had enough room.

Joe suggested while drinking his beer, "You should probably buy some new work clothes, Sonny. The ones worn by the drivers down here are different than the ones you wear in the woods. A lot of guys wear blue-and-white striped overalls. They also wear long-sleeved collared shirts, buttoned down the front. They all have gloves and wear hats. Some guys wear flat caps. Others wear peaked caps with a leather bill. Haggen orders them a couple of times a year for the drivers who want them, and the company will pay for them. Whatever hat you buy, stick your union button on it. It answers a lot of questions, and you, as a new guy, don't want to answer a lot of questions.

Now I need some sleep. I'm bushed. Would you drop me off at my apartment?"

Sonny paid the check, dropped Joe off, and was driving across the trestle east of town fifteen minutes later. He was back up at Wallace just before 11:00. Lise was waiting up for him.

"You're awfully late, Sonny. I was getting worried."

"I had supper with Joe. I got the job. Start Monday after New Year's. It'll give us more money and stability. We will be moving to Gardiner as soon as I find a place to rent. In the meantime, I am moving in with Joe during the week and will back here on weekends. Now let's go to bed. It's been a long day."

Heavy hauling at Haggen Trucking was everything Sonny wanted in a job. Each hauling job was unique in one way or other, with its own set of problems because of the size and weight of the equipment or its location. The three other heavy haulers and Sonny were given authority to experiment in resolving them, and because of their frequent successes, they received considerable attention and encouragement from Eric Haggen, who often visited heavy hauling job sites, either loading or unloading.

Sonny loved the big equipment and being the center of attention. Unknown to the other drivers, Haggen had bought Sonny one of the peaked hats with a leather bill and the company's nickel-platted emblem in front. Joe warned him that some of the other drivers were calling him Eric Haggen's "fair-haired boy" behind his back.

"That might be," Sonny retorted, "but I am making him money. And with the overtime pay, I'm making more money than I ever thought possible."

Lise and Mark moved down to Gardiner in April, after Sonny found a two-bedroom house in the north end of town in a middle class neighborhood, one street east of Main and two blocks south of 19th Street. Moving inevitably has its challenges, and Henry was the first of them for Sonny and Lise. He could not understand why Sonny would leave his high rigger job in the woods for a job driving an "auto truck" in a town forty miles away. Why would he and Lise leave Wallace after all the work they did "fixing up the little house across the street?"

"What are they thinking?!?" he would exclaim.

After Henry had repeatedly expressed his misgivings, Katie responded impatiently: "Sonny sees more opportunities than you and I, and he is blessed with confidence and youth so he can seize them. Let him and Lise make their own decisions on what is important to them."

"But what about the money and work we put into the little house to make it better?"

"Rent it to someone else!" she said sharply.

Joe was the second challenge. As a result of a dispute with his landlord, he was told to move out of his apartment by the end of May. Lise and Sonny agreed that he could move in with them until he found something suitable.

"After all, Lise, it was Joe who put me onto my job at Haggen. I owe him something, and he is your brother." Joe lived with them for nearly six months, during which a stormy relationship with a woman friend evolved into a difficult marriage destined from its inception to fail, which it did three years later when Joe returned from working in Alaska to find the money he had been sending her to be deposited in a joint savings account had been spent. It was all gone.

Lise's pregnancy was the third challenge. She and Sonny had their second child, a boy they named John, in mid-November of 1941. Twenty-one days later, Japan bombed Pearl Harbor, and the United States declared war on Japan. War was declared on Germany and Italy almost immediately thereafter. The world would never be the same again.

***

Tom and Clara began to reassemble the shards of their lives left by the Depression and the foreclosure on their ranch. Tom's job was steady, more so than it had been at any time during the Depression, and the money was good. Clara was spending it almost as fast as it was made, however. Things they had left in Salkum needed to be replaced, like a table, chairs, and beds. Eddie, their remaining child at home, needed new clothes and shoes. Hand-me-downs had reached their limit with him. Most of all, they wanted to put away some money so they could make a down payment on a house. Tom was fifty two, and Clara, forty three. Like everyone else, they wanted to own their own home in their old age, and this was fast approaching.

Logging technology changed rapidly during the late 1930s and early1940s. Steam-powered engines lost out to gasoline-powered engines before Tom's eyes. Virtually every logging outfit in the Skagit Valley used a high-lead cable yarding system and either a McClean boom or a heel boom to load logs—big changes from Tom's logging days in the 1920s. Power shovels equipped with gooseneck heel booms were being developed as mobile loaders. They would require fewer men in a loading crew. Log trucks were everywhere. Almost as many logs were coming out of the woods on log trucks as on rail cars. Many of the technological changes required increased operator skills and manual dexterity, and Tom's missing thumb was a problem from time to time, but he adjusted.

Clear Lake had several advantages in Clara's eyes. She liked the stores in Mount Vernon, and the produce and dairy products yielded by the farms of the Skagit Valley, which were abundant, varied, and of impressive quality. Clear Lake was not home, however. Neither was Salkum, actually, not with all the adversity the Depression had inflicted on Tom and her. Their children had moved away from the Suquamish Valley one by one. Only one was left, recently married Madeline, the youngest girl. So Clara was restless, unable to put roots down, as she had been most of her life, accentuating her flinty edginess. She didn't want to be that way, but circumstances made it so.

The crew Joe Zach had put together in 1940 was doing well by the middle of the following year. He was making money, and he bought two more log trucks. He told everyone he was out of the railroad logging business for good. It was a thing of the past. Joe routinely drove a log truck to work each morning and another home at night, occasionally boasting his was the last load of logs off the landing at night and the first truck on the landing in the morning.

The last time Joe Zach hauled logs off a mountain, he was being followed by Tom and another crew member in Tom's pickup. The brakes on the truck failed. To slow the momentum of the truck, Joe swung the trailer and the load of logs against the cut on the inside of the road. As the tractor came out of the drainage ditch at the base of the cut, it struck a log and mass of rocky debris, which caused the tractor to jackknife. The inertia of the load launched the logs past the tractor cab, tipping it on its side. The driver's side of the cab was crushed, and Joe's face and chest were mashed into the steering wheel, which had been broken in the wreck.

Tom and the other crew member were able to pull Joe out of the tractor cab, but to do so, they had to cut the steering wheel apart with a hacksaw. Joe's face and chest were lacerated and bruised, and his tongue was almost severed. He was bleeding profusely from his mouth and could barely talk. Once he was pulled out of the tractor cab, Joe insisted on walking to Tom's pickup on his own. They helped him climb into the back after Tom had cleared a place for him and had laid out their coats for a bed. Tom drove the rest of the way down the mountain with Joe being tended by the other crew member in the back. They stopped at the first place with a telephone, called an ambulance, and arranged to meet it on the way to the hospital in Sedro Wooley. When they met, Joe was transferred to the ambulance, which raced back to the hospital while the attendant tried to staunch the bleeding. Once there, Zach insisted he get off the gurney by himself. He was helped into the emergency room, where he died from his injuries.

Tom and the other crew member had tried to keep up with the ambulance in the pickup, but couldn't. They got to the hospital only in time to hear the doctor say Joe had died. His wife, Adele, hadn't arrived yet. When she came through the door about ten minutes later, everyone was standing mutely with ashen faces. The doctor stepped past them to meet her, and took her into the emergency room.

When she came out, she obviously had been crying. When Tom and others who had come to the hospital after hearing about the accident started toward her, she held up her hand to tell them to stay back. Then she motioned Tom over to her.

"I am sorry," he said.

She said, "I know you are, but I have prepared myself for this. Working in the woods is dangerous. Now go to work tomorrow morning and meet the crew. Tell them we are going to continue to operate. Pay day is Friday. I have been doing the payroll and paying the bills for Joe for years. You are the woods boss until I get someone else, which will probably be Joe's nephew, Leroy. Maybe Joe mentioned him to you. Clean up the mess at the accident. Bring down anything worth salvaging. Go home now and tell Clara."

"Okay."

"One more thing: we will shut down for Joe's funeral, which I will arrange for tomorrow."

Two weeks later, Leroy Zach showed up and said he was the woods boss. He looked the part and never did anything stupid to indicate otherwise. Zach Logging Company operated without interruption from Joe's death, except for the day of his funeral.

***

The summer of 1942 was hot and very dry. Wildfires were a threat, but logging was going full tilt on the ridges and mountains south of the Skagit. There was a war going on, and lumber was needed. While everyone in the area was aware of the fire danger, no one was taking unusual precautions. The Zach Logging crew was yarding logs about 700 feet from the bottom of a set. The friction of two large Douglas-fir logs being dragged across some downed trees ignited some logging debris about 500 feet from the landing. The fire quickly spread and started moving up the slope. Whistles blew, and crew members ran for firefighting tools. Those below the fire moved across the set to the access side of the landing. Climbing across all the logging debris made for slow going. Tom worked quickly to bring the logs toward the landing so the chokers could be unhooked and the lines slackened. Leroy Zach told the crew to save the equipment on the landing and the timber on the log deck by moving off the landing and log deck, and building a fire line below, a reasonable tactic given the size of the fire and its speed moving upslope.

The men worked feverishly, and the heat was becoming unbearable. All the while, the fire moved steadily uphill, crew members eyeing it as they worked, not wanting to get caught in any "blow up," their worst fear. The fire line held in the end, but its making required a furious and backbreaking effort.

Sweating profusely, Tom became short of breath, and he climbed, stumbled, and crawled back to the landing, the pain in his chest now shooting down both arms. He collapsed on the hot, dusty ground about the same time someone poured water over him. He saw it bubble on the surface of the hydrophobic soil as he was both breathing and eating the fine dirt and dust. He fought for control, but it would not happen. He lost consciousness.

When he awoke several hours later, he understood that he had had a heart attack and was in the hospital in Sedro Wooley, but he was unable to speak coherently to the doctor and nurses because he was terribly, terribly tired. Tom knew he was in trouble, and in the midst of his calamity, he dreaded Clara's coming to the hospital. He had failed again.

It took him some time to gain enough strength to go back to work—not in the woods, which would never happen again, but for someone who would pay him a reasonable wage. Regardless of what the doctor had told him, he knew he had to find something. They needed the money. Clara's resignation to the situation was unusual in its quietness. Tom expected that underneath it all, she was frantic, not knowing what was going to happen.

Finally, on one rainy November morning, Clara blurted: "Tom, are you up to going to Gardiner tomorrow to look for work? We could take Eddie out of school and spend the day. It is the closest place from here where industries are located with plants and mills, and I saw advertisements for workers in the paper when I was in town yesterday. Both you and I should go to work. Sonny is living in Gardiner; so is Suzie. We are in a fix right now, and they would be able to help us."

"We can drive down there tomorrow, Clara."

Tom got a job in the shipyard as a steam engineer in the power plant at the end of the week. Clara got a job as a cook in a nursing home. They went back down to Gardiner the following two days, located a house for rent, and enrolled Eddie in a nearby elementary school.

"I never seen so many things move so fast and well for us," Tom remarked. "I guess we put ourselves in a place where we could be a little lucky."

"Maybe," Clara responded. "But there is a better chance of getting a job if you go to where the jobs are, where business is growing. We stayed too long on the hill in Salkum, Tom. We were waiting for the jobs to come to us. We would have still been up there waiting for a job if we hadn't lost the ranch."

"Yeah, but I sure liked it up there," said Tom.

"But to stay there, you'd have to have a job that earned us a living, and we didn't have one. By the way, how many more miles are left in this old Hudson Six? It is six years old."

Tom shook his head and spoke with quiet resignation. "Enough to drive around Gardiner for a few years, while we put away enough money to buy a new one," he responded.

"Never liked a maroon-colored car. The paint oxidizes more than any other color."

"I know, but the price was right, and the car runs well."

"Are you feeling okay?"

"Sure. I'm okay. Sonny got us a truck, and he will help us move on Sunday."

***

The winter of 1943–1944 was unremarkable in western Washington State, raining a lot and snowing a little. The war effort was the overriding circumstance. Tires, gasoline, meat, sugar, coffee, and butter were rationed. Metallic consumer appliances had disappeared from stores. General Dwight Eisenhower had been designated Supreme Commander of Allied Forces in Europe in January 1944, and in that same month, allied forces had landed on the Italian coast at Anzio, thirty miles south of Rome. Haggen Truck Lines had all the business it could handle, including its heavy hauling operation.

Sonny and Lise had bought a two-bedroom house on the south end of town. They were able to buy it largely because Sonny had taken a six-month leave of absence from Haggen to go north to work on the Alcan Highway. Why Eric Haggen was receptive to him going was never clear to Sonny. And because of the miserable working and living conditions, the reasons for going there often became equally unclear. A normal work day was twelve hours, and the normal work week was six days. Mud and snow were everywhere, and at the same time. Miserable! But he had made money, and he had avoided the draft. Deferments were given for working on the Alcan Highway because it was viewed by the local draft board as essential to the war effort.

Lise was in the kitchen when she heard the mailman, and she went to answer. There was more mail than she expected, two bills and two letters, and one of the letters stuck out. It was from the local draft board. She opened it, and it was an "Order to Report for Induction into the Army" for Francis Claude Dubois. She broke into tears, and then she began to weep aloud, startling the children. She went to the telephone, called Haggen Trucking, and asked for Sonny. She was surprised when the office said they would get him. She thought he would be on the road. She told him of the draft board letter and asked him to come home, which he did.

They both cried for a time, Sonny because Lise was so distraught. Finally, he said: "Lise, getting a draft notice has been looming over us for months. My number just came up in the draft lottery. So I am going to be inducted. It doesn't mean I am going to die. But it does mean we are probably going to be apart for a while until the war is over. I have ten days until I have to report, and we have a lot to do during that time. Let's make the best of it."

Lise sobbed once and said quietly, "Okay."

"I am going back to work now and tell Eric Haggen. I'd like to tell my folks tonight, and go up to Wallace and tell your folks this weekend after I round up some gas."

The response of Sonny's parents was predictable. There was a long, awkward, emotional pause.

Tom cleared his throat and quietly began: "I suppose if ever there were a time when a war was justified and a draft made sense, this is it. So go and do what you have to do. Just don't take any unreasonable chances. We need you back whole."

Clara sniffled and, with her chin quivering, added: "Be careful son. I…" Before she finished her sentence, Eddie burst through the front door.

"Hi, Sonny. Hi, Lise. What you doing here?"

"I've been drafted, Eddie."

"No kidding? Wow! So when do you go?"

"Wait, Eddie," interrupted Clara, "Sonny, I just wanted to say Poppa and I will take care of, look after Lise, Mark, and John, while you are gone. She can call on us anytime."

"That would be nice, Mom," responded Sonny.

The conversation settled, Eddie asking most of the questions, Sonny answering. They didn't stay long, however; the boys had to get home to sleep. As they left, Sonny and Lise assured his parents they would see them again before Sonny reported.

Sonny and Lise arrived in Wallace at 1:00 on Saturday. Katie was in the kitchen, preparing dinner, which was nearly ready: cabbage rolls, canned green beans, and bread. Lise hugged her mother. So did Sonny. Hearing the commotion, Henry came into the kitchen. Sonny greeted him and shook his hand. Lise kissed him, and he nodded.

"So why do you come?" asked Henry.

"We came up here to tell you I have been drafted. I report for induction into the army in seven days."

Katie gasped and started to cry, her hand over her mouth.

"This is not good," said Henry. "How will Lise and *der Jungen* be cared for?"

"I am going to work, Poppa," said Lise.

"*Mein Gott*, Lise, what can you do?" Henry nearly shouted.

"I am going to work at Boeing. Well, I am going to apply for a job at the Gardiner plant as soon as Sonny is inducted. They are looking for workers."

"Lise, Boeing makes airplanes. Even I know that. How can a woman make airplanes?"

"Poppa, they break things down so women can do the work, one piece at a time. Then they put them together with machines and the women working together."

"But who is going to take care of the children?" asked Katie.

"I can hire a woman. She can live with me and the boys," responded Lise.

They struggled with their questions and responses as the boys ran back and forth between the dining room and kitchen, Lise telling them to stop running or taking things out of their hands when they had grabbed what they shouldn't have, Katie putting her hands to her head in anxiety, then to her mouth to hide her trembling lip, Henry shaking his head, attempting to make sense of it all.

Then Sonny said, probably louder than he should have, "Listen, I am not the only guy who has been drafted. Two hundred thousand men a month are being drafted to get the army up to strength to win the war. I don't know how Lise and

I are going to do all the things you are asking. But we will one way or other, like all the other families whose fathers, husbands, and sons have been drafted."

Katie said, "Good. And we will help. The food is getting cold. We should eat now."

After dinner, Sonny and Henry were having coffee at the dining room table while Lise and Katie were in the kitchen cleaning up. The boys were outside playing by the chicken pen. Henry was silent, obviously reflecting and wanting to give Sonny the benefit of his knowledge and experience.

After several slow, melodic slurps, he put his saucer down and said, "It is more important you stay alive than win the war."

"What?" asked Sonny quizzically.

Henry went on, ignoring Sonny's question; "Stay away from the Russians. They have experienced brutality beyond anything you have known. Stalin has debased and corrupted them by killing millions of people through forced famine, mass starvation, pogroms, purges, deportations of entire populations to remote and forbidding places, and sending hundreds of thousands to forced labor camps operating under the direst conditions. He is a cruel monster."

"I thought Hitler was the monster, Henry?" Sonny asked, barely catching himself from being a fool by teasing his father-in-law, who was completely serious and well intentioned.

"He is. And he is a terrible leader. But Stalin is a monster in his cruelty to his own people. I am sure he killed—murdered—my brother Rudolph in a forced labor camp and sent what was left of his family to Siberia. Hitler is a monster in his cruelty to non-Germans like Poles, Ukrainians, Jews, and Gypsies. Both are crazy, rabid dogs. But Britain and the US are not naming Stalin for what he is because of politics, because his armies are fighting the Germans. He is an evil monster, regardless of whether his armies are fighting the Germans."

"What are you saying, Henry?"

Henry went on as if he had not heard the question. "The war in the Eastern Front is over with the defeat of the German army in Stalingrad. The German army is now like a wounded, savage beast, a wolf, being hunted down by an equally savage beast, a bear. It will be a long and ugly ordeal. But there will be more than enough time for an Allied invasion of Europe in the Western Front, during which there will be terrible fighting and atrocities." Then his eyes focused on Sonny. "You will probably be a part of this fighting. If you are, look out for yourself. No one else will. They will be too frightened."

"I will, Henry. You can be sure of it."

7. War

Sonny had never been so cold. It was Christmas Day, and he was driving north in an M8 armored car on an icy, snowy road in southern Belgium. Everything was white except for the dark grey forms of farmhouses, barns, sheds, and trees. The scout jeep was about 100 yards ahead with its driver, scout leader, and machine gunner. The M8 and its four-man crew—commander and gunner up in the open turret, radio operator and driver seated below and forward, side-by-side in the hull—were covering with its 37mm gun and 30 cal. machine gun. M8s were easily recognizable by their six wheels—three to a side—with one axle forward and two axles in the rear. They were small tanks with wheels instead of tracks. Behind the M8 was another jeep with a 60mm mortar and crew.

The three vehicles and their crews made up one section, and three sections composed one reconnaissance platoon. Three reconnaissance platoons together with the headquarters and service elements made up one cavalry troop, a company-sized unit of about 110 men.

The reconnaissance vehicles moved at varying speeds because they were part of a much larger, coordinated operation led by the 4th Armored Division to relieve the 101st Airborne Division in Bastogne, which had been surrounded by German army units in their Ardennes Offensive, begun nine days earlier on 16 December. The 6th Squadron of the 6th Cavalry Group (Mechanized) was assigned to screen the right flank of the 4th Armored Division, while the 28th Squadron of the 6th Cavalry Group was assigned to screen the division's left flank, and when that mission was completed, to move north toward the town of Recogne, twelve miles southwest of Bastogne, to assess the limit of the German advance. C Troop of the 28th Squadron, with its three reconnaissance platoons, was forward and fully deployed. Sonny had seen the other sections of his platoon at times during the day. Their movements made them stand out, for everything else was still. Nothing stirred about the farmhouses, not even smoke coming from the chimneys. No farm animals were out in the weather because it was too cold and there was too much snow.

Sonny was a replacement who had arrived at the squadron headquarters with three others and a load of K-rations in the back of a two and a half-ton truck near the German village of Karlsbrunn on 12 December. He was assigned to 3rd Platoon of C Troop as an armored car driver. His previous eight months had been a swirl of NCOs and officers; military posts; an unending variety of training activities—day and night—without stop, with all sorts of firearms and equipment, including jeeps, trucks, armored cars, half-tracks, and tanks. Sonny had shipped out of Baltimore to England, then across the English Channel to France and a replacement depot. He had no idea where it was or what route was taken to deliver him to his unit. All he had roiling around in his head was a chaotic assortment of words and phrases and a crazy mix of exaggerated images, like a broken movie newsreel. He was disconnected from everything he knew and cared about, unable to articulate his experiences in a coherent set of thoughts. His attention was focused on keeping the M8 on the icy road, while listening to the instructions and frequent criticisms of the vehicle commander, Sergeant Corson. Bastard!

C Troop pulled into a village late in the afternoon, a cluster of nine farmsteads about an intersection of back roads. It was quickly cleared under the cover of the M8s. The recon platoons were oriented to the north, east, and west, and the headquarters section to the south. Inhabitants of the village were confined to their houses—actually their cellars, with one person per family allowed out to care for farm animals. There was no protest. Everyone was too scared: scared of the Germans, scared of the unknown. The vehicles were pulled up alongside or behind buildings. It would have been more desirable to disperse them among the trees in nearby forests, but they would have been impossible to get to because of the snow and the poor off-road capability of the M-8s.

Sonny ate his K-rations cold. No fires were allowed. He was not sure what he was eating, could have been corned beef hash. No one in the platoon was particularly friendly, which was to be expected. He was the replacement, and it was too cold to do anything but accept the aloofness and drive the M8. Later, Sergeant Sack, the platoon sergeant, came by and told the men what they would be doing tomorrow: screening the left flank of the 4th Armored Division and reconnaissance, attempting to locate the enemy. They would be in Recogne tomorrow, or thereabouts.

Sonny was on guard from two to three in the morning. Well before first light, the vehicles were cranked and they were back on the road. It was snowing; the beginning of the third straight such day since they'd left Karlsbrunn. The platoon moved cautiously, with the roads as slick as they were the day before. If the brakes of the M8 were applied hard, the combat vehicle would skid uncontrollably for several yards. Sonny often heard shelling in the distance, northeast of the direction they were heading.

As the 28th Squadron neared Recogne in the afternoon, B and C Troops were sent northeast to Moircy and Remagne along the Ourthe River approximately eight miles due west of Bastogne. A defensive perimeter was formed at day's end, with the vehicles up against the sides and behind the buildings. For the next four days, the 28th Squadron conducted reconnaissance and screening missions and established communications among scattered units. Nights and days were difficult to distinguish. Both were cold and varying combinations of white, grey, and black. The shelling in the distance was almost continuous.

The 6th Squadron rejoined the 6th Cavalry Group at Recogne on 28 December and was immediately sent into action west of the 28th Squadron. The next day, a 6th Squadron reconnaissance patrol made contact with British forces to the north, which fixed the limit of the German advance. That night, Sonny could hear vehicles, mostly trucks. Someone said they sounded like our army trucks, and that they probably belonged to an infantry outfit that was getting ready to move through and engage the Germans.

Food was a problem, and Sonny and the others in his platoon were always hungry—sometimes more hungry than cold. They had taken to "liberating" food wherever and whenever they could find it. Sausages and bread were prized and were quickly gathered when clearing a village or a farm. Wine and cognac were good, too. Alcohol helped with the cold. Most nights they would commandeer a farmhouse or barn to sleep in. One night they slept in a shelter made from the snow, which was miserable. No sleep; just shivering with their eyes shut and wondering why the army didn't have better cold-weather clothing, equipment, and food.

Both 6th Cavalry Squadrons were moved, during a snow storm, about twelve air miles east to a location south of Bastogne at the end of December. The 28th Squadron was attached to the 35th Infantry Division to fill gaps in its front that had occurred as a result of heavy fighting around the village of Lutrebois over several days, and the 6th Squadron was put in reserve, patrolling between the 35th and 26th Infantry Divisions and providing rear area security. (The 6th Cavalry Group, the 35th Infantry Division, and the 26th Infantry Division were all components of III Corps, which in turn was a part of the Third Army, commanded by General George Patton. Other components of III Corps during the Ardennes Offensive included the 4th Armored Division, the 6th Armored Division, and the 90th Infantry Division.)

A few days later, the 28th Squadron was ordered to rejoin the 6th Squadron for an assault through a portion of the front that had opened up between the 35th and 26th Infantry Divisions. The mission was to close in on and destroy a regiment-sized pocket of German soldiers, located near the villages of Harlange and Watrange in Luxembourg, a short distance to the east.

Lieutenant Parker, the platoon leader, told the 3rd Platoon that the mission of the 6th Cavalry had been changed from screening and reconnaissance to direct assault and pursuit of the enemy and that C and B Troops were going to make a dismounted attack on the villages of Harlange and Watrange. Covering fire would be provided by the 6th Squadron, reinforced by two tank troops and a self-propelled tank destroyer platoon. Once the towns were secured, the 6th Squadron would move through in a mounted attack northeast through the village of Tarchamps, destroying the German pocket and shutting off possible German escape routes.

Lieutenant Parker went on, "We will coordinate with A Troop in bringing up our vehicles once the reinforced 6th Squadron has moved through and out of Harlange and Watrange. Then we will rejoin the attack." Lieutenant Parker concluded, "We are going to punch through whatever German units are in front of us. No stopping. Haul ass and bypass. Make sure all vehicles are topped off and have three days of rations in them, and that each of you has an automatic weapon, preferably a Tommy gun. And lots of ammo. There won't be much need for long shots tomorrow. Everything will be close and personal, so we want fire superiority. We are to be at the line of departure at 5:30 a.m. Any questions?" No questions were asked.

The next day was grey and cloudy with a heavy snowfall. C and B Troops entered into the southwest corner of the Harlange Pocket on foot. Harlange and Watrange were secured by 11:00 a.m. with occasional intense fighting and covering fire. The reinforced 6th Squadron was committed through them, and the fresh cavalrymen were soon engaged in ferocious battle, which the 28th Squadron joined, mounted in their vehicles. They continued the fight, mounted and dismounted, in the snow all day, through most of the night, and well into the second day without letup. The fighting was fierce and decisive with the 6th Cavalry prevailing. Once Tarchamps had been seized, and seeing that he had the advantage, the 6th Cavalry commander, at his own discretion, ordered the cavalrymen to continue the attack northeast to the tactical ground around the village of Sonlez, where they linked up with the 90th Division, closing the pocket and finally eliminating it. A reported 500 German soldiers were killed, and over 300 surrendered in the assault. Also, eight 88mm guns and five *Nebelwerfer* rocket launchers were captured.

The third day was exhilarating for the cavalrymen, even though they were terribly fatigued from the fighting. Like his comrades, Sonny was elated, in part because he took a Thompson submachine gun with two 30-round magazines and an FN Browning M1922 semi-automatic pistol from a surrendering German officer. Sonny knew where the submachine gun had come from. It had to have been from a soldier of an American airborne outfit. And he got it back.

While the cavalrymen were clearing the area around Sonlez, Sergeant Sack and Sergeant Corson "liberated" several pounds of wurst, loaves of bread, and many bottles of cognac for the 3rd Platoon, which the men noisily wolfed and gurgled down well into the night. Sonny thought better of Corson. Maybe he wasn't such a bastard after all. He still didn't know about Sack.

The two cavalry squadrons improved their defensive positions until fresh infantry troops came through. Afterward, the 28th Squadron moved south to a reserve position where vehicles and equipment were repaired and resupplied. The cavalrymen even got some sleep—and, surprisingly, mail from home. Sonny hadn't thought of home in days, if not weeks, and he didn't open his mail. It would only sharpen the pain of his being away at war. The damage Sonny's M8 had sustained during the Harlange Pocket battle was more than he had expected. All its equipment, including crew bedrolls and personal gear strapped onto the exterior, were gone, shot, or blown off. They had even lost their cable towlines. The other two M8s in the platoon were also damaged, more or less. It was nerve-wracking to see. At one point, Sonny hid behind his M8, uncontrollably shaking with a kind of fear he had never experienced before.

An artillery battery and a tank destroyer company were attached to the 28th Squadron on 18 January, indicating it would soon move into battle. When Sonny was sent to the rear with Phelps, the M8 gunner, to get cable towlines for the M8, he heard a familiar voice singing "I'm an Old Cowhand." Sonny, remembering the winter dance in Salkum in 1936, walked in the direction of the singing. He didn't get far before he was stopped by a sentry.

"Who's that singing?" he asked the sentry. "Sounds like somebody I know."

The sentry responded, "Oh, that's our C.O., Lieutenant Barton. He does that sometimes."

"Frank Barton?"

"Yeah."

"Frank Barton from Tualco, Washington?"

"I don't know about Tualco, Washington, but his name is Frank Barton. He received a battlefield commission about five months ago and now he commands this tank destroyer company, part of the 134th Infantry."

"Can you get a message to him?"

"Sure."

"Tell him 'Sonny Dubois, C Troop, 28th Squadron, 6th Cavalry Group, says he is glad he can still carry a tune after all this shootin' and to look him up sometime when he is able. It'll surprise the hell out of him."

"I'll tell him."

"Gotta go. Thanks." He returned to where Phelps was waiting. And they moved further to the rear to get the towlines.

The reinforced 28th Squadron moved out before first light the next morning, moving rapidly north, relieving two infantry regiments, and surging across the Wiltz River. After forming a bridgehead, the squadron then captured the small town of Winseler and also Wiltz, a larger town a mile to the east. Intense fighting was involved, but nothing like at Harlange.

Both squadrons of the 6th Cavalry Group advanced, screening the right flank of III Corps. The cavalrymen drove northeast and east, across the uplands between the Clerve and the Our Rivers. The steep, twisted inclines down into and up out of the narrow, sinuous river valleys were fearsome, particularly with Germans anywhere and everywhere. Road mines were a constant concern. The floor of Sonny's M8 was sandbagged because of the thinness of the bottom of the hull, like all the other M8s in the troop. None of the crew members were sure a layer of sandbags would work, but it was better than only one inch of steel in any case. The mountains and hills were mostly forested. Indeed, forests were everywhere, and there were Germans in them, which meant Germans were everywhere, attempting to slow the advance of the American army toward their damn, bloody homeland.

The 6th Cavalry Group was assigned a five-mile stretch on the west side of the Our River, from the town of Vianden north to the village of Gemund, with the 6th Squadron to the north and the 28th Squadron to the south. It was the extreme southern end of the sector assigned to III Corps. Vianden was still held by the Germans and would have to be cleared because it was on a main road east into Germany and the Siegfried Line.

C Troop was deployed in a forest on a hill overlooking the Our River northwest of Vianden. Platoons were instructed to dig in because 88s were expected to be in the woods across the Our. When 88 shells started whistling that night, Sonny was glad his foxhole was covered with the logs that he and Hermann, the M8 radio operator, had found and put over the top. He yelled that to Hermann, who was sharing the foxhole with him, almost every time a shell came whistling in. Hermann nodded, too frightened to say anything. They dug the hole deeper the next day and reinforced the top with more logs and dirt.

That first night's firing was largely harassing fire. C Troop subsequently learned how accurate German 88 crews could be—and also that forward observers were nearby on the west side of the Our River in Vianden and had registration points on road intersections, critical terrain features, and major physical structures. It was bloody horrific when someone blundered into them.

***

Lise walked up to Carlton, one of three main north-south streets in Gardiner, with two friends from work. They were bundled against the cold and wet, normal for a February in the Pacific Northwest. Two of them were riveters working on the assembly floor of the Boeing plant. Lise worked in the tool room, checking equipment in and out. It was a little after 11:00 p.m. and they had just got off working the swing shift.

"Brrr. It's cold. Heard anything from Sonny?" one asked.

"Nothing, which worries me. I haven't received a letter since way before Christmas. The paper says the Germans have been pushed back into Germany, and I thought I would have heard from him by now. How about you?"

"Bob is in the artillery, and he writes often. I have been getting letters almost every day, except for twelve days in late December and early January. Apparently his unit does not move around like your husband's does. What unit is your husband in?"

"6th Cavalry."

"Your husband rides horses?" she asked, puzzled.

"No, no," she laughed, "it is a mechanized cavalry unit. He drives an armored car. He says it looks like a tank only it has wheels instead of tracks."

"We have got to turn here. See you tomorrow."

"See you tomorrow," Lise called back over her shoulder. She was weary after working an eight-hour shift, but the swing shift was kind of nice. Much better than working nights, which she hated, like everyone else. The only good thing about working nights was working days the following week.

Two more blocks, she thought as she crossed the street and started down the sidewalk of the long hill to her house. A few minutes later, she unlocked the door and flipped on the light switch. Nothing stirred. The boys were staying with her folks, who had moved down from Wallace and were living across the alley. It was a welcome surprise that they had moved to Gardiner.

Lise had told her mother how wonderful and what a help it was, and all she said was: "*Ja,* I asked Pa, 'Why are we living in Wallace when all our children are gone, when four of them are living an hour away in Gardiner and two need help? What use are we here?' Pa went outside for an hour or so like he does. When he came back in, he said, 'We sell the house and move to Gardiner. I can find work there.'"

The house in Wallace was sold quickly, although at a lower price than it should have. By June, Katie and Henry had rented a house in Gardiner, across the alley from Lise, and Henry was working at the shipyard.

Lise tried to maintain her independence, but it was more effort than it was worth and so she and her parents soon combined households. She would buy the groceries. Her mother would take care of the boys, who ate and slept at their grandparents'. Lise ate there, too, but slept at home across the alley, regardless of the shift she was working. She cared for the boys whenever possible. Her mother did it the rest of the time.

Lise had sold their white Chevrolet Special Deluxe Coupe. It seemed an unnecessary complication, with a grocery store and meat market three blocks away, the Boeing plant six blocks away, and the center of downtown Gardiner eight. Henry had also sold his car. Driving an automobile had not come easy for him, and he hated to spend money on things like insurance and licensing.

"The car runs as well without these things as it does with them, so why should I buy them?" was Henry's logic.

Lise was saving money, which gave her a great sense of accomplishment. Her and Sonny's combined annual income, including government allowances for his military service, was about $2,500, and she had saved $500 since he had left for the service. The sale of their Chevrolet coupe had netted an additional $400. So now, combined with their earlier savings, they had a little over $1,700 in their savings account. *A huge amount,* she thought. *By the time Sonny comes home, we could have $3,000 in the bank. The war should be over soon, within the year maybe. I hope so. Everything is so boring. All everyone does is work. All they talk about is the war and rationing. I hope Sonny is safe. I wish I would hear from him.*

***

In early February, a combat engineer battalion, the 1255th, was attached to 28th Squadron to improve defensive positions along the Our River. Several troop units, including Sonny's C Troop, were repositioned and dug in. Minefields were laid. The engineers had no sooner completed their work then they were assigned the task of clearing Vianden with the 28th Squadron and attached artillery covering. It was an expedient tactical decision. An engineer battalion could place more dismounted troops in the town than could a cavalry squadron. After seven hours of intense urban fighting on 12 February, with seemingly unending automatic gunfire, the town was captured—at a heavy cost. One of every seven engineers had been lost in the battle, but Vianden was cleared for establishing a bridgehead on the eastside of the Our. That task was assigned to the 28th Squadron a few days later.

The 6th Cavalry Group's attack across the Our River into Germany was part of the larger offensive to breach the Siegfried Line, which began on 18 February. The 6th Squadron in the north was successful in getting the entire unit across the Our on the first day. The 28th Squadron, however, got only a small bridgehead established amid fierce fighting, with B Troop losing twenty-seven men. The next day, the bridgehead was expanded a little at a time, while beating back several German counterattacks with withering automatic gunfire. German resistance broke on 24 February, and both squadrons of the 6th Cavalry immediately pressed to the northeast.

Four days later, the 6th Cavalry crossed the Prum River and assaulted German forces east of Waxweiler. Two days of very tough fighting were necessary to clear the town and tactical ground around it. The 28th Squadron, including Sonny and the crew of the M8, was physically spent, but it was ordered to press on across the Nims River, and another two days of fighting followed in taking the town of Lasel.

By Sonny's count, and looking at the map, the 28th Squadron had covered thirty-four miles in fourteen days of virtually continuous combat. The cavalrymen were finally given a respite when they were ordered back near the Belgian border for resupply, repair, and recuperation. Sonny's ears were still ringing from the large caliber round his M8 took back near Vianden after crossing the Our. He couldn't hear unless people shouted, and his hands were shaking again. When they reached the assembly area, he was dead tired, like everyone else in the squadron. They all stumbled out of their vehicles, some immediately falling asleep on the ground among the forest trees while drivers refueled their vehicles.

Sonny got four letters from Lise. He didn't read them. He stuck them in his pocket instead. They would make him think of home, about her and the boys. This was not the time. Later, maybe.

***

Henry was working the swing shift and eating his lunch/supper at the shipyard. Since it was winter, everyone wanted to get out of the cold, damp, and drizzle to eat. The small, temporary wooden building along the dry dock under construction had a woodstove and six eight-foot wooden tables and benches. Henry usually ate alone. He did not know anyone, and he was older than most. Some others in the room were in the same situation. So they ate with their eyes focused on either their sandwiches or some spot on the table, saying little.

A hand tapped him on the shoulder, and the voice behind it asked: "Mind if I sit here?"

Henry responded, "No. Help yourself."

The man sat down and opened his lunch bucket. He was a small, wiry man with a ruddy complexion. He looked familiar. Removing his meal, the man looked back at him and smiled.

"Aren't you Henry Hofmann, who used to live up in Wallace?"

"*Ja,* this is me."

"You have a daughter named Lise?"

"*Ja*."

"I am Tom Dubois, Sonny's father."

"Lise told me you were working here. When did you start?"

"Two years ago. You started about six months ago, I heard."

"*Ja*."

"Nice of you and Mrs. Hofmann to move down to Gardiner and help Lise and the boys while Sonny is overseas."

"They needed help," shrugged Henry. "Have you heard from Sonny?"

"A couple of times. The last letter we received was written when he got to France. We haven't heard from him since early December, before this Ardennes Offensive. Has he written you?"

"No. We hear from him only through what he has written to Lise. It is too much to ask a soldier to write home to his in-laws."

"I suppose. Oops, there goes the whistle. Time to go back to work. Let's eat lunch together again," said Tom.

"*Ja*. That would be good," responded Henry.

"Henry," Tom's voice grew quiet in its sincerity, "It was good of you to help Sonny and Lise the way you have. Clara and me should have done more. You are a good man, Henry."

"*Ja*, okay."

"Remember Joe Zach?"

"*Ja*, sure. Sonny got me a job working for him."

"He died from a logging truck accident about four years ago. A load of logs crushed him in the cab. We got him out, and he was still alive, but he bled to death. Died in the hospital."

"I remember him. He was a good boss."

"Yeah, his death was a big loss." Tom shook his head and got up from his seat. "Well, we have to get to work. See you, Henry."

They closed their black lunch buckets and parted ways, walking out into the drizzle in different directions.

***

The 6th Cavalry Group crossed the Rhine at Boppard on 27 March. Their mission was to push east through the widened bridgehead and seize the autobahn south of Geissen, about fifty air miles east, as soon as possible. Its two squadrons covered approximately forty-five miles and fifteen towns and villages on the first day, moving along different axes. Each town was cleared by the scouts in jeeps, backed up by M8s, tanks, and 75mm self-propelled assault guns, as the cavalry units moved through, often dismounted. Many houses had white sheets hanging from windows, and some German citizens cheered the American soldiers.

The second day, 28 March, promised more. Both squadrons had advanced about thirty-five miles, clearing nine towns and villages with several hours of daylight left. The 3rd Platoon, C Troop approached the town of Schmitten, fifteen miles northwest of Frankfurt. The scouts had scoped it from the west. White sheets were hanging from several windows and nothing looked awry. On the way back to the main road, where the rest of platoon was waiting, the scouts met a middle-aged man with a bedraggled military uniform who surrendered immediately. They asked him if a German military unit was in the town or nearby. He indicated a military unit was somewhere in the woods to the east, but it was shot up, understrength, and ready to surrender.

"It shouldn't give you any problem," he said in German.

The scouts moved down into the town from the west with their jeeps, followed by one tank, three M8s, and a 75mm self-propelled assault gun. They joined the main road, which ran from the southwest to the northeast. The town was nestled in a small valley at the base of three big hills, big enough even to be called mountains: one to the north, one to the south, and one to the east. A third road from the southeast joined the main road in the center of town, making an inverted "y" or the Greek letter lambda. When they reached the town center, the tank pulled through and blocked to the northeast, the first two M8s turned south and blocked the road coming from the southeast, and the third M8—Sonny's—remained at the intersection, protecting the rear of the 75mm assault gun, which had turned 180 degrees and "blocked" the road to the southwest, the road on which they had come into the town. The scouts, having moved through the town to the northeast, came back on the shoulder of the north hill overlooking the town center and scoped the hill to the east. It was quiet. While several white sheets were hanging from second-story windows, few people were to be seen.

Sergeant Corson yelled to the crew that he was going to get some "groceries," that a *Bakerei* or *Metzgerie* had to be nearby.

He added: "Everything on the battlefield is ours, boys—just for the taking."

Hermann yelled, "Wait, I'll go with you, Sarge."

After they left, Sonny grew restless and eased the M8 forward so he could better see up the road to his left. After a few minutes, he saw a woman come out onto the balcony of a large building below which the tank was idling and lob something into the turret. She ducked back into the building, and there was a fiery explosion from inside the tank. Before Sonny could react, another explosion came from the woods above and behind the buildings to his front. A larger explosion came from his rear almost instantaneously. He knew the 75mm assault gun had been hit. Sonny slammed the M8 into reverse and backed it up several yards as Phelps, the gunner, spontaneously cut loose with a continuous burst from the .50 cal. machine gun in the turret. Sonny swung the M8 forward and down a side street to the right. Two-story stone buildings provided cover from gunfire from the east. The noise of automatic fire was now incessant.

"Where the hell are Corson and Hermann?" he yelled to Phelps.

"I don't know. We'll wait a few minutes. They'll be back," Phelps yelled in return. Sonny saw an M8 cross in front of him with another close behind. The second M8 turned onto the road Sonny was on and came directly toward him. It pulled past Sonny's M8 and covered to the north; Sonny eased his M8 ahead and covered to the south. The third M8, which had crossed in front moments before, backed in from a side street and covered to the southwest. A secure perimeter had been established, for the moment.

Phelps yelled: "I am going back to the other M8. Cover me to your front. Stay in the driver's seat." Sonny already had his Thompson submachine gun in hand.

Sergeant Corson came through a doorway at the back of a building, dragging Hermann, obviously dead. They had been on the other side of the building when the tank caught fire and exploded. Corson was the second-ranking surviving NCO. Sergeant Sack, the platoon sergeant, had survived and was assessing the situation with Phelps. The tank and crew were gone. The 75mm assault gun and crew were gone. Three M8 crew members were dead. So was Lieutenant Parker, the platoon leader. There was no radio contact with the scouts, and no one knew where they were.

Sergeant Sack called the troop commander and told him the situation.

The troop commander said a platoon would be sent to get them out of the town. "It'll be there in less than a half hour. Stay put. Locate the scouts and retrieve them."

"Roger, out," said Sack. Nothing else he could say.

The four surviving scouts were actually less than 200 yards away. A two-man patrol was sent out to locate them along the overlook, and they were successful, which they signaled, but it was obvious there was no way the scouts and the patrol could come down from where they were hiding and cross the road. German troops were already moving southwest along the north hill, and more were coming up from the southeast along the south hill. The main road into Schmitten was being covered by at least one infantry assault gun as well as machinegun fire, making it impossible for the M8s to use as an escape route. Their best way out was in the forest along the north slope of the south hill.

The scouts and the two-man patrol began working their way west back out of town to where they could cross the main road safely. Sergeant Sack and the surviving M8 crew members wanted to move in the same direction using a service road in the forest along the north slope of the south hill. But to get out of town and into the forest, they would have to expose themselves for thirty to forty yards as they moved from the edge of town, past some barns, and up into the forest. Covering fire from the relief platoon would be needed to do so successfully.

Sergeant Sack redistributed the M8 crews so that the first M8 had a full crew, including himself; the second had a driver, Sonny; and the third M8 had a three-man crew, which included Sergeant Corson and Phelps. The four dead cavalrymen were stuck in the turret of Sonny's M8.

When they had finished preparations, Sergeant Sack said: "At least we can get these guys out of here. Dubois, move when

I move, and stay dead on my ass. Corson, when the second M8 is in the woods, you go. Stop for nothing."

The relief platoon came on too hard and too fast, and it exposed itself to flanking fire from the north. At the same time, it distracted the Germans from the M8s, which quickly moved to the southwest edge of town. The relief platoon responded with all the automatic gunfire it could muster, enough to gain fire superiority and maneuver room to provide covering fire for the M8s. On cue with the commencement of the covering fire, the M8s raced out of town, past the barns, and up into the forest and down the service road. When M8s had gone far enough for protection from enemy fire, they turned about and provided covering fire for the relief platoon, allowing it to pull back.

The 3rd Platoon M8s rendezvoused with the scouts and two-man patrol, and then moved west in coordination with the relief platoon. After several terrifying moments, both platoons were able to fully disengage from the enemy and move north to a position a few miles away that had been designated by the troop commander via radio, who was there when the two platoons arrived. By the time a defensive perimeter was established, the first sergeant had arrived with medics, fuel, and ammo. The medics tended to the wounded and the dead, including the four that had been stuck in the turret of Sonny's M8.

The two platoons had sustained 36 casualties and lost one light tank, one 75mm assault gun, and four jeeps. The C Troop commander combined the two platoons into a "reinforced" 3rd Platoon, commanded by the surviving platoon leader. Sergeant Sack continued as platoon sergeant. Vacant vehicle crew positions were filled by shuffling the men, and the few extra troops who remained were jammed into vehicles wherever they could fit. The troop commander told the cavalrymen to continue east on the middle axis of the assault, then drop down to the south axis well east of Schmitten until they reached the objective, the high ground east of the autobahn.

"We got bloodied today, men," he continued. "But no sense in going back to the west because we would be going right into the face of the entire Third Army. So we will continue the attack east against these *Kraut* bastards. Your route has already been cleared by the 1st Platoon until you cut down to the south axis. So move out. See you on the other side of the autobahn." Minutes later, Sergeant Corson, Sonny, Phelps, and a new radio operator moved their M8 into its assigned spot in the column as the platoon moved forward.

Schmitten was bypassed, left for an infantry unit to subdue later. The 3rd Platoon, it was later learned, had driven into the middle of the 6th SS Mountain Division, which, however understrength it was at the time, still had a lot of fight left in it. Surviving members of the 3rd Platoon, including Sonny, never forgot the bloody afternoon in Schmitten.

The 6th Cavalry reached the autobahn south of Geissen the following afternoon, 29 March. It had covered fifty air miles, about 150 ground miles, in a little over two and a half days. Everything was in a rush, however, to cover more ground to the east. After resupplying, repairing, and resting, the cavalrymen moved northwest near Bad Hersfeld, and were immediately assigned the task of clearing the autobahn of enemy combatants from Eisenach to Erfurt to Jena to Gera, where they arrived ten days later on 15 April. Their next assignment was another clearing mission south toward Plauen in southeastern Saxony by the Czech border. On 7 May, the 6th Cavalry attacked east and seized the towns of Adorf, Markneukirchen, and Erlbach. The war in Germany was over the next day. Further movement of the 6th Cavalry to engage the enemy was terminated.

The intensity of the war lessened during its final days, offering the cavalrymen an opportunity to look around them—cautiously, of course. They soon became aware of—even stunned by—the sheer scale of the devastation. They were also moved by the escalation—an almost daily increase—in the number of refugees, mostly women and children, fleeing westward along the roads, often pulling or pushing wheeled conveyances, such as wagons and pushcarts. Many were ethnic Germans (*Volksdeutsche*) who had been expelled from countries such as Czechoslovakia, Poland, and Romania. Others were Germans who had lived in eastern Germany (*Reichsdeutsche*), who were fleeing from the advancement of the Russian army. Later, there were peoples from the Baltic nations—Estonians, Latvians, and Lithuanians. All of them were pathetically frightened, hungry, and vulnerable, and all of them were fearful of Russian soldiers, who were now in Berlin, about whom horrific stories were told.

Sonny and his fellow cavalrymen did not know how to respond. The experience at Schmitten had made them bitter, vengeful, and wary of Germans. The behavior of some of the troops in taking advantage of the vulnerability of the refugees and local Germans occasionally rose to unconscionable levels, which Sonny found appalling, especially when it came to girls and young women.

"Get off her for chrissake, Sarge. You're hurting her!"

"She is a fucking *Kraut Whoren*, Sonny!"

"She's just a girl, asshole. Get off her."

Sonny began writing Lise letters, realizing he had gone for weeks if not months without writing her, much less thinking about her. He had prided himself on being unfeeling, as much as he could, like when they ran over a *Kraut* who got in the way of the M8 as he raced for cover from flanking machine gun fire. Drinking helped a lot because it numbed. Guys who were overcome by their fears, by their emotions, and who didn't pay attention, who were not alert, got hurt. Many died.

After several days of vehicle maintenance and repair and running mounted patrols out of Markneukirchen, the troop commander assembled the C Troop cavalrymen and told them that some 6th Cavalry units, including C Troop, would be road-marching the following week to Berlin to be part of the US honor guard for a conference of allied leaders in Potsdam, a suburb bordering southwestern Berlin. The conference would be attended by President Harry Truman, USSR leader Joseph Stalin, and the new Prime Minister of the United Kingdom Clement Attlee. He said the conference would be held around the end of July, and the US cavalrymen making up the honor guard would be there for about three months.

"Afterwards, he added, "We will road march to northern Bavaria, where the 6th Cavalry Group will be based at the town of Sonnenberg. Those 6th Cavalry units who are not part of the honor guard will be there when you arrive."

"When do we go home, Captain?" someone shouted.

"About when I do, and that will be after the conference," he answered. "Not before. So figure probably in September, depending on your points. By the way, there will likely be mingling with Russian and British troops while you are in Berlin, and you are going to have to mind your manners. Everything will be political. You might have your wives or girlfriends send all the Mickey Mouse watches they can get ahold of. Russian soldiers are supposed to be wild about them and will pay a good price for them."

***

Lise knew Germany had surrendered by the time she had walked the six blocks to work on the morning of 8 May. There had been nothing in the paper the night before, and she seldom listened to the radio. But the mill whistles were blowing almost continuously when she stepped out of the front door, and people were yelling, waving, and honking their horns as they passed by in cars along Carlton Avenue. When she got to the Boeing plant, everyone was talking and cheering, and they all moved to the biggest assembly area after they clocked in. The plant manager came on the floor and said in three or four different ways what a great day it was and how grateful everyone should be.

He went on to say: "Many of us have loved ones fighting in the Pacific area, and the war is not over for them. So it is not over for any of us. Germany's surrender must spur us on to even greater efforts to make our victory complete, complete on all fronts. Let us resolve to redouble our efforts to crush the Japanese. Let us resolve to stay on the job, to buy war bonds, and to work harder than ever before. This is not the time to celebrate, not the time for revelry, for men are still dying. This is the time not only to thank God for the great victory we have won, but to ask for the strength to make the ships and planes necessary to destroy the enemy in the Pacific. This is the time we must all come together with our men in uniform to defeat Japan and the Imperial Japanese Army and Navy, completely and unconditionally. Let's have three big cheers now and get to work."

There was a half-hour celebration, and afterward shift workers got their tools and went to work building B-29 components.

When Lise walked over to her mother's for supper that evening, everyone was excited. The boys asked repeatedly when Daddy would be coming home. Lise tried to explain the war was only partly over, that we had to the beat the Japanese in the Pacific next and that would take some time. She tried to tell them that when the war in the Pacific was over, Daddy would be coming home soon thereafter.

"Well, where is Daddy now?" they asked.

"He is in Germany."

"Well, how come he isn't in the Pacific?"

"Because the war in Germany just got over," she responded.

"When is he going to the Pacific?"

"I don't know, and I don't know whether he is going to the Pacific. Actually, I don't want to him to go," she said.

"How is the war going to be over if Daddy doesn't go?"

"Someone else can do the fighting, like the Marines, who are very tough and can do it."

After the boys went to bed, Lise put the Lincoln Logs away in the front room. Katie, sitting back in her rocking chair with her head back against the headrest and her legs spread and stockings rolled down, asked: "When do you think Sonny will come back?"

"I don't know, and I am not sure anybody does. It depends on how long it takes to defeat Japan, how many troops are needed. Surely, part of the army is going to stay in Germany to keep order. The country is not going to be given back to the Nazis or left to the USSR and the communists."

"What are you going to do until he comes back?"

"I am going to work, Mom. I am going to work as long as I can at Boeing and save as much money as possible. We need so many things, a car being the most important. And our savings could actually be worth less than we think because of inflation. We pay more for things than we did a few years ago. At the same time, the economy could decline when the war is over. I read it does after most wars. I think Sonny will get his job back. Eric Haggen told him he could. But if the economy goes bad like during the Depression, how long will he be able to keep it?"

"That is good, Lise. But Pa and I are not going to stay here after the war. You know that. We are going to buy a house in town, somewhere on a bus line, so we can get around. Your father is sixty-four, and I am sixty. We have to settle down, and you are going to have to find someone to care for the boys."

"I know. I will work until Sonny comes home. Then I will stay home with the boys."

"That makes sense, Lise. Your father is easier with your boys than he was with your brothers. But he told me he has had enough of having children around, especially when he is working nights."

***

Tom's work in the power plant at the shipyard was going well. The only problem was that he was easily fatigued and often had shortness of breath when he exerted himself, which was embarrassing when he was with other workers. He would be panting, and they would not be, to the extent that some of his fellow workers would look at him as if to say, "Are you all right, Tom?" Sometimes his heart would beat very rapidly, skip a beat, and then pound heavily for several beats afterward. It frightened him. But the fatigue and shortness of breath when he exerted himself was the most troubling.

He didn't want to tell Clara. She would be impatient and disparaging, seeing his health problems as another thing in the way of their finally earning a decent living.

Tom made a morning appointment with a physician during the week he was working swing shift. He was also able to keep the appointment without Clara's knowing. Her being there would just complicate things.

After Tom told the physician how he was feeling, the physician examined him closely, poked and prodded. When he put his stethoscope to Tom's chest, his eyes narrowed. He had Tom lie on his left side and listened for a long time. He went back through the routine with the stethoscope twice more. Then he had Tom sit back up, and the physician listened to his lungs. He took the stethoscope from his ears and sat down in a chair.

"Mr. Dubois, you have a heart murmur. Has a doctor ever told you that before?"

"No."

"Were you sick for a lengthy period as a boy?"

"What do you mean by that?"

"Spend a long time in bed once or twice?"

"Yes."

"Tell me about it."

"Well, when I was about ten, I spent several weeks in bed with a sore throat much of the time, and a high fever."

"Did your joints ache?"

"Yeah. Very much so. That was what I remember most about it."

"Were you under a doctor's care?"

"Yes. But I only saw him a couple times. My mother didn't have the money for us kids to see a doctor."

"Mr. Dubois. I think you have mitral stenosis, which is a narrowing of the mitral valve in the heart. I am going to make an appointment for you to see a heart specialist here in town to confirm my diagnosis. But I am fairly confident it is correct."

"How bad is it?"

"It is as serious as it gets in this office. The disease tends to weaken and enlarge the heart. You may also have more intense periods of irregular heartbeat. You could also have blood clots, which might lead to a stroke, and congestion in your lungs. In the end, the disease is fatal."

"What can I do?"

"Rest when you are tired, and don't overexert."

"Should I quit work?"

"It's up to you. But like I said, rest when you are tired, and don't overexert. Now, put your clothes back on, and the nurse will be in here in a few minutes with an appointment with the heart specialist I am going to refer you to."

"Is it really necessary, Doc? You sound pretty confident."

"Yes. I am sorry."

On the way home, Tom decided he would work as long as he was able. There was nothing to lose. He would go home and pack his lunch for work. Then he would drop off the car for Clara at the rest home where she worked as a cook, and walk the rest of the way to the shipyard.

A little closer to home, he asked himself: "Why in the hell did I ever buy this ugly old Hudson Six? Clara's right. Maroon paint oxidizes so easily. Looks like hell."

***

Atom bombs were dropped on Hiroshima on 6 August 1945 and on Nagasaki on 9 August, killing thousands of Japanese, and however horrific, shortening the war in the Pacific and saving thousands of American soldiers' lives. The terms for Japanese surrender were set during the Potsdam Conference and accepted by Japanese Emperor Hirohito on 15 August 1945, and it was subsequently declared "V-J Day" by the Allies. World War II was over. The formal surrender of Japan was made on the deck of the USS *Missouri* on 2 September.

Sonny was dozing in his seat on a troop train heading west. It was packed. Someone said 480 officers and enlisted men were on the train comprising fifteen sleeper cars, two kitchen cars, and three baggage cars. The enlisted men's compartments were two three-person seats facing one another, which were folded at night. The seat bottom became the bottom berth, the seat back became the middle berth, and the top berth folded out from the compartment wall for a total of three berths on each compartment side. Sleeper cars had a lavatory with a toilet, urinal, and two washstands at each end. The train also had a kitchen car in which meals were prepared. The troops were served their meals in their seats on metal trays that arrived on wheeled carts.

The train was okay the first day, but it was now the fourth, and everyone was tired and bored. Conversations had an edginess to them. War stories—those they were disposed to talk about—had all been told. Card hands had been played. Everyone was pretty quiet and wanted to get home. The canteens set up by civilians at stops along the way were welcome relief. It was usually just a cookie and a smile, but it was a personalized cookie and a smile from a real home, not a barracks or a mess hall, which made a big difference.

Crossing the North Atlantic was more than twice as long, and much more confining. Sonny sailed on a converted Navy cruiser that embarked from Le Havre, France. Enlisted men were put below decks in makeshift troop compartments, where they slept on canvas hammocks two feet wide by six feet long and tiered three high, with about two feet between the tiers. They ate two meals a day in the equivalent of a mess hall with chest-high tables—standing room only. Enlisted men were allowed go topside for a few designated hours a day, weather permitting, and on several days in the late fall and winter it wasn't. Enlisted men also had access to a couple open areas on the ship with some furnishings like tables and chairs. Sparse in number, the troops competed for their use. Luxury was an armchair.

After landing stateside, Sonny moved from boat to train, which switched from a steam locomotive to an electric one before going over Stevens Pass through the Cascade Tunnel and then back again on the other side. The familiarity and beauty of his home country embraced Sonny: the mountains, the forests, the rivers. God, he loved and had missed them all. He left his compartment and got between cars as they rushed down the valley, taking his breath away. He saw the Suquamish River, Wallace, Salkum and Gardiner. Everything was so beautiful, if maybe a little cold. After all, it was late November, and rainy.

The train arrived in Ft. Lewis in the mid-afternoon, about four, and the personnel were well organized, having processed thousands of soldiers on many troop trains before this one. Everyone went to the baggage cars and got their duffel bags as they were identified. Officers were segregated from enlisted men, and enlisted men were divided into alphabetical groupings according to their last name. Sonny was in the "ABCD" group. Then each soldier proceeded one by one through the respective stations behind each alphabetical group. At the last station, each soldier was directed to one of several buses that would take him to a public transportation depot for the final leg home. He stowed his duffle bags in the baggage compartment and got on the bus, which was full less than a half hour later. The driver got in the bus, started it, closed the door, backed it out of its slot, and headed north to the nearest public bus station. Sonny arrived in the bus station in Gardiner a little after midnight. He looked for a cab, but there wasn't one.

He shrugged his shoulders and said aloud, "Shit, I'll walk home. It's only six blocks. I would be there before a cab gets here."

He crossed the street carrying two duffle bags, one on his shoulder and one to his side. The light drizzle actually felt good on his face. Before he had walked a block, a car stopped, and the driver, a shipyard swing shift worker, asked: "Need a ride, soldier?"

"Sure."

"Put your duffle bags in the back and hop in."

Sonny thanked the man as he got out six blocks later.

"Thank you, soldier. Proud to have helped you."

Sonny walked around to the back porch and rapped on the window of the back door, calling to the boys, whose bedroom was closest. If he could wake them and get to them to answer the door, he might be able to surprise Lise. No response. He rapped the window and called to them again. No response. He rapped the window of the door a third time, and he heard them stir. They ran into their mother's bedroom, Mark saying, "I think I hear Daddy." Lights came on, and Lise, Mark, and John rushed into the kitchen to the back door, unlocked it, and leaped into Sonny's outstretched arms. He was home. The war was over.

8. Picking up the Pieces

1946–1949

Katie was beaming with joy because most of her children had come home for Christmas Eve. Melvin and his wife, Betty, a nurse he had met in France during the war, were there; so were Martha and her second husband, Ralph; Elmer and his wife, Katherine, also a nurse; Lise and Sonny and their boys; and Juliana and her boyfriend. Joachim or "Joe"—the latter the name he went by at work and around town, which he preferred and about which he would quickly correct family members when they called him otherwise—had arrived late, unaccompanied, and maybe a little tipsy. It was clear his second marriage was *kaput*. *Good riddance!* Katie thought. *What was he thinking when he married her?*

It had been years since she had seen Henry so happy. *I wonder if he has drunk some schnapps*, she questioned. He, Sonny, and Joe were in the basement for a long time. They had left Juliana's boyfriend in the living room with Ralph and Elmer, the two men with whom he probably had the least in common. How impolite.

She called everyone to the table for the Christmas feast: roast turkey, dressing, mashed potatoes and gravy, canned string beans, and pickled beets. She asked Henry to give thanks, which he did *auf Deutsch* as was his practice, a routine prayer, which never acknowledged it was Christmas Eve, or gave thanks for the safe return of Melvin and Sonny, or acknowledged the recent marriages of Martha, Elmer, and Melvin. It was just the German equivalent of the traditional prayer "Bless us O Lord and these thy gifts which we are about to receive from thy bounty through Christ our Lord." It could have been so much more, but grace was over almost as soon as it had begun, and dinner plates were being passed. Katie started to cry, partly because her children were home safe, partly because of the effort she had expended in the making of the Christmas feast.

She wiped the tears from her eyes before anyone noticed and passed her plate toward the turkey on which all eyes were riveted.

"Look at this wonderful food," exclaimed Mel. "Isn't it great to be home, Sonny? I know I feel that way. How many months were you overseas?"

"Six months of combat; five months after the fighting stopped," Sonny responded. He added with obvious pride: "My outfit was in the Battle of the Bulge, the crossing of the Our River, the breaching of the Siegfried Line, the crossing of the Rhine, and the drive into Central Europe. We were part of the honor guard for the Potsdam Conference after the war. I saw Field Marshal Zhukov and a bunch of other Russian generals, and have photographs of them."

"You were drafted and came back to the States about the same time I did. How did you get the additional points?" Mel asked. He had gone to Officer Candidate School in 1942 after serving a three-year enlistment. By war's end, he had been promoted to the rank of captain in the Medical Service Corps.

"Remember, he got twenty-four easy ones with the two boys, Mel," offered Betty. Then she blushed and said: "I am sorry. I spoke without thinking. I didn't mean anything."

"Sure, I got some points for the boys, but none of us who were in combat—actual fighting—got any points for it under that damned advanced service rating system. Which was not right, compared to guys who sat on their asses in the rear echelon throughout their time overseas, who never fired or even heard a shot fired in anger," said Sonny pointedly.

"I said I'm sorry. We all served, just in different ways," Betty responded, quietly yet firmly. Betty had separated from the army as a captain in the Army Nurse Corps.

"Sure, Sonny, I knew enough about the Army by the time the shootin' started to serve in the safest place possible and where the food was the best, which was in the rear. No one was looking out for me, and so I looked out for myself. I am glad it worked out the way it did. No regrets. An officer's pay is pretty good, too."

"You've always been lookin' out for yourself," Sonny sharply countered.

"You might try it, Sonny," Mel laughed. "Life would be a lot easier for you."

Elmer interrupted the silence that followed by announcing: "I am going to have some more turkey. It is so flavorful and moist. Done to perfection, Mom." Lise admired once again his knack for shifting difficult conversations to easier ones.

After dinner, gifts and holiday greetings were exchanged. Everyone was happy and stuffed with food.

Walking home across the alley, Sonny carrying their sleeping boys, Lise asked if he'd had a good time.

He laughed, "Hell yes! It was a lot better than last Christmas by a damned sight."

"I don't know if I like Betty after what she said about the point system tonight.

"Who gives a shit? It's water under the bridge. She's your sister-in-law."

"She pissed me off, Sonny."

"She did?

"She didn't bother me. I'm just fucking glad to be here."

"Sonny, please don't use that word around me and the boys."

"Oh. I'm sorry. I am just really, really glad to be here, then," he responded in a mocking tone of voice.

"That's better, Sonny, even if you don't mean it. Did Mel's comments bother you?"

"Naw, Mel is Mel. I would have done the same if I were in his shoes."

Opening presents on Christmas morning was memorable for Sonny, Lise, and their sons, Mark and John. Each of the boys got a nice toy and a stocking filled with oranges, candy, socks, and underwear. Sonny and Lise exchanged gifts, of course, and everyone was incredibly happy. Afterward, Sonny scrambled eggs and made hotcakes.

His happiness waned as he was sitting in the front room watching the boys play with their new toys while Lise washed the breakfast dishes. He shivered at the thought of Christmas a year ago. *It was so goddamned cold, and all that chaos and confusion,* he thought. *Nobody knew what the hell was going on.* His shivering became virtually uncontrollable. He got up and walked to the bathroom.

As he passed the kitchen, he announced to Lise, "I am going to take a bath."

He filled the bathtub and climbed in, adding more hot water. Then he scooted down and submerged his head bit by bit until it was covered, holding his breath, his eyes closed. When he came up out of the water, Lise was there.

"May I wash your back?" she asked.

"That would be nice," he smiled.

He sat there in the intimacy of Lise and the watery warmth of the bath. The residual chill and fatigue of the war began to wane.

Then, without any warning, a fearful panic seized him, contorting his face and compelling him up and out of the bathtub. He grabbed the towel from the towel bar, almost bowling over Lise, and went into the bedroom to dry and dress alone. He sat on the edge of the bed for several minutes, blindly staring into the dresser mirror. Lise was surprised by what had happened, sensing he was, too. *It must be part of his adjustment to being back home*, she thought.

Several friends from work, drivers and their wives, came over in the late afternoon. Sonny and Lise couldn't go anywhere because they were still looking for a car. Each driver brought a bottle of whiskey of some kind, mostly bourbons. Three of the wives were in the kitchen, and the drivers sat in the breakfast nook around the table with their bottles in front of them. The conversation was ribald and the laughter spontaneous, greater than warranted by the wit and humor. Still the party and laughter went on and on, and most of the wives retreated into the front room.

War stories were inevitable because two of the five had served in the Army in Europe, and one had served in the Navy in the Pacific. Only snatches of the stories were accurate, unguarded, or emotionally sensitive. They were there to laugh, forget, and be with friends. They had their jobs, homes, and hopes. The Depression and World War II were over. Anything beyond their illusions of the moment was incomprehensible.

When the bottles were empty, the drivers and their wives began to leave for home, couple by couple. Sonny was in his cups, obnoxiously aggressive, slurring his words, virtually every other one profane. His eyes were slits, irritated by all the cigarette smoke, and he lurched and stumbled when he walked. Twice he had threatened another driver.

"Let's go outside, and I'm going to whip your ass, you sonofabitch." Lise did not know what the problem between them was. No one else did either.

One of drivers said several times, "For chrissake, Sonny, calm down. Take it easy." Lise had never seen or heard of Sonny behaving this way before.

She emptied ashtrays, threw empty bottles into the garbage, and picked up dishes and took them to the kitchen sink. They didn't speak a word to each other, and at some point, in his stupor, Sonny staggered off to bed. Lise began to cry as she washed the dishes, and she cried as she dried them. She cried when she took the garbage out to the can in the alley, and she cried when she swept the floor. She cried until she went to bed and lay beside him. Who is he? Who has come back from the war? How could he have done what he did tonight? It was Christmas, for goodness sake.

Sonny was up at 5:30 the next morning, frying bacon and eggs. Lise listened as he "kerploped" about the kitchen in his heavy work boots. She put on her bathrobe and went out to the kitchen. Sonny looked up at her expectantly through blurry, bloodshot eyes.

"I will never have a party again if you behave like you did last night," she said evenly.

Sonny looked at her coldly. "It's my house, and I will have all the parties I want, when I want them. That is the way it is."

"Read the mortgage loan, Sonny. It's our house. You have been gone for almost two years. Everything is 'ours.' You don't have a pot to piss in without me."

"I don't need your crap; I got enough of my own," he sneered as he grabbed his lunch bucket, jacket, and peaked hat from where they hung on the porch and then walked the six blocks to Haggen Truck Lines.

Lise was distant when Sonny came home that night, but she fixed a dinner plate for him. She and the boys had already eaten. Sonny looked at the food and the kitchen around him. He listened to the boys playing in their bedroom. Her resolve and commitment were obvious. Whatever accomplishments he had or might achieve, they would be partially hers. She was no longer the young, naïve girl from Wallace.

"I'm sorry, Lise."

"Yes, I know, and you should be." Was all she said.

New Year's Eve fell on a Monday, and of course, Sonny and Lise were invited to another holiday party, to which they were taken by a Haggen driver and his wife. Sonny and Lise were still without a car. From the moment of their arrival, Sonny's engagement in the festivities was full and frenetic. He was everywhere all at once, talking, drinking, laughing, singing, and flirting. Lise could not keep up, and she didn't want to because he would inevitably embarrass her, himself, or both of them. Sonny was beyond obnoxious when twelve o'clock arrived. He and another inebriated driver attempted to shoot a double-barrel twelve-gauge shotgun they had somehow come into possession of in the backyard. Fearing a serious accident, the party quickly retreated back into the house and left the two wrestling over the gun. Suddenly there were two shotgun blasts in quick succession, and everyone in the house was fearful as to what had happened. When both of them came back indoors—shirts torn, muddy, wet, and holding the shotgun aloft—there was a spontaneous and relieved cheer.

Sonny's response was to attempt to give each of the women at the party a long and inappropriate New Year's Eve kiss, "backbenders" someone called them. One of the husbands attempted to stop Sonny from kissing his wife. Sonny, in full embrace, blindly stuck out his fist and struck the husband in the nose, which began to bleed profusely. A brawl ensued, concluded by both Sonny and the offended husband being held back from one another by the other drivers. Sonny's shirt was torn further.

"What the hell is the matter with you, Sonny? Are you goddamn crazy?" shouted one. Lise was mortified and asked to be taken home. She went into the bedroom, grabbed her coat off the bed, and left.

Sonny followed her about an hour later. Lise exploded in a combination of reproach, anger, and retaliation when he came into the bedroom. "You could have killed someone tonight, Sonny."

Knowing he was wrong and drunk, Sonny said nothing.

They spent New Year's Day home alone with the boys, even though they had been invited to a New Year's Day dinner. It was quiet in their house; the tension between them was deep. The boys avoided it by playing outside for most of the day. When they came in, they retreated into their bedroom.

Sonny and Lise bought a used 1941 Chrysler Royal five-passenger coupe five weeks later. Buying a new car required being on a waiting list for months, and they could no longer wait. A used car would have to do.

Sonny, Lise, and the boys drove out to visit Sonny's folks on their first weekend with automobile transportation since the war ended. Tom and Clara were elated that they had dropped by. His father appeared more tired and thinner than Sonny remembered. When the conversation settled, Sonny asked his father if he would like to go outside and look at his Chrysler coupe.

Tom replied without hesitation, "Sure, let me get a jacket." Outside, Sonny lifted the hood to show the six-cylinder L-head engine, which he started. Tom looked at it with obvious interest.

"You okay, Pop?"

"I don't know, Sonny. I feel awfully tired," he said without looking up from under the hood.

"Looks like you're losing weight, too."

"Suppose so. I'm not eating much. Have no appetite. The thought of food makes me nauseous. Then again, it might be I can't stand the thought of eating rabbit. Eddie started raising them damned things during the war for meat to help out. We eat fried rabbit every night, it seems, with no cows, chickens, or hogs."

"How long you been feeling poorly?"

"Since before the shipyard shut down."

"Have you seen a doctor?"

"Not lately. Every time I go see one of 'em, I get bad news, and your mother gets all kicked out of shape."

"You had better go see one again. You look awfully pale and peaked."

"Sure. Let's go in now. It's cold and raining. Good car you bought."

***

Henry and Katie began looking for a house to buy after the shipyard closed. It was difficult because of the housing shortage after the war. After several months, they were able to locate a two-bedroom wood-frame house with a detached garage and chicken coop on a large lot that provided ample room for a garden. The house was also on a street on a city bus line, important because Henry had concluded he was not going to buy a car again. Automobiles were too expensive to operate.

The main reason the house was priced so cheaply was because of its dilapidated condition and rotten wood foundation.

"We can use some of the money we save by buying and fixing it up," Henry argued to Katie. "We can have a better house for less money and have more savings for our old age."

Katie shook her head. "Are you sure you want to do this, Henry?" she asked. "You are much older than you were in Wallace when you remodeled the old house."

"I am not working. So what else am I going to do?" Henry asked. "I can increase our wealth by making a more valuable house. We will start by putting in a basement, which will solve the foundation problem and provide storage for canned fruits and vegetables, like I have done before."

Within a week after the sale, water, electrical, and sewer lines were disconnected, and all the skirting was removed from the perimeter of the house. Timbers were inserted underneath, and the house was raised by jacks. The dirt was excavated in sections by shovel, pick, and wheelbarrow, accelerated on those weekends when Joe, Sonny, and Melvin helped. Cribbing was put in place as the excavation went along. Two months later, with the entire house on cribbing, concrete walls were poured. After they had cured, and the forms and cribbing were removed, the house was lowered onto the walls. A concrete floor was poured, followed by basement steps.

When the water, electricity, and sewer were hooked up, Henry and Katie moved in. They used a hotplate to heat their food, usually soup and bread. It was rough living—no heat and no hot water—but Katie was persevering and Henry was relentless. And they were paying no rent.

Joe helped part-time. He was working for a local contractor, having picked up plumbing and electrical skills during his work in Alaska and Gardiner. He also knew what to do and where to go when his or his father's capabilities and knowledge were lacking. Building permits and inspectors were a problem Henry had never dealt with before. So Joe got Henry's permits and arranged to be at the house when the inspectors came. Whenever Henry started to object about the permits or the inspectors, which was frequently, Joe's response was direct.

"Pa, forget it, dammit. Inspectors need jobs, too. And they can shut you down. I will talk to them. You keep quiet and just say you don't understand English if they ask you anything."

Mutual respect had grown between the two men, father and son. Henry needed the plumbing and electrical skills Joe had acquired, and he respected that Joe was employed all through the Depression, even though he worked a lot of different jobs and had to move around a lot, which probably contributed to his first divorce. Joe was willing to help Henry because his father had frequently helped him with the house he was building in his spare time. Most important, Joe had come to understand that his father had treated his mother about as fairly and honorably as he was capable, which was important to Joe because he was aware that while the failure of his first marriage was only partly his fault, he could have treated Lorna, his first wife, better. After all, she was the mother of his children.

Henry and Joe usually spoke to each other in German while working together. They usually swore in Russian, which Henry had learned while in the Russian Army and Joe had learned as a youth, working in the fields in North Dakota with Germans from Russia. Joe was Henry's only son with whom he would have a drink. The reason might also have been merely because Joe drank more alcohol than the rest of Henry's sons combined, and usually had a bottle around.

Remodeling the house took almost two years, the last major accomplishment of a man of meager means, common skills, and much perseverance. Henry and Katie's children were unusually impressed by his work. Not only was the house finished well, far better than the Wallace house, with lots of storage space for a two-bedroom home, their mother had a wringer washing machine, an electric stove, a refrigerator, and a floor furnace. Joe and his sisters had seen to that.

The gardens and flower beds were extraordinary, raised and leveled in many places by dirt coming out of the basement, thoroughly amended by manure from the chicken coop. The vegetables were abundant, and the flowers—over a dozen long rows of gladioluses and many beds of daffodils, tulips, and irises—were dazzling in their colors.

When his daughters asked for cut flowers to take home, Henry would normally decline and say, "They are for your mother, so she can have some beauty in her life."

"But Dad," they would protest, "There are so many flowers here to enjoy, and their blossoms will wilt soon."

"A flower's beauty is greater and longer on the stem. Leave them."

***

Tom died 22 October 1946 at the age of fifty-seven, old for his years. An autopsy indicated the cause of death was liver cancer and mitral stenosis. Reverend Caleb Shifley of the First Baptist Church of Gardiner conducted the funeral service, and although Tom had never actually attended a church service over which the Reverend Shifley presided, he got it about right when he said: "Tom was given very little in his life, but he was always hopeful and optimistic and kind, and he struggled through a great economic depression and two terrible wars. In the end, he put his children in a place where they could be successful, and he was at peace with God. He did the best he could with what he had."

When Sonny and Lise came home, Mark asked: "Is granddad dead and buried now?

"Yeah. We can start living like white people," Sonny responded.

"What does that mean?"

"It's just an expression. Go play. I got things to do."

Clara remarried ten months later to a man named Clarence, who sold J. R. Watkins Home-Care Products and Medicinals door-to-door. It was a part-time job for him. He also worked for the county at a gravel pit, and he played the organ at a roller skating rink on Friday and Saturday nights for pocket money. He was a good person, but he had a lot of children by his first wife, who had died. Three were still living at home on his five-acre stump ranch four miles south of Gardiner. Eddie moving in with his mother would seriously complicate living arrangements at the house, so, with Clara's manipulation and encouragement, Eddie made it easy for everyone by asking his oldest sister, Becky, if he could live with her and her husband, Lawrence, and their two children. They had moved from Salkum to Idaho, where Becky's husband worked as a fireman at an Air Force base. It all made sense somehow, and Clara wasn't going to spend the rest of her life working as a cook in a damn nursing home.

***

There was more heavy hauling work at Haggen than the company could handle by the late spring of 1948. They had purchased a new Kenworth three-axle tractor along with a two-axle, low-boy trailer and had hired two additional experienced drivers. No one complained. Everyone was getting as much overtime as he wanted. Sonny, still Eric Haggen's fair-haired boy, was assigned the new Kenworth tractor. His knowledge of cable rigging set him apart from the other drivers. So did his cockiness. Some called him "hot shot"—though not to his face.

Sawmills and shingle mills were running almost uninterrupted after the war, many running double shifts. They needed sawlogs, and so the logging industry was thriving, even expanding. Sonny got a couple of calls asking if he would be interested in coming back and working in the woods. It was flattering to be offered a good job back home up in the Suquamish Valley, but steady, well-paying work was something he could not afford to give up, like the proverbial bird in the hand. He said no to both offers. Lise was miffed that he would even consider the jobs. She liked him driving at Haggen, for the most part. They were living better than they ever had before and were saving money. The only problem was the rough element among the drivers, which seemed to be concentrated in the heavy hauling crew, or so thought Lise.

Sonny was either attracted to them or was one of them, Lise was not sure which. They drank too much and often went to a local bar after work. When they were on big jobs away from home for days at a time, Lise knew Sonny drank heavily. The drivers joked about it on the side when they were together with their wives on social occasions. Lise would pretend she didn't hear, but when she raised the issue with Sonny when they were alone, he would become enraged, and a terrible fight usually followed.

Sonny was not the same fellow she'd met at the dance in Salkum in 1936, the man she married in 1938, the man with whom she came to Gardiner with two small children in 1941, and the husband who went to war in 1944. He had evolved into a more complicated man than his years, marriage, children, work, and war experience would suggest. He could no longer be described as optimistic and fun-loving. He was cynical and arrogant, and increasingly envious of the advantages others had had while growing up that he had not. The deficit made him uncomfortable with himself and occasionally insecure. He was embarrassed by his father's inability to provide better for his family during the Depression. They had been poor, much poorer than they had to be, and his father had lost the ranch in a bank foreclosure. That, too, didn't have to be. Surely, he could have come up with $300 from someone. He was embarrassed to have gotten a fifteen-year-old girl pregnant. He was embarrassed by his lack of education. He was embarrassed by his fear during the war—sometimes a nearly uncontrollable fear—of his M8 hitting a mine or running into an ambush, of the image in his mind of a row of frozen German soldiers stacked like cordwood at least 200 feet long in the snow alongside a road in Luxembourg. He would compensate for all of it with aggressiveness, a short temper, and occasionally belligerence, which could reach a level of frightful nastiness when he was drinking.

Lise saw it when he thrashed a fellow during a scuffle at an Elks Club picnic they'd attended the summer before. He did not have to hit him so hard and so many times.

"What the hell are you doing, Sonny?!" she'd screamed. "Do you want to kill him?!? Stop it!" Sonny's head had snapped around angrily toward her, with a look she had not seen before. Lise had gone to the car and sat until he came long after the picnic was over. When he did, not a word was exchanged between them, either then or the rest of the way home. They hadn't stopped to pick up the boys at her parents. She would have been embarrassed if her mother and father had seen Sonny in such a state.

When they were in bed, she'd asked him through the dark: "Did you win, Sonny? Did you prove anything, accomplish anything, or gain anything?" He responded with an obscenity, but soon was asleep and snoring.

The next morning, after Sonny had gone to work, she'd driven over to her parent's to pick up Mark and John.

Her mother asked, "Why didn't you pick them up last night?"

Lise had expected the question and replied, "Because the picnic ran later than I thought, and I didn't want to wake you up."

"You know that I don't sleep well, that I was probably awake."

"I have given you my answer."

"Is Sonny drinking too much?" her mother had asked, her eyes unblinking and her voice unusually controlled.

"More than I would like," responded Lise. "But I think his drinking might be because of his war experience, and I think he is working his way out of it."

"Are you sure?" her mother'd asked.

"Sonny is a prideful man. If he loses the boys and me, I am sure he would see himself as a failure, like he sees his father as a failure. He knows I will leave him when I can no longer tolerate his drinking. I am not sure when that will be, Momma, but he would be a fool to test me, and he knows that, too."

The Elks Salmon Fishing Derby was a major fall event in Gardiner. Whoever caught the biggest salmon won first prize, typically a Chevrolet four-door sedan, provided by the local Chevrolet dealer, who was also an Elks Club member. Second prize was an outboard motor, and third prize, a new first-rate salmon rod and reel.

Sonny and two other Haggen drivers were out on the water before daybreak in a rented skiff and a borrowed five-horse Johnson outboard motor to catch the incoming tide over Cultus Bar. Trolling with herring, they caught some cohos midmorning—five of them—and Sonny's fish was of competitive size. The weigh-in was at 1:00 p.m. in the Elks parking lot. So they left the bar at 10:30 for the long run back.

The banter among fishermen at the docks was animated, and Sonny and his fish were the focus of much attention, which only increased as they neared the parking lot. Sonny reveled in all of it. After the fish was officially weighed and tagged, Sonny and the two Haggen drivers went to the bar for drinks and a smorgasbord for all official derby entrants. The banter grew in noise and intensity as the time for announcing the prize winners neared. So did the number of drinks consumed, scotch in Sonny's case.

In the end, Sonny's coho, at twelve pounds, two ounces, came in fifth, less than a pound from the third-prize fish. No prize, of course. Sonny was given a lift home by his fishing partners and dropped off at the street. He stumbled to the back of the house, having sense enough even in his sotted condition not to drag his fish and fishing gear through the front.

Lise had spent the day painting the kitchen and had taken but one break to make a sandwich and open a can of soup for the boys for lunch, who were somewhere, she really didn't know where, playing outside. Sonny staggered through the door from the back porch to the kitchen, holding his fish in front of him and smiling stupidly.

"I caught a fish; fifth place," he slurred.

Lise, holding a paint can with one hand and a paintbrush in the other, screamed, "Sonny, you *arschloch,*" and hurled the paintbrush at him. It struck him in the chest just above the head of the fish he was holding. At the same time, Sonny lurched to avoid the paintbrush, but his feet got tangled in the drop cloth put down to protect the linoleum floor from paint splatters. He fell, dropping the fish and pulling the drop cloth out from underneath an open can of paint, upsetting it.

"You're stupid drunk, Sonny. Beyond that, you're a self-centered, arrogant, thoughtless asshole, who is going to destroy everything we have put together if you don't get a hold of yourself. And don't give me any shit about the war and the terrible things you have seen. Deal with it goddamn it! I am tired of it all. I have seen more blood giving birth to Mark than you ever have, and it was my own. Now pull your share of the load, goddamn it!" she screamed.

Sonny tried to get to his knees. He put his hand in a pool of paint spilled on the drop cloth, and, in his stupor, tried to wipe it, pathetically, from his hands onto his shirt and trousers. It was a sorry effort at best, and it enraged Lise.

"Go out on the porch and take off your clothes," she yelled. "I will try to get the paint out of them. Sit in this chair," and she flung a chair from the kitchen table out into the back porch, which caromed off the wringer washing machine. A clean drop cloth and the fish soon followed out into the porch.

"Wrap yourself in this and sit out there with your goddamn fish until I get this mess cleaned up. I don't want to hear another word from you. I have had enough! Enough, Sonny!" she shrieked.

***

Sonny and Lise and the boys went down to Bill and Ida Mae's for Thanksgiving, arriving early in the morning in the rain, in the middle of Ida Mae getting the turkey ready to go in the oven. Lise immediately began chopping and sautéing onions and celery for the dressing, while Ida continued working on the turkey. The boys were sent outside to play in the barn amid loud objections. The lone girl in the family was told to either go upstairs to her room or out in the barn with the boys. Bill took Sonny down to the equipment yard and shop of Pappas Logging, five miles away.

The yard contained all kinds of logging equipment, including four three-axle truck tractors and pole trailers, an old donkey on log skids, a Koehring shovel, excavator buckets, a Caterpillar crawler tractor, a couple of bulldozer blades, grapples, tongs, and cable spools. The shop was filled with tires, wheels, an engine block, radiators, hoists, a mélange of tools, welding equipment, compressors, grease guns, and a couple of fifty-gallon drums of lubricants. A smaller part of the shop, an add-on, was loaded with cable yarding equipment and supplies, including butt rigging, chokers, and blocks as well as cables, clevises, and clamps. It was impressive and exciting to Sonny, conjuring up grandly distorted memories in which he was the heroic figure on top of the spar tree. Bill saw it more pragmatically, in fact a jumbled but still organized collection of logging equipment, tools, and supplies getting ready to move.

All of it was partly his, he told Sonny. "Ole man Pappas and his sons made me a partner. I'm no longer slingin' riggin' for a wage. They got a big cutting contract out of Long-Behr Lumber in Cowlitz County, and they want me to be part of the operation down there. Ida and I bought a place outside of Amboy, and we're moving there after Christmas. It's a bad time to move for the kids, but it's also too good of an opportunity for me to pass up."

"That's great, Bill!" exclaimed Sonny.

"Pappas Logging is a good outfit. Three family members are partners, including Nick Pappas, the old man, and his son, Louie. There is a fourth partner outside the family. He is a good, capable guy. They all do different things in the company, and they all earn their money. I will be the fifth partner. Hope that won't be like a fifth wheel."

"So what are you going to do for 'em?" Sonny asked.

"Nick wants to me to handle the planning for the logging for the Long-Behr contract. We're going to be logging old growth on some pretty steep, rough ground, and we could lose our ass if roads, landings, and settings are not laid out right."

"When did you learn to do that?" Sonny asked.

"Learned it along the way from ole Nick. He doesn't want to do it anymore, and nobody else wants to because it's complicated and takes a lot of time. But it's mainly a matter of breaking things down into steps and using some rules of thumb. I can hire a civil engineer if I have a serious problem. Anyway, when I am through with that, I'll probably be operating a side.

We will have two sides going in Cowlitz County and one up here, at least for a while, until our contract is completed."

"You got it made, Bill."

"I don't know about that. Most of us will have few breaks in our lifetimes, and we have to recognize them when they occur. I was pretty sure this was a break for me, and I grabbed it."

"I sure would if I had an opportunity like you had," Sonny said.

"You will, Sonny. Don't rush it. It will come when it is ready. You just want to be sure you are capable of recognizing an opportunity when it comes. We had better be going back to the house. It's getting close to dinnertime."

***

With Lise's insistence, Sonny and she worked to develop friends outside of Haggen drivers and their wives. Sonny joined the Elks and the Veterans of Foreign Wars after he returned from the war. Several of the drivers were members of both. They offered entertainment and a place to meet people. The Elks had more members and was bigger. Its lodge had become the principal meeting place for middle-class residents of Gardiner. There was the country club for the well-to-do, but nobody Sonny and Lise knew belonged to it.

VFW members had the common experience of having served abroad during wartime. Sonny was willing to share his wartime experiences, but not frequently or in much depth, and he seldom mentioned the names of places like Harlange, Wiltz, and Vianden. Nobody knew where they were, anyway. Many VFW members were Marines, having served in the Pacific Theater. Their experiences were very different from his, he learned, and he was glad he had not fought in the jungle. He had nothing in common with Navy veterans who'd been on ships at sea. His membership in the VFW lasted two years.

Sonny's membership in the Elks, on the other hand, was enjoyable, and his participation in club activities grew. He and Lise liked the bimonthly seafood buffet dinners and the professional entertainers who performed throughout the year. The lodge also had a gymnasium and a swimming pool, which Sonny regularly used. He played in one of the volleyball leagues. Conversations at the bar in the "Members Only" room, regardless of occasion and level of sobriety, were genial and appropriately superficial. In other words, members were friendly and they usually kept their noses out of other members' business. Sonny was getting to know several beyond simply putting names with faces.

He also tried to reach out to people he had known before the war. For one, he called Frank Barton, brother of his brother-in-law Bill, who had returned to Tualco after the war and was back working in the woods. Over the telephone, they arranged to meet on the following Friday night at the American Legion at Tualco, where Frank was a member. Sonny initially wanted to bring Lise with him, but he sensed early on in the telephone conversation that she might not be comfortable, given that Frank gave no indication he was married or had a woman in his life. Furthermore, Sonny reasoned, Frank was known to be pretty wild in the old days before the war, and there was no telling how he would be now. It'd be better if Lise stayed home.

Frank served in the 134th Infantry Regiment, 35th Infantry Division throughout World War II, beginning with the landing at Normandy and ending with the German surrender. The Division suffered 15,822 casualties, including 2,485 men killed in action during the war. Frank commanded a tank destroyer company for most of the war as a result of a battlefield commission received in late July 1944 after D-Day, after a battle with the equivalent of a German tank battalion in which most of the company's commissioned officers were either killed or seriously wounded and had to be evacuated.

Later, with some modesty, Frank would argue, "It is not that I was that good, but there were not many left of the company after that battle." He saw some of the bloodiest fighting during the Battle of the Bulge at Loutrebois, some of it alongside the 6th Cavalry Group at Harlange, Tarchamps, and Sonlez. Frank was a genuine war hero, having received two medals for valor, including a Bronze Star, and the same number of purple hearts.

The war had taken a serious toll on him, which became increasingly obvious to Sonny as the evening wore on. The conversation, the laughter, the drinking were at a frenzied pace, and soon Sonny was overwhelmed by Frank and his demons. He had to get away from Frank to get control of his own fears and insecurities, and he left as soon as he was able. The one good thing that happened to Sonny that night was learning that the sentry, to whom he had given the message for Frank, had indeed given it to him. In relating his own side of the story, Frank starting singing "I'm an Ole Cowhand," and he was immediately joined by virtually all the Legion members at the bar, who had obviously heard Frank sing it many times before. It made Sonny tear up.

Driving back over the trestle to Gardiner, Sonny caught glimpses of his own reality. He saw his mind too often clouded by alcohol and too distracted by the banalities of everyday life—especially the damn war—to know what was actually going on around him. There was too little time and space left to recognize an opportunity, even if it came up and bit him in the ass. He had to change that.

When Sonny and Lise went to the Elks the following night, they met Jack Dwyer and his wife, Janice. Actually, Sonny and Lise had met them before at the home of one of the Haggen drivers, and Sonny had talked to Jack several times at the bar in the "Members Only" room. His was one of the more familiar faces.

Jack, five years older than Sonny, was a big man with an easy laugh and an excellent sense of humor. Janice was the daughter of Norwegian immigrants, attractive and a good conversationalist. Jack's employment seemed to change every time Sonny met him during the first year of their acquaintanceship at the "Members Only" bar, odd because he seemed to be a capable kind of guy, certainly capable of holding down a job. Jack hadn't served during the war. Some medical condition prevented it, which was of no concern to Sonny—if he hadn't been drafted, he wouldn't have served, either.

Jack, like many of his Irish ancestors, drank a lot, not at any one sitting but consistently, usually beer, occasionally gin and bourbon. He was as comfortable at a bar as he was doing his toilet in the morning. He was unencumbered by guilt, in part because his family had long given up the Catholicism common to his heritage. And the only connection Janice had with her traditional Lutheranism was a strong dislike of Catholics. Religion was never a problem with the Dwyers. Neither was Jack stopping off at a bar nightly.

What would irritate Janice was being at home alone with their two young daughters at night. She preferred being at the bar with Jack, listening to him telling stories. A lot of people liked the stories Jack would tell. Jack's father, Dan Dwyer, a successful lumber broker in his sixties, was not among them. He thought his son's stories, however amusing, were complete bullshit and a thorough waste of time.

Dan was shrewd, as he had to be in a highly competitive business operating on very small profit margins. He had tried to set Jack up in business a couple of times and had failed. Jack was not good with numbers, not "quick" in Dan's estimation.

"For chrissake, do you have to figure everything out on paper? Use your goddamn head for something more than a hat rack." And Jack was easily distracted, which was a problem when you bought and sold lumber on freight cars rolling hundreds of miles away.

"You got to know your costs, margins, and where your product is all the time. Forget the being funny crap. It doesn't matter. Pay attention; pay attention, for chrissake."

The two were a study in contrasts: The father, small, nimble, feisty, and shrewd; the son, big, a little clumsy, amiable, and almost guileless. The father had been a lightweight boxer in his twenties. If Jack had boxed, he would have been a heavyweight.

Jack's insecurities would manifest themselves most strongly whenever Dan was on a tear. And Dan could be cruel. After the war, Dan, though not having read John Steinbeck's book *Of Mice and Men*, took to occasionally calling Jack "Lenny." Some friends of Dan and his wife had been discussing the book during a dinner conversation at Dan's home. Dan observed "Lenny" seemed to be a lot like Jack, from what he had gathered, and everyone nervously laughed, a fact which had eluded Dan. Jack hadn't read the book either, but he knew being called "Lenny" was not good after it became clear to him during a bar discussion one Saturday night at the Elks. Jack told Janice, who was in the dining room with another couple, that he had to leave for a bit, and he drove over to his father's house, less than a mile away. Jack walked in without knocking, grabbed his dozing father out of his chair, and, while he was suspended, told him never to call him "Lenny" again, that he wasn't a goddamn lummox or whatever the goddamn hell "Lenny" was supposed to be."

Dan said, "Okay, okay. I was jokin' with you."

Jack roared back, "Like hell you were, you son of a bitch." And he threw him back into the chair and returned to the Elks.

Dan didn't call Jack "Lenny" again. But Janice did, and many times, usually when they were drinking, when she knew

Jack was vulnerable, when she could inflict the greatest damage. He could almost tell when it was coming.

None of them—Dan, Jack, or Janice—ever read *Of Mice and Men*.

Sonny and Jack talked about their fathers from time to time when they were together and after having a few drinks. Sonny was troubled not only by his father's early death, but by what the Depression did to him, particularly the loss of the ranch. Underlying most of it was Sonny's difficulty in understanding his father's acceptance of, even submission to, adversity. His father was a failure, to his way of thinking. There was no good reason for him to have lost the ranch. The bank to which he was indebted even offered Sonny and Lise the ranch if they would pick up the remaining monthly payments. They seriously considered it, but declined the offer. Lise did not want to live "up on the hill" above Salkum.

Jack was also troubled by his father's behavior, particularly his feistiness, which could readily descend into viciousness, and his shrewdness, which was more self-absorbed cunning. The two fathers, Jack's and Sonny's, were virtually opposites at the extreme. They only thing they had in common were their small physical statures.

Dan and his wife, Enid, lost a daughter, a stewardess, in an airliner crash in Denver in 1949. It was tragic, their worst fear, but she was adventuresome and had her own mind, different from Jack. When the catastrophe occurred—almost unimaginable in their minds—Dan and Enid were stunned. Dan wrestled with his grief for weeks, and in the process, he reached the conclusion that if he were going to do anything for his surviving children, he should do it now while he could. Red-eyed and resolute, he drove over to Jack's house. Janice met him at the door and told him Jack was at the Elks. Without entering the house, he said "goodbye" and drove down to the lodge, where he found Jack sitting alone at the bar.

"Have you eaten tonight?" Dan asked Jack.

"Well, yes and no. Janice isn't a very good cook, and tonight was really bad. The kids were screaming, the house was a damned mess, and the food was terrible, and so I just left."

"Let's go eat then," said Dan. "I'll buy. It's on me. I want to talk to you about something."

They walked to a small diner a block away and ordered chicken-fried steaks and two beers. After a long swallow, Dan began.

"Jack, I want to set you up in a business where you can make a living. You haven't got shit going for you right now. I am probably responsible for that in some way or another. So listen to what I have to say. Gardiner is growing. People want houses, and they are going to need lumber and all sorts of other wood products. The town can only grow to the south because of the Sound and the Suquamish. I bought eight lots on the highway about a mile south of the city limits before the war. I'm thinking of putting a lumberyard on it where I could operate my lumber brokerage and wholesale business. You could operate a lumber retail business. The yard would be well located for people going home from work and stopping off to buy building materials. We can work out of the same building and use the same yard. What do you think?"

Jack looked at the old man and saw he was sincere. "Same yard, same building; you, wholesale; me, retail. Is that it?"

"Yeah. What do you think?" Dan asked.

"How much money will it cost me?"

"Nothing."

"Good, because I haven't got any. But there is another problem. You and I don't get along."

"Too goddamn bad, Jack. Have any of your bullshit, boozin' buddies down at the bar made you a comparable offer? If they have, take it, and be sure to 'get along' with them for chrissake. This is a business arrangement, not a goddamn fraternal organization. I am trying to help you, do something for you."

At that point, the waitress tried to set the plates of chicken-fried steaks, mashed potatoes and gravy, and cut green beans in front of the two of them as Dan's arms were flailing about.

Dan said to her without pausing, "I thought I said no gravy on the potatoes."

To which she replied, "I will get you plain mashed potatoes, sir."

"Good, good." he replied dismissively.

There was a long pause. Finally, Jack said: "Dad, I cannot work with you alone. I need someone between you and me."

"Like who?"

"Like a friend of mine, Sonny Dubois. He is a truck driver at Haggen Truck Lines and a smart, hard working guy."

"Shit! A truck driver! What can he bring to the business?"

"He is a go-getter and smart. And he will provide me some relief from you."

"Does he know the lumber business? Do you have any ketchup?" he asked the waitress, interrupting himself.

"Here," the waitress said.

"Can he put in some money?" Dan asked, as he unscrewed the cap and began slapping the bottom of the bottle.

Jack shook his head: "No to the first question, and I don't know to the second. I can ask him."

The conversation paused while Dan applied the ketchup.

"The green beans have been cooked too long," he muttered.

"I know, Dad. But at the moment, does it matter?"

"All right, talk to your buddy. See if he wants in. It will cost him some money, three grand, minimum. And I want to talk to him. You can be there, too, of course. I want to know who the hell I am going into business with."

Finished, Jack shoved his plate to the center of the table.

"You through?" Dan asked.

"Yeah."

"Well, go see your buddy, Sonny whatever-the-hell-his-name-is. He had better not be a boozer. I don't want any of your drunken buddies in this venture. Oh, I will get the tab when I am through eating," he said with a wave of his arm.

Jack drove over to Sonny's house eight blocks away. He had just finished his supper, having worked late, getting home a little after 7:00.

Lise said, "I'll put the kids to bed while you guys talk."

After she left the kitchen and Jack had taken a long swallow of a beer that Sonny had given him, Jack began.

"I had supper with my dad tonight, and he made me a business offer, which I would accept if you would come into the business with me. I can't work alone with my dad. He pisses me off."

"What's the offer?" Sonny asked.

"He owns eight fifty-foot lots along the highway south of town, and he wants to put a lumber yard on them with a building. He would operate his brokerage and wholesale business out of it, and I would operate a retail lumber yard. I told him I wanted someone—you—to come in on the retail side with me. You don't know the business, but you're smart and hardworking. You can learn, and I just don't want to be working alone in the same building with that crusty ole bastard day after day."

"Where are the lots?" Sonny asked.

"It'll only take a few minutes to drive out there. I'll show them to you if you like."

"Lise," Sonny yelled toward the boys' bedroom, "Jack and I are going out to look at some property for a few minutes."

"Okay," she yelled back.

Ten minutes later, Sonny and Jack stopped alongside the highway.

"This is it, Sonny. What do you think?" Jack asked.

"Great location. Let's walk it."

Jack turned off the engine, and they got out. A misty rain was falling, which caused them to quicken their steps.

When they got back into the car, Jack shivered and asked, "What do you think?"

"I would be a partner. You said that, right? One third? How much would it cost me?" Sonny asked.

"Three thousand dollars. Can you get it?"

"Just so happens I asked my father-in-law for some money to buy a house on an acre south of town. It's in the bank along with money we have saved while we work out a mortgage loan."

The next day, Dan, Jack, and Sonny met for supper at the same diner as the night before. After ordering the meatloaf special, Dan began.

"Here is the deal. I own property south of town. It's a great location for a lumber yard. I will build a one-story, wood-frame building, forty by eighty feet, at the south end of the property. It will have office space for me to run my brokerage business. Jack and maybe you, if it works out, will run a lumber retail business, buying at least some of its lumber inventory from me, I would hope. The retail lumber business will be a three-way partnership: Jack, me, and you. I would be a silent partner. The brokerage business and the wholesale business are mine. The retail business will lease the land and the building from me with an option to buy. It will cost you $3000 to come into the partnership, which will go into inventory and a truck. There you have it in a nutshell. What do you think?"

"How do I fit in with the two of you?" Sonny asked.

Dan laughed, "Probably not very well, and I recommend you not try. Jack's and my relationship is typical family crap, which should have nothing to do with the partnership of the three of us. Dwyer family stuff has to be kept out of the business, understand me, Jack? I will do my best to keep it that way. You have my word on it, Sonny."

Sonny looked at both of them, one at a time. Their nods and smiles suggested it was workable. Their meals arrived: meatloaf, mashed potatoes and gravy, and cut green beans with a little bacon added for flavor. The waitress had held the gravy on Dan's order, and she brought ketchup after she had laid down the plates. They ate their meals with only small talk.

Dan, finally, said: "I think it will work, Sonny. When can you have the money?"

"I want to talk it over with Lise, but in a couple of days. I'll bring a check over to your house on Friday night. You write up a partnership agreement like we discussed between now and then, and I will sign it with the two of you. I would like to have a lawyer fine-tune it later, after we have written down what we agree to."

"Good," Dan and Jack replied almost simultaneously.

With the meal over, Sonny drove home with an excitement he hadn't felt in months.

"I am going into the lumber business! Wow!" he kept saying to himself aloud. "My ship has come in." *Hey,* he thought, *does that sound too much like my dad?*

Lise looked up from her sewing when he came in the door.

"How did your supper with Jack and his dad go?"

"Good. Real good, actually."

"Why do you say that?"

"They asked me to go into business with them."

"What business?" she asked.

"The lumber business!" Sonny responded as if she should have known.

"What? This is news to me," she said as she put down her sewing. "You had better explain, Sonny. Things are going pretty well for us right now. You have a good job, we are buying a house, and I am pregnant. Going into the lumber business now really complicates things, especially when you really don't know anything about it."

"Opportunity does not always come at the 'right' time or at a 'good' time. But when it comes, you have to recognize it and seize it," retorted Sonny.

"You read that on a matchbook cover?" she sniffed.

"Dammit to hell, Lise, you are just trying to put me down," Sonny replied, his voice rising.

"No I am not, Sonny. I asked for an explanation, and you gave me a slogan. So start from the beginning, and let's work our way through it."

Sonny began to explain, too impatiently at times, and at other times a little patronizingly, quickly signaled by the narrowing of Lise's eyes and the pursing of her lips. He needed her support, so he forged ahead through the maze left by their disagreements and conflicts of the past.

"Where you are going to get your lumber?"

"Buy it from local mills. Dan has lots of contacts at sawmills around here. He is a broker, you know, and very successful."

"Hmm. So Dan is putting in his highway property and building a building, what are you and Jack putting in?" she asked.

"Our labor." Then he blurted: "And they want me to put in $3000."

"Where are you going to get that?"

"The money your mom and dad have loaned us," he responded.

"But Sonny, that is for the house," she stammered with astonishment.

"Listen now. I think we can get the mortgage loan through the VA and use our savings for the down payment on the house. We can use the money your folks lent us for the lumberyard. This is a once-in-a-lifetime deal, Lise; once in a lifetime."

"Sonny, we would not be using the money they lent us for the purpose we told them we would," she said.

"Your dad doesn't need to know," Sonny objected.

"But he will find out sooner or later, and he is bound to ask. I won't lie to him; I can't."

"Well, don't then. But I want to go in with Jack and Dan. This is my big chance, like Bill's with Pappas Logging. This is my opportunity to be in business for myself. I want to take advantage of it."

"Sonny, I am not sure this is the only opportunity you will have. You have put me in a difficult position of either supporting you and deceiving my folks or not supporting you and being honest and respectful of my parents. I don't like it. This is not a way to start a business. It isn't fair."

"I am going to do it, Lise," Sonny said emphatically.

***

Easter fell on the 17th of April in 1950, and Henry and Katie invited their children home for Easter dinner, including an Easter egg hunt for the grandchildren. All of them who lived in Gardiner came: Joe, Nellie, Martha, Mel, and Lise, and their spouses. After dinner, with the grandchildren either outside in the yard or down in the basement, the adults were seated around the table, expanded by two table leafs, enjoying their coffee and a rare moment together in Henry and Katie's newly remodeled home. While modest in size and plain in style, Henry had done a remarkable job, and he was proud of the quality of his work, as was Katie.

Joe was feeling particularly good because he had recently married for the third time. His job was also going well, and a new house he was building on his own out in the Soundview area was now framed, plumbed, and wired. He and his new wife and stepdaughter would be in it by the end of June. Joe hadn't seen Sonny or Lise since Christmas Eve, and then for only a part of the evening.

"So how is the new business going, Sonny?" he asked directly, but entirely innocently.

Sonny winced; Henry snapped his head toward Sonny, Katie paused halfway in lifting her coffee cup to her mouth, and Lise slumped into her chair. All the eyes around the table were turned toward Sonny, except Lise's and Joe's new wife's, who was smiling brightly and without guile, enjoying her first meal with Joe's family, having no idea what was going on.

"Good," Sonny responded quietly, hoping against hope that Henry had not heard. But to no avail.

"Business? What 'business'?" Henry asked.

"Yeah, Henry," Sonny said quietly, "I went into the lumber business with Dan and Jack Dwyer."

"You quit your job at Haggen Truck Lines?" Henry asked incredulously, his voice rising.

"Yes." *No use in lying to the old man,* Sonny thought.

"You have money enough to go into business, but not enough to move into the bigger house you were planning to when your wife is having a baby in a month?"

"It's going to happen, Henry. I am getting a mortgage loan through my veteran's benefits. It is just taking longer than I expected."

"Wasn't the money I lent you enough?" Henry asked. "You said it was. I don't understand."

"I used the money I borrowed from you to go into business. So we had to make a different arrangement for the mortgage loan for the new house."

"You deceived me?" Henry asked.

"Not really. When I borrowed the money from you, I was going to use it for a down payment for the house. But then this opportunity with Dan and Jack Dwyer came about, and I took it."

"You deceived me."

"Not at the time, but later I did, at least I suppose I did," Sonny looked down at the table, then up at Henry, and then to Katie.

Lise got up and said: "Excuse me."

"I am deserving of more respect than that. I worked hard to accumulate that money, and I have helped put you in a position where you can succeed, helped you to be able to provide for your family, accumulate some things, and be taken seriously by the people around you. I didn't lend you the money to go into business. I want my money back."

"I understand, Henry, and I will pay it back."

Katie got up from the table and went to the kitchen where Lise was cleaning up. She said: "It would be better if you and Sonny and the boys left now. Leave the rest. I want you to leave before your father or Sonny says something stupid." Then she put her hand on Lise's shoulder and said: "You are the only one of our children who your father and I have lent money."

"I know, Mama."

The chatter around the table had resumed its former volume. And Lise began to gather up the boys.

As they left, Joe wished Sonny success in his new business. So did Mel, now working for the federal government in the Bureau of Indian Affairs, with ten years credit toward federal retirement.

A few blocks away, Sonny said, "Your dad didn't say goodbye when we left."

"No. I didn't expect he would." A few blocks further, she continued: "The only thing you can do is pay him back his money as quickly as possible and make a success of the business. Time will do the rest." Almost home, she added: "And Sonny, you make arrangements for the boys to stay with your mother when I am delivering the baby. We have worn out our welcome with my folks for a while."

"I know I have," Sonny responded quietly, almost contritely.

9. Lumber Business

1950–1957

Sonny and the boys regularly went to his mother's to watch Monday night wrestling on television. She and Clarence had bought a television set, uncommon in 1950 in the Pacific Northwest for ordinary people. There was only one channel. Sonny wanted to see what "watching TV" was like. He had been satisfied listening to the radio on Sunday afternoons, programs with comedians like Fred Allen, Jack Benny, and Red Skelton. It was difficult for him to imagine anything more entertaining without leaving the house.

Watching wrestling seemed to be a good start. It was a farce, which Sonny knew. But the kids liked it, and so did his mother. Clarence was low key, pretty much liking everything. He reminded Sonny of his father. Both were small and wiry. Both had rather small, rectangular heads, square jaws, and ruddy complexions. Both parted their hair on the left side. Clarence wasn't nearly as good as a mechanic as his father. But he was a steady worker and one of the most patient and agreeable men Sonny had ever met. He never raised his voice. He just chuckled a lot as Clara flailed away at activities she had undertaken, one of which being another attempt at commercially raising chickens for eggs.

It was going well. They had built a large chicken house out of used lumber from a neighbor's barn and had a flock of 400 chickens in full production, and plans for more. Clarence was even thinking of quitting his job with the county. He had already stopped his gig playing the organ on Friday and Saturday nights at the nearby roller rink. He was too involved in cleaning and candling eggs.

Clara had become a fan of wrestling. Her favorites were Frank Armstrong, Gorgeous George, the Masked Marvel, and Rufus Jones. One or more of them were featured virtually every

Monday night. Armstrong was a local college football hero, now long out of college, who was trying to make a living and who apparently did not have many other options. Gorgeous George was a big man with long blonde hair and an affected manner. He would preen in the ring before his matches and between rounds to the boos and catcalls of the audience. The Masked Marvel was more or less an antihero. Virtually all his opponents would try to rip off his mask, which he would defend with a vengeance. He carried more weight than he should, with his blubbery stomach and back. Clara would raucously jeer at him during his matches, calling him a "masked tub-of-gut." Sonny would call him "fatback," a name that drivers at Haggen called one of the guys who had a physique similar to the Masked Marvel. The last—Rufus Jones, a negro—would, at some timely moment in a match, grab opponents by their ears and butt them until they fell to their knees, stunned. Then Jones would leap on top of them for a pin. For some reason, Jones, whom Clara routinely called "that darkie," was her favorite. Sonny thought it was maybe because Jones was typically cast as the underdog. The boys also liked Rufus Jones, especially Mark.

Monday night wrestling started at 7:00. Sonny would get home a little after 6:00, eat, and go out to his mother's with the boys. Clara and Clarence would have popcorn ready when they arrived. Wrestling was over at 8:00, and Sonny would be home at 8:30. It was plain and maybe a little homely. But it gave Lise, who was working for a dentist during the day, some time with the baby. It also gave Sonny a reasonable distraction from the lumberyard, which was getting off the ground, which he had not told his mother about, and which he had warned the boys not to talk about to Grandma.

"It is none of her business," he told them. Neither of the boys was sure of what "none of her business" meant, but they did as they were told, or what they thought they were told.

So the conversation between mother and son was mainly about wrestling and raising chickens, sometimes about Sonny's sisters and brother, who, seemingly, had scattered with the wind. Sensitive matters—the events of their lives that occurred between 1937 and 1950, in other words, anything connected with losing the ranch, the circumstances of Sonny and Lise's marriage, Mark's difficult birth, Tom's illness and early death, Sonny's World War II experience, and Clara and Clarence's marriage—were ignored. If they were even hinted at, they were dismissed by feigned interest in Monday night wrestling.

Clara would routinely ask Sonny shortly after his arrival, "How are Lise and the baby?"

Sonny would say "Fine," and no more.

Clara would also ask at some point, "How is your job going, Sonny?"

And he would give her the same response he gave her inquiry about Lise and the baby: "Fine."

Sonny had his own question for Clara. "How is Eddie?" Her answer was always short, and she would first look at Clarence before she gave it, more or less.

"I expect he is fine. I haven't heard from Becky."

The lumberyard was succeeding beyond what Sonny had expected. The part-time bookkeeper Jack and Sonny had hired, Randall, also the bookkeeper for Dan's lumber brokerage business, gave them an income statement, a cash flow statement, and a balance sheet for the first six months of operation in early July. Jack handed them to Sonny as he asked whether they were making any money.

When Randall assured him they were, Jack asked, "And all the bills are paid?"

Randall nodded and replied, "So far as I have them."

Jack said, "All I need to know." He continued over his shoulder to Sonny as he walked toward the door, "One of us has to get out the deliveries. It's Friday, and I don't want to be working here after seven o'clock tonight. You take care of Randall and the customers."

Jack had little use for Randall, whom he considered his father's lackey. He had apparently worked with Randall in some earlier business ventures with his father before the lumberyard, and more than once, when Jack had difficulty in understanding a financial statement, Randall had become impatient and even sarcastic in providing his explanations. Randall laughed at Jack in front of his father, who joined in the mirth with his own laughter and sarcasm.

Dan had blurted: "I have never seen a man so goddamn slow when it comes to numbers." To Jack, this was a double insult. Both his intelligence and manliness were being challenged. His dad was good at doing that kind of thing.

Sonny began to look over the three documents, shuffling through them without any apparent logical sequence. Randall stopped him.

"Go to your income statement; look at your sales, cost of goods sold, and gross profit; then look at your operating expenses. Gross profit minus your operating expenses will give you your net profit. See, you're doing pretty well. Sixty-two hundred dollars net profit in the first six months is a good start, especially with the inventory you have put in during the past six weeks and the fact you are paying yourselves weekly wages."

"Yeah. Sure it is," said Sonny as he tracked down the statement with his finger to the net profit line.

"Go to your cash flow statement. It shows the flow of cash in and out of the business—where your cash is coming from and where it's going. It shows the ability of your business to pay its bills. Watch your cash flow and where it is going, up or down. Most small businesses get in trouble because of their cash flow."

"Okay."

"Then go to your balance sheet. It shows the assets, liabilities, and owners' equity at a given point in time. Look at your accounts receivable. You are extending credit to some of your customers, which is reasonable. But don't let the accounts grow old. You are not a bank. I will start aging them—thirty days, sixty days, and ninety days—by the end of the year."

"Sure," said Sonny, exposed for a sixth time in as many months to a quick and practical explanation of financial statements. He was beginning to understand where the lumberyard stood as a business and how it was operating financially. It was much more than lumber, customers, trucks, and drivers.

"You have come quite a ways in the past six months," Randall concluded.

"What we wanted," Sonny responded.

"Won't be long before you should be thinking about hiring a bookkeeper full time."

"You interested?" Sonny asked.

"Not until I have a better idea about what goes with the job, where I would be doing the work, and what office equipment I would have. Not much of that around here at the moment. I can't work over a counter."

"I know. Jack and I will have to work on that. We still have some time," Sonny responded.

"I would probably still have Dan's books to do. I have done his books for several years now."

Randall left, and Jack came into the office as a loaded truck pulled out on the highway with the first delivery of the day. It was 8:30 in the morning.

"So are we making money?" Jack asked.

"Sure. You want to go over the income statement?"

"Naw. I'll leave it to you. We have too much to do in the yard."

Dan's phone rang in his cubicle. "Where in the hell is my ole man? I am not going to answer his damn phone. He should be here by now."

"He's probably talking to Randall about the books," Sonny said, "You know he doesn't like talking about his brokerage business in front of us."

"I hope the numbers Randall gives us on the yard are the same numbers he gives my dad," Jack muttered skeptically.

"Jack, we are too far into this to be talking like that."

Dan came in two hours later with a cheery, "Morning, boys." Sonny and Jack greeted Dan in return.

"Morning, Dan."

"Morning, Dad."

Jack asked, "You talk to Randall?"

"Sure did, me boys."

"And what did he say?"

"The numbers are right where they bloody should be if you two are worth your salt." With that he went into his cubicle, sat down, and began separating the mail into stacks: one of envelopes with apparent checks in them and the other of envelopes with apparent bills. When he was done, he took out his letter opener and began opening the checks. Then he proceeded to open the invoices. The unvarying pattern of his opening the mail intrigued Sonny.

Dan looked up and saw Sonny watching him. "Now aren't you glad you didn't go signing on with the Army Reserve like you were thinking a few weeks ago—for a bloody few extra bucks a month—with this invasion of South Korea. Focus on business, Sonny. It's all about inventory, margins, and service. Take care of them, and you will make money." He went back to opening envelopes.

***

Business increased throughout the remainder of the year. And there were some major changes. The big three-axle heavy-duty army surplus truck had been replaced by a two-axle medium-duty Chevrolet truck and a Ford pickup. They were more flexible in making deliveries and cheaper to operate than the larger army truck. Further, a bookkeeper-salesman had been hired to do the journal postings, purchasing of business supplies and equipment, reconciling accounts, and handling sales taxes. When the yard was busy, he doubled as a salesman—at which he was not particularly good. He even made deliveries from time to time, at which he was also not good because he had no interest in being a truck driver. Randall still did the payroll, paid suppliers, and prepared financial statements.

Sonny found the profit margins in finished lumber, moldings, and siding were much larger than they were for common lumber, and so he wanted to build a large dry shed to hold bigger inventories of these items. Jack agreed with the idea. Dan was lukewarm. Sonny was also pushing to buy a gasoline engine fork truck with pneumatic tires—a Clark Yard-lift 40 was what he really wanted—that would make unloading lumber and plywood from the mill faster and easier, as well as putting up deliveries. Jack also liked this idea, but Dan was harder to convince.

"Jesus, this is a lumber business, not an equipment company," he argued.

Jack and Sonny worked well together, and their friendship deepened during their first year of business. They would often socialize together with their wives, since the hours at the lumberyard were long and their pay was low. Jack's customary seat at the bar at the Elks Club had been filled by someone else, and while he was home during his non-working hours more than before, his intake of beer, gin, and whiskey remained about the same. He was a steady drinker. Sonny's intake of alcohol, however, had increased, which was of serious concern to Lise—when Sonny drank, it didn't conclude until the available alcohol had been consumed. He was a different man in many ways after he returned from the war, and probably the most pronounced difference—at least in Lise's view—was his drinking behavior. An evening or weekend with Jack and Janice almost inevitably saw a drunk Sonny and an irritated, anxious, angry Lise. Sonny could be mean when he was drunk.

None of this was lost on Dan. He saw it as the most serious problem in the functioning of the partnership. Jack and Sonny were doing well, but the drinking had to be controlled.

Dan, Jack, and Sonny met after work with Randall for year-end financial reports. Like all their meetings, they gathered after work around the potbellied woodstove in the middle of the store, in which ends trimmed from sawn lumber and other wood scraps were burned. They didn't gather all at once. Sonny was there all along because he had the last customer and the responsibility for locking up. Jack had run down to the local grocery store for a case of beer a half hour before closing time. Randall and Dan came in precisely fifteen minutes after closing time, in separate vehicles.

Jack drove in after them. When he came through the door with the case of beer, Dan was put off. "Why the beer? Isn't this a business meeting? Probably the most important of the year?"

"Since when can't we have something to drink during a meeting after closing hours? I have been working all day," explained Jack.

"And you are still working, for chrissake," Dan retorted sharply.

Randall, familiar with Dan and Jack's issues with each other, interjected: "May we get started? My wife and I have a dinner with some friends this evening." He passed out the draft accounting documents and began with the income statement. Sonny was pleased when he read that net income was over $15,000. Randall went rather quickly through the cash flow statement. Then he went through the balance sheet: assets, liabilities, and owners' equity.

"So what number is the pot that is to be split up at the end of the year?" Jack asked.

Randall started to speak. Dan interrupted him.

"We are going to get there, Jack. Please be a little patient."

"Patience my ass," Jack snarled. "Unlike you, I have been living on starvation wages the past year, with a wife and two kids to feed. So has Sonny." Jack opened a third bottle of beer.

"We can go to that now if you like," Randall said evenly. "I show retained earnings to be…"

"Why not split net income three ways and be done with it?" interrupted Jack.

"Because we want the business to grow," Dan responded. "You take out all of the net income, and we are about where we started last December. Don't you understand that?"

"Hell, yes. But can't you understand Sonny and I have just got by this past year, and it was hard?. We made no more money than ordinary truck drivers, and we went into business for more than that."

"Do you understand you didn't have jack shit last December," Dan retorted almost sneering. "Now you are a partner in a thriving business, which has the potential to get bigger, be more profitable, and make you more money. Use your bloody head for something other than a fucking funnel for a bottle of beer."

The room was silent except for the snap and crackle of the wood burning in the potbellied stove. Jack took a long swallow of beer. Dan, his father, had insulted him once again. He wiped his mouth with the back of his hand.

"Okay, how much are we going to split?" he asked in a rage barely under control.

Randall went through some possible numbers. Dan turned to Sonny: "What do you think, Sonny? How much?"

Sonny answered, "About a fifth of net income. It will give us some retained earnings and a nice balance sheet for the year for dealing with the bank, and it will give Jack and me a reasonable increase in income."

Dan said, "That's agreeable with me."

"I am not finished," Sonny blurted. "For this year, 1951, Jack and I each should get a salary increase of a hundred dollars a month."

Randall inserted. "That would be a business expense..."

"I know. The business can handle it," Sonny countered.

Dan paused and looked at Jack. "Would that be satisfactory with you?"

"Yeah. It is enough for the moment. I'm agreeable. Now if that's it, I want to get something to eat. I haven't eaten since breakfast." There was another long silence, save for the snap and crackle of the burning wood.

Finally, Randall stirred and said, "If there is no more business to do, I will leave. When do you want your checks?

"Tomorrow," Jack quickly responded.

Dan stood up. "This old potbellied stove sure puts out a lot of heat. The end of the week will do. I'm going home." He paused, "You got a good thing going here, guys. Don't fuck it up." He was out the door. Randall was right behind him. Jack put some more ends from the wood box into the potbellied stove and opened another bottle of beer.

He sat down, and after he took a long swallow, he said, "Sonny, let's you and me buy out my ole man."

"Suits me. Would you pass me another beer? How would we do it?"

"Borrow money from the bank, I suppose."

"I think it would be easier than that," Sonny said as he took a gurgling swallow and burped. "I don't think your dad is interested in the retail lumber business. He wanted to set you up in a business, and the retail lumber business was the best available fit. I think he would carry the contract for a purchase agreement for his share of the yard. It would be an important part of his retirement income. The problem will be over the price of his share of the business."

"You think my dad is going to retire?" asked Jack in disbelief.

"Yes, and what he wants after all the problems between you two, is the satisfaction of having set you up in a successful business," Sonny answered. "To keep respect, he wants a reasonable return on his investment in this property. He would be free from blame for any wrongs he might have done to you and still be a respected businessman."

"Kind of sounds like him."

"I will talk to the bank during the next few days. Get some idea of the terms of a loan to buy out your dad and what the interest rate would be. Also I need to find out what your father paid for this property, and how much it might be worth currently. There is a lot of inflation in the economy, I read nine percent, and it will probably continue with the war in Korea going on. We get these numbers, and we have a basis to negotiate with your dad."

"Do it. I can't stand working with him. He makes me out the fool."

Sonny and Jack offered to buy Dan out two months later, after concluding their monthly business meeting.

"Oh, do you now," responded Dan. "And you boys want to be taken seriously, I suppose."

"Yeah," said Sonny. "Thirty-three thousand."

"How in the hell did you come up with that number?" he asked almost amusedly.

Sonny noted Dan had not rejected the offer. "We started by looking at the balance sheet and by projecting net income for the year divided by the return we expect. Each gave us a value of the business, and we divided by three," Sonny stated. "Then we adjusted it based on information we got from the bank and from a couple commercial real estate agents we know."

"I think the lots and building are worth more, which is what I put in."

Sonny held his ground. "They are part of the business and can't be easily separated out. The success of the business is part of their value, and you bought the land over ten years ago."

Dan scratched his chin. "I put more into this business than you guys, more than a third. Actually Jack, you didn't put a damned thing into the business except your fat ass."

Ignoring the insult to Jack, Sonny countered: "All you are saying is you want more money for your share, more than a third. If that is it, how much more do you want? Give us a number."

"Yeah, give us a number, Dad," Jack chimed in.

Dan scratched some numbers on a tablet on his desk. He bowed his head, closed his eyes, and tapped the desk with his fingers.

"Thirty-six hundred dollars more."

"Will you carry the contract?" Sonny asked.

"Sure, why not? I would be better for you than the damned bank," responded Dan.

"What terms?" Sonny asked.

"Three years at five percent," Dan quickly responded.

"No penalty for early payoff."

"No."

"I suppose you are the one to have the contract drawn up?" Sonny asked.

"Yeah. It will take a couple of days. Look to Friday for signing. I will be out of here by the close of business on the day we sign.

"Good. We need the space," Sonny stated quietly. Then he asked. "It is agreed?"

Dan nodded. Jack let out an audible breath.

Lise was thrilled when Sonny arrived home and told her he and Jack had bought out Dan.

"Wonderful, Sonny! Really wonderful!" she exclaimed.

"Yeah, it is, but it means you will be working a little longer. We need the money."

"Yeah, we do, because I want another house," Lise countered. "This one is too much work. I have been trying to fix it up room by room, but I cannot make enough progress working full time. And you were going to plant a big garden and have a flock of chickens, which hasn't worked out alongside the lumberyard. Buying this place was probably a mistake. Let's sell it and buy a lot in the Soundview development. We can build a house, a three-bedroom rancher with an attached garage."

"Jeez, Lise, give me a moment to appreciate Jack and I buying out Dan."

Sonny got his moment. And the house was on the market in May, freshly painted white with green shutters in the front. While there was considerable interest in the house, it didn't sell until the fall. But they almost got their asking price.

***

The economy was growing in the US in the middle fifties, and unemployment was low, disproportionately in cities and towns on the West Coast, to which people from the Midwest were migrating in increasing numbers. Lumber and plywood manufacturing mills were operating multi-shifts because of the post-war boom in home building, dramatically in evidence in the Puget Sound region. Gardiner was thriving, and Sonny and Jack were profitably selling all the building materials their yard was capable of at any particular moment.

There was also tension. While Sonny was expanding inventories and product lines, investing in more equipment, and hiring more employees, Jack was bossing the yard crew and drivers with the comparatively mundane details of loading and unloading trucks, making deliveries, and trying to keep some semblance of order in the warehouse, dry shed, and yard. It was not easy for Jack, who had come to realize he would always be a step or two behind Sonny, who always seemed to have a new idea, which always cost money to implement and which usually involved borrowing from the bank.

They now had five delivery trucks, two fork trucks, and a crew of seven. They had also built a large dry shed and had paid off Dan several months earlier than required in their purchasing agreement.

After going over the books for the month with their new bookkeeper, Sonny thanked him and asked him to leave, saying, "I gotta couple of things I want to talk about with Jack."

Sonny opened another bottle of beer as he waited for the bookkeeper to close the front door of the store. He began, "I think we should remodel this building, Jack, expand the merchandise display area and enlarge the sales counter so at least four salesmen can operate easily behind it. I want to build a second story and a warehouse all the way back to the alley. In other words, I want to quadruple the size of this building. The purpose of the warehouse would be to inventory panel products; roofing; metal products, like downspouts, flashings, vents, et cetera; coatings and insulation. We would have to get a loan from the bank to do it, but that shouldn't be a problem."

Jack winced and asked, "We want to go into more debt? Jesus! We just got through paying off my dad. Why don't we accumulate some capital for a while? Then we wouldn't always be going to the bank. Ahh, hell, let me sleep on it a few nights. It is awfully disorganized in the back.

What else do you want to talk about?

Sonny, undaunted by Jack's rejection, responded, "I want to hire Eddie, my brother. He is getting out of the Coast Guard and needs a job."

Jack exploded: "Not a good idea! We had too much family involvement here a few years ago, and we took care of it. Now you want to start it all over again, go in the opposite direction."

"Eddie is a good kid, a smart kid, and a hard worker, Jack," Sonny pleaded.

"Eddie might be able to walk on water, but damn it, sooner or later, there would be a hard decision to make of which he would be a part, and it would be confounded by the fact he is your brother. You wanted to hire him right after we opened the yard, and my ole man nixed it, and he was right for doing it.

"He would be a good employee, Jack," Sonny argued.

"Sure, I know, Sonny, I'm fucking tired tonight, and I have been working too damned hard for the money I take home. I don't like the amount of debt we are in and out of. Scares the shit out of me. I am arguing with Janice about it all the time. She can't figure how the hell you bought a lot in Soundview; built a brick house; owned four different cars, two of them Buicks; and bought a beach lot during the time we have been in business together. I can't either, frankly. We make the same amount of money, and I haven't accumulated anything like that."

"What are you saying, Jack?" Sonny asked evenly.

"How come you and Lise got all of those things, and Janice and I are still living in the same house we lived in four years ago and driving the same damned old Ford?"

"You keep bringing up my house. I worked nights and weekends on that house, and the cars I have bought have all been used. You should talk with Ralph Condon at the used car lot down the street. He'll get you a deal. That's his business. Finally, Jack, Lise has worked, has a good job as a dental assistant, and your wife hasn't worked a day except around the house."

"Tell me again, Sonny," Jack began, looking pointedly at Sonny, "How you got a fly-by-night contractor like Don Morgan to build you a house and how the yard came out on that."

"Ahh shit, Jack, I've told you dozen times. He owed the yard money for the houses he built on spec, and he worked for me building my house. He would bill me for his work on the house, and I would pay down his account for the spec houses. All the materials for my house were charged to me, and I paid for them."

"At cost, right?"

"Yeah, at cost, and the same thing would be done for you if you were building a house," responded Sonny.

Jack rubbed his forehead, looked up, shook his head, and said, "It's too close, Sonny. You are always out on the edge. Maybe I am not getting screwed, but I am sharing the same risks you are, and I don't think I'm getting the same benefits."

Sonny watched him, looking closely at the changing expressions on his face, sensing Jack wanted to say something else.

After a long moment of silence, Jack blurted: "Buy me out, Sonny! I am not a businessman. I want to work from eight-to-five and go home and sleep at night without worrying about meeting a payroll, about the bank loaning me money or foreclosing on me. Buy me out, and hire your brother. Make your goddamn fortune! I hope you don't go broke in the process. You probably will. I have never seen a rich man who didn't go broke a couple of times getting his fortune."

Sonny stirred. "You're serious, aren't you?" he asked.

"I am. Make me an offer."

"Something like the one we did for your dad?" Sonny queried.

"Sure, why not. I want some money up front though, enough so I can make a big down payment on a new house."

"I will work something up, so we can talk with some numbers in front of us."

***

A little drunk, Sonny got out of his car unsteadily to raise the garage door. When it was up, he motioned to Lise to get out. She seemed tipsy too, so he helped her through the garage to the back door into the kitchen. They had gone out to dinner that night, celebrating Sonny's purchase of Jack's half of the lumberyard. Sonny went back to the idling Buick. While walking around the open car door, he stumbled off the driveway into a shrubbery bed, jamming a small branch of an ornamental tree into the corner of his eye.

"Shit!" he exclaimed. He got into the car and turned on the interior lights to examine his right eye and side of his face. It was scratched and bleeding. Nothing serious. "It just doesn't look good," he said aloud. "And I bet Katie is awake, waiting for us to come home." He drove the car into the garage and closed the garage door. The garage was dark, and he stumbled into the lawnmower and a rake, knocking over an empty galvanized water bucket that had been left along the garage wall. He had seen all of them as he drove into the garage, but he thought he could get around them.

"Shit!" he said again. "I told those kids to put that stuff on the other side of the garage. What in the hell is the matter with them?"

Finally, Sonny got to the door of the kitchen and opened it, just as Lise was coming out to see what all the commotion was about.

"Are you okay?" she asked. Then, "Oh, your face is scratched and you are bleeding from the corner of your eye."

"I know, I know, it is nothing," he responded. "I just walked into a tree branch in the flower bed getting into the car."

"I will fix an ice pack. Mom is up. She couldn't sleep. She is darning socks in the living room. Sober up a little before you go in."

"Hell, I am all right. Get me some ice. I will use my handkerchief for the moment. This is a big day for us, among the biggest in my life. I sure as hell can take my wife out to dinner and have a few drinks to celebrate, can't I?"

"You can. But you have had more than a few, so sober up before you go into the living room," she whispered.

"I'm okay. It is my house, dammit. She is just staying here for the night," he whispered noisily back. "Get me some ice," he ordered, as he walked into the dining room from the kitchen toward the living room, dabbing at his eye with his handkerchief.

"Hi, Mom!" he said too loudly. "Big day for us. Cause for celebration," he chortled before she could greet him.

"Yes it is, Sonny," she responded as he plopped himself into a wingback chair.

"Well, I worked hard for it, and now it is all mine," he asserted.

"Yes, it is. And that's good. What's the matter with your eye? It's bleeding."

"It was dark outside, and I walked into a tree branch opening the car door. Lise is getting me an ice pack." He paused. "Yep, great day! Shows what hard work can accomplish."

"Remember what the Bible says, Sonny. 'Remember the Lord your God, for it is he who gives you power to get wealth.'"

Sonny was rolling his eyes as Lise came into the room and applied the ice pack. She looked at her mother and said: "Sonny worked for it, Mom."

"Yeah, I worked for it, and I earned it," Sonny said with obvious self-satisfaction, holding the ice pack to his face and squinting at Katie.

Katie put her darning down and looked directly back at Sonny. "You take credit for your success too readily. Hard work is not enough for success. You know that. Henry worked hard, and your father worked hard. Neither of them had the success you have had."

"I worked for it, Mom," Sonny repeated.

"Yes you did. And so did Lise, and I admire you both. But never have I seen such an easy time and easy place to make a living. 'Working hard' does not explain everything about making money or being successful."

"I admit these are good times, and Jack and I had a few breaks. Sure."

"Education helps, too, Sonny. Henry and I were 'dumb Russians' when it came to education. We should have pushed our boys harder to go to school, extend themselves, so they could do something and get good jobs. We didn't. We wanted our children out of the house on their own. Having big families made sense in Russia, where they could work in the fields. Here a child is only another mouth to feed."

"Mom, what a terrible thing to say," Lise retorted.

"Lise, I am not a fool. Your father and I didn't know what we were doing. I had no control over anything. When children came along, we met our responsibilities, his as a father, mine as a mother and wife, *Pflichten einer Ehefrau in der deutschen Tradition*. (Duties of a wife in the German tradition.) We even learned to love them, some more than others."

"Mom!" Lise gasped.

"I didn't have any more education than Elmer or Mel," Sonny inserted.

"So what does that mean, Sonny? Maybe you would have been even more successful if you had a better education? Sonny, your willingness to step out and take a reasonable risk is something special, something to be respected. I have learned that taking risks is necessary to be successful in life. It is part of how we as human beings adapt. Henry wasn't a risk taker. Russia, North Dakota, and, finally, the Depression beat it out of him. He wasn't always like that. I have talked too much. I am going to bed now." She put her mending down and stood up. Then she hesitated and said: "Sonny, you and Lise have had good fortune, which is wonderful. Now the challenge is for you to keep it, which probably will be an even greater challenge than getting it in the first place. A good start would be to follow the words of the sages who tell us to 'seek moderation in all things.' Good night."

Sonny said "Good night." He removed the ice pack. The bleeding had stopped. *The old lady is relentless,* he thought. *She is not going to let up on me until she dies.* As she was walking away, he added: "I suppose that includes drinking."

"How could it be otherwise, Sonny?" Katie responded.

"I am not drinking as much as I used to," Sonny said defensively.

"Good. But is it under control?" she asked.

"It's better. Ask Lise."

Lise looked at him, then her mother.

"Yeah, it's better, Mom. For sure, but he still has a ways to go."

"Good." And Katie turned down the hallway to the bedroom where she was staying.

***

Sonny had taken a small delivery to a shipyard that catered to small commercial fisherman on the waterfront. He wanted to talk to the owner and see if he couldn't get more of his business. Afterward, impulsively, he decided to swing by the rest home where old Henry was staying. It was on the way back to the yard, and he had not seen Henry for months. He had been too busy, or he had not taken the time, or whatever had been his excuse at any given moment.

Henry had had a "heart stroke," as Katie called it, three years earlier in the middle of the night. Mark was staying with them, recuperating from rheumatic fever, and he'd had to call Henry's doctor and the ambulance. The stroke had evolved into Parkinson's disease, with symptoms that worsened over time, gradually leveling Henry. Now the old man could not take care of himself, could not walk for any distance because of partial paralysis on his right side, and had a severe tremor in his right hand and arm. He had resigned himself to dying—the sooner, the better.

The rest home was a converted single family dwelling, a big Craftsman house out of the 1920s. It had been remodeled with its rooms partitioned into smaller spaces to hold patients. This was where you went when you were poor, when there was no one strong enough to care for you at home who could help you eat, urinate, and defecate. Sonny was assaulted by the smell of piss, shit, and death when he entered the front door. *How in the hell could anyone be involved in this kind of business*, he thought. *How in the hell did they get a license to operate it? Surely it must be regulated by some government agency. If ever there were a business needing regulation, it is health care for old people.*

Sonny found Henry in a hospital bed in what once was one half of the dining room of the original house. He appeared to be sleeping, pale as his sheets, with his mouth agape. Sonny sat down next to him. The old man breathed noisily as Sonny watched him.

"How you doing, you ornery old *Kraut*?" Sonny asked.

After a moment, Henry stammered, "H-H-How do you think, h-h-hot shot?" His eyes remained closed.

"Oh, I thought you were sleeping, Henry. I didn't think you could hear me."

"N-N-Not sleeping. Y-Y-You could have helped me more with my house," he stammered again.

"I was busy making a living. I am sorry."

"I-I-I helped you with your house."

"You did, and I am grateful, Henry. Thank you. But I didn't help you more because I needed to make a living for me and Lise."

"Y-Y-You deceived me, too," stammered Henry.

"No I didn't. I might have tried," Sonny chuckled, "but I wasn't able to."

"I-I-It's okay. Took chances I couldn't, and you paid me back." Henry stammered. "Y-Y-You made many good things happen."

"Yeah, good things have happened since I went into the lumber business, Henry. You may have heard. I own the whole damned show now."

"Good. B-B-But leave. I am s-s-sick and want to d-d-die."

Sonny rose from his chair and touched Henry's arm. "See you, old man." And adding quietly: "I've taken care of Lise, you know."

"D-D-Die Pflicht. G-G-Gehst du. I want to d-d-die." Sonny left in his pickup. He was back behind the counter at the yard ten minutes late.

10. Making a Living

1969

Twelve years had elapsed since Henry's death, and they had been good years for Sonny and Lise nonetheless. The lumberyard had prospered, swept along by the strong economic growth of the 1960s in the region. Sonny was engaged in a variety of business ventures in addition to the yard. He liked "putting things together," and more often than not, Sonny's ventures succeeded. Success was defined by Sonny as being profitable, a standard to which he arbitrarily added more flexibility than was customary under ordinary accounting practices. But by any calculation, winners offset losers. Some losses were serious, however, usually the result of Sonny acting impulsively. And Lise wanted fewer losers. She struggled to articulate what Sonny's ventures lacked to her way of thinking. When she came up with the word "coherence," it set Sonny off.

"What in the hell do you mean?" he angrily retorted.

"I mean your business ventures seem to be scattered in every direction, not directed toward a common goal. You invest in building lots in eastern Washington one day, selling a new line of windows the second, and going into the roofing business on the third. There doesn't seem to be an overarching plan."

"The 'overarching' plan, Lise," his words dripping with sarcasm, "is to make money!"

"I understand," she responded with icy determination. "But shouldn't your business investments fit together toward some end? I don't see that."

"God, woman, I don't know what in the hell you expect of me," snorted Sonny.

"Well, since you asked in a way, I will tell you. I am concerned you are not tending to business as closely as you should. You play a lot—fishing, hunting, golfing, and skiing—

more than you used to do. You want to go to the beach a couple of weeks, a couple of times, every summer. You buy season tickets to Cougar football games. You want to go to Hawaii and Sun Valley a couple of weeks every year. Maybe you play too much. And when you are at work, nobody knows where you are, often as not. I get calls, Sonny, a couple of times a week from people trying to reach you, wondering where you are. I agree you work hard when you are not out playing. But in the end, aren't you supposed to?"

"You got it all out?" he snapped.

"Sonny, you have made a successful business and a good living..."

"You're damn right I have," Sonny interrupted, "and I am entitled to a little fun, to enjoy my success. And you get to enjoy it, too. You are right there with me in Hawaii and Sun Valley. So what is your bitch, dammit? Tell me one more time."

"Sonny, I am worried you are going to lose what we have acquired because you are distracted too often. I fear hard times are coming back, and we are spending too much and saving too little. We are not preparing for that eventuality. I am not sure we are as aware as we should be of things going on around us, the big picture, the forest instead of the trees."

"Why in the hell do you have to exaggerate so? We are living better than we ever have. And you know it!" he yelled.

"Sonny we can live even better if we operate a little more wisely, think things through, have an eye to the future."

"What in the goddamn hell does all that mean?" he yelled again.

This conversation, monthly in occurrence on average, would be suspended without resolution or agreement, like similar conversations on Sonny's drinking—which had significantly decreased through the years—and the extra weight Lise was carrying—which had not. They swirled around like the undercurrents of a major wave after surging ashore in a heavy sea.

Lise initiated the conversation again during supper on a rainy winter evening in 1969.

"I read that the county has grown very rapidly in the last few years; pretty obvious, I know. Actually, the article said the county is one of the fastest growing counties in the country. I wonder whether the lumberyard has grown as fast as the county."

"I don't know, probably at a lesser rate," Sonny replied while chewing his food.

"Shouldn't you know?" she asked pointedly.

"I don't know, Lise, for goodness sake," Sonny answered, scoffing. He continued after he swallowed the food in his mouth. "I can say, however, we have all the business we can handle because of the size of the yard and our parking situation. I am worried about a lawsuit from somebody getting hit backing out and trying to get onto the highway. I am also worried our location is not the advantage it used to be, now that residential home construction is going on further to the south of Gardiner and east across the river."

"So why don't you invest in a lumberyard where the location is better?" Lise asked.

"What? I thought you didn't like my business ventures, that they were scattered in every direction and lacked 'coherence.' Are you suggesting I go out and invest in a new yard at a better location?"

"Sonny, don't mock me. My concerns have been how your business investments fit together as a whole, and how often you are distracted from business by your participation in leisure activities. What I am suggesting is that if the current yard is inadequate in size or location, do something about it. Buy or build another yard. You have proven you can establish and successfully operate a business over a long period of time. Now the challenge is to prove you can grow one and take full advantage of the extraordinary opportunities going on around us."

"That actually makes some sense," Sonny replied. He was quiet for a bit, ate several more mouthfuls of food. After excusing himself, he got up and added, "You've got a point, Lise, and good timing. Thank you. I think I am going to look into some property for sale north of Tualco tomorrow. It is an old lumberyard sitting on a lot of acreage."

"Just think it through, Sonny. Don't be impulsive."

***

Sonny and Lise agreed their sons were moving through their respective lives with an appropriate number of significant accomplishments, about which they probably extolled too long in conversations with friends. All three sons—Mark, John, and Mike—had completed high school. Mark and John had finished college, and Mike was well along in the process of doing so. Mark and John were married, and Mike had a serious girlfriend. No doubt, he would be married soon.

The boys were more different from one another than Sonny and Lise had anticipated. Mark had confounded them when, after completing his military service, he told them he was going to graduate school to study economic history. Sonny and Lise were skeptical of the wisdom of his decision. Their idea for him was much more practical: he was married; he and his wife had a child; he should get a job and settle down.

Mark received his Ph.D. in a little over four years and was, unexpectedly, appointed to a temporary faculty position at the same university from which he'd graduated—none too soon in terms of their depleted savings and meager family income. The year before, Wendy had given birth to a second child, a baby boy.

"Why would they be having a baby while they are still in graduate school?" Lise and Sonny asked each other many times.

One substantial benefit of having a temporary faculty position without having to move was that it gave Mark time to engage in a systematic search for a permanent position in economic research, which he did effectively. He got a first-rate job in Washington, D.C. after ten months of reading position announcements, sending out resumes, and interviewing. He and Wendy were elated.

The telephone rang, and Lise answered it on the fourth ring. She wasn't as agile as she used to be.

"Hi, Mom. How are you?" It was Mark.

"Good. And you and your family?" Lise asked.

"Fine. I have called to tell you I have taken a job in Washington with an economic research institute."

"Good," she said. "Time you moved." Then without hesitation, like it was something she wanted to say for some time, she added, "You can't grow any more where you are. And the university is not paying you what you are worth."

Mark, put off by her frankness, responded, "Well, it is not that bad, Mom, compared to salaries in my field at other universities in the region." His conviction waned as he spoke, as he looked about his 120-square-foot office and its grey Steelcase desk, chair, and file cabinet and wooden five-shelf bookcase. He wondered how an office space could be so sterile. Was it designed that way, to be so plain, or was it because of him and his lack of interest in decorating it?

"That may be," his mother went on, "But what you are earning, at least what I think you are earning—and I know it is only a temporary position—is not what it should be given the time and money you spent getting a Ph.D. Look at what your uncle makes as a physician, and what your brother makes with his civil engineering degree."

"Ah, Mom, Uncle George is a medical doctor, and John is a civil engineer. I am an economic historian. Salaries are higher in their professions than mine. You know that." By this time, Mark was out of his chair and looking out through the sliding-glass aluminum windows onto the asphalt parking lot below, with red maples regularly spaced along the adjacent parking strip. He looked beyond the parking strip to the street and onto the tennis courts, where college students and a few faculty members were practicing serves and strokes. *Almost idyllic,* he thought.

"Your father and I are proud of what you have accomplished in your education. That aside, you have to earn enough to make a living and take care of your family."

"Jeez, I know that, Mom. I am taking care of my family."

"Good. You should. It is your responsibility. So congratulations on your new job. When are you moving? By the way, your dad isn't here, and I don't know where he is. I called down at the yard a bit ago, and no one knew where he was."

"We are moving next month. Have Dad give me a call when he can."

"Okay, and, did I say congratulations on your new job?"

"Yes you did. Thank you, Mom."

Standing, he placed the telephone in its cradle and looked again out the window.

"I won't regret leaving this place," he muttered aloud. "The aesthetics of this building are awful, little more than that of a modern jail house."

His mother often irritated him, making him feel guilty. She always was giving advice, usually hackneyed and parochial. Now and then, however, she had extraordinary insights, which impelled him to listen to her. He knew his irritation was mostly his problem. They both wanted him to be successful: he, so he would not be the embarrassment he felt he was, and she, so her son could be somebody who provided for his family and was deserving of respect.

Unqualified success to his mother's mind meant being a physician. She would have allowed for a dentist, but she had worked for a dentist and found them to be little more than mechanics in lab coats, with about the same lusts and frailties of other men. She was unsure about engineers. They didn't wear suits to work, and while lawyers did, they basically were whores who would represent anyone, good or bad, for a fee. Schoolteachers and coaches were poorly paid and didn't deal with the real world. Foresters were a lot like engineers, but they were closer to loggers, and you didn't have to go to college to be a logger. So she was suspicious of the education of foresters and their profession.

Mark vividly remembered telling his mother shortly after his return from the army that he wanted to go to graduate school to study economic history. She was quiet for a while, chopping onions on a cutting board on the kitchen counter.

Finally, she said, wiping her eyes with the back of her hand, "I don't know what that is. Would you be an economist or a historian? You can't be both? I do not know what economists do, but a historian is basically a history teacher, and teachers are a dime a dozen and don't make beans. Of course, you are paying for it, aren't you? I hope so. What does Wendy say?"

"Too many questions, Mom. Only two are relevant so far as you are concerned. By the way, their answers are: yeah, I am paying for it; and yeah, Wendy is okay with it."

"Oh," she quietly responded and went back to chopping onions. Mark remembered watching her from where he was sitting at the kitchen table with a coffee mug in hand. He regretted being sharp with her. But he could not bring himself to say he was sorry, which, he was sure, would only lead to more discussion on his going to graduate school. He and Wendy had already made the decision. He was just looking for his mother's approval, like her unrequited love, her unquestioning approval. Maybe he was asking too much.

Later, when it was almost time to leave his office for the day, the telephone rang.

Mark lifted the receiver to his ear and before he could answer, he heard, "Hi, Mark! So you are going back east to work for some economic research outfit. So tell me, what you are going to do? Research on what? Who are you working for? When do you leave? I want to know everything."

Mark heard himself responding. He admired the enthusiasm of his father. Sonny Dubois was the man who never met an opportunity, a challenge, he didn't want to engage.

Optimistic, confident, and forceful, his father continued, "Someplace in your decision-making, you have to ask yourself, what is the worst that can happen? The answer is usually not that much—if you've got your act together. And hell, if that's the case, go for it! Like I told you before, you will be sorrier for the things you didn't do than the things you did."

He was not sure his father had heard or understood what he had told him. But it didn't matter. It would not change anything, so he asked: "So what have you been doing today, Dad? Mom said you were out gallivanting."

"She would say that," Sonny responded with obvious and instantaneous irritation. "I was out working, making a living. You know the lumberyard I bought from Homer Brandt over at Tualco. Remember? I took you there to look at it with me when you were over here last. Well, I was looking it over to put in a truss plant. Engineered wood components are the coming thing in home construction. There is room enough for a truss plant, lots of room, room for everything, and ole Homer had a lot of the necessary equipment, saws, and tools. It just needs to be thought through in terms of layout and how many people to hire."

"All the equipment I saw seemed awfully worn and dated. Aren't you going to put in more advanced technology?" Mark asked.

"Equipment might be a little old," responded Sonny. "But ole Homer maintained everything pretty well. He was a good mechanic. I might have to put more labor into the operation than I otherwise would, but much of the equipment came with the yard, and I want to take advantage of it."

"What about your rule of running everything one man short? Doesn't it conflict with using old equipment and hiring more labor?" Mark asked.

"Maybe. Could. Then I would just have to make up a new rule," said Sonny laughingly. "It'll all work out, Son. Never mind." Success in business and its attending affluence had softened Sonny. He was less driven and more pleasant to have a conversation with.

"So what do you think of me getting a new job and moving to Washington?"

"Good. If you are happy and can make a living at it, fine," responded Sonny. "But it's about time you started to accumulate some things. You need to have something to show for yourself and all that education."

Ahh, there is the Sonny Dubois we all love and remember, Mark thought.

"Oh, I should tell you I think Eddie is coming back to work for me. He would run the Tualco yard, which is great. Never had anybody as smart as Eddie work for me."

"Dad, you fired him three years ago!" Mark blurted in disbelief.

"Oh hell, I didn't really fire him. I might have said that. But he actually quit because he was pissed at me. Said I didn't live up to my promises. Imagine that? I gave him a job! But we got that all ironed out. He's startin' first of the month."

"Jeez, Dad. You've got to get your stories straight."

"Straight for whom? Eddie didn't have much of a chance, being born in the bottom of the Depression, my dad losing the ranch, him dying young, and my mother remarrying and having no place for Eddie to live at home. I am glad I was in a position to give him a job when I bought out Jack. Eddie's smart and very good with numbers. Best man I ever hired with numbers."

"Whatever you say, Dad. Good talking to you. I have to get home now. I'll be in touch." Mark hung up.

***

Moving from Washington State to Washington, D.C. was much easier than anticipated in terms of the physical requirements, and much harder in terms of breaking away from family and friends. Mark was in his small office at his desk, examining data he had assembled on community stability, when a fellow researcher, the occupant of the office a few doors down the hallway, knocked and poked his head in.

"Hi, I am Rick Contini. Wasn't the landing on the moon something? I watched it on television most of the day. Too hot and humid to do much else."

"Yeah, it was memorable," Mark responded. "Although I am still not sure what Neil Armstrong said about 'steps for mankind.' Maybe it was the sound system in my television set."

"How important do you think landing a man on the moon will be in thirty years?"

"I don't know. There are so many extraordinary things that have happened in the last year and a half, with the war in Viet Nam, the King and Robert Kennedy assassinations, civil rights demonstrations, rioting on college campuses, the Soviet invasion of Czechoslovakia, the riots at the Democratic National Convention, and the presidential election. I do not seem to be able to put them in reasonable perspective, but it seems unlikely that landing men on the moon and returning them safely to earth—while a spectacular engineering achievement—will ease the social conflict in the country." Mark immediately knew he had gone too far with his answer. He was the new guy in the office, and no one wanted to know his opinion, especially a lengthy version, about anything. *Why didn't I just say something like "very important" and let it go,* he wondered to himself. *Ask a question in return like the Brits do.*

Contini smiled, "Well, maybe it will be more important in the future after everything sorts itself out. Have you unpacked all your boxes at home?"

"No," Mark responded and pointed to the boxes distributed about his office, "I haven't even unpacked all of them here, as you can see."

Contini laughed, "I still have several boxes of books in my office, and I have been here for two years." He continued, "I remember you are an economic historian, but I have forgotten what your research interest is?"

Mark reminded himself to be concise and to the point. "I am analyzing and comparing case studies on the economic development of small, single-resource-dependent communities like the mining towns of West Virginia and Montana, the logging towns of Oregon and Washington, and the fishing villages of Alaska."

"What have you found out?"

"Generally, they can be nice places to live, but difficult places to make a living over a sustained period of time. The mine plays out, the sawmill shuts down, the fish stocks become depleted, and people don't want to leave because it is where home is. So they flounder about trying to make a living."

"I got it. All you have to do is to find the commonalities, develop a partial equilibrium model, and run some simulations, applying a few remedial public policy alternatives. Sounds like a couple of years' work!" And he laughed. "Good luck. I have to go. Let's go to lunch some time." He turned to leave Mark's office.

"Are you interested in this area of research?" Mark asked.

"Mildly, to be honest. My interest is in longer term problems."

"Like what?"

"Like facilitating movement and optimizing employment of capital and labor in an economy," Contini responded. "For example, your resource-dependent community maybe should die out because the resource on which it is based is economically exhausted. So then the question becomes how workers and capital might be more efficiently redistributed. My evidence pretty convincingly suggests that the market solution is best, and the correct public policy is simply 'benign neglect.' Let the market operate unfettered."

"With all the human costs? People living in small resource-dependent communities usually have a very strong sense of place. Where they live really matters to them, as it did for my family, loggers who lived in the foothills of the Cascade

Mountains. They tend to value economic stability more than income or wealth. They feel left behind and excluded when they see the rest of the country prospering, feel their work is being arbitrarily devalued—by whom, they are not sure."

"Yes, even with all the human costs," Contini answered. "While they can be significant, the benefits of the market solution are usually significantly greater. I must go now. Like I said, let's go to lunch sometime. *Ciao*."

Mark responded, "Nice to meet you again." As he did, he understood the value of his research as perceived by a colleague down the hall, which was very little. He also regretted the awkward terms and language of economists he used. He would have to think this through. *I should call home,* he thought. *I need a dose of reality.*

His mother answered the telephone. "Hi, Mom, how are you?"

"Not good. I was going to call you today. My mother has been diagnosed with cancer and has only a short time to live, weeks, a few months at most."

"I am sorry to hear that. But she has lived a good and long life, Mom."

"Don't give me a cliché," she bawled. "My mother is the most important human being in my life. You wouldn't be alive if it weren't for her. She is sick and dying, and I won't have her to talk to and be with. I haven't been as good to her as I should have. I was always too impatient with her. But it is too late now to do anything about it."

Silence followed Lise's outburst. Mark felt his lips tightening, remembering the bad times after the war and the early years in his father's business, when he was binge drinking and there was often fighting and bitter words that made his mother cry.

He finally stammered, "Mom, I am sorry for my poor words. And I am very sorry about grandma. Is there anything I can do?"

"No, there isn't." Lise answered. "She is going to die shortly. She is going to be gone, and there is nothing anyone can do about it. She has been a wonderful mother, and the inevitable is about to happen. I have such terrible guilt."

"She has been a wonderful grandma, too, Mom."

"Mark, please don't say anything if you have nothing more to say than a bromide. Just listen. Let me talk. My mother is dying," she sobbed. "And I wasn't as good to her as I should have been, wasn't as respectful as I should have been. In many ways, you are the only person I feel I can talk to. I am terrible. I am not even sure if I ever told my mother I loved her."

"You have time to fix that," Mark offered.

"Just listen, Mark."

"Okay, Mom.

"By the way, have you unpacked all your moving boxes?"

"Most of them."

"Unpack all of them. You will never get the boxes unpacked if you don't do it soon."

"How do you know, Mom? I have moved more times than you have."

"Because I know more people who have moved than you do," she replied. "I have to go now. I am an emotional wreck."

***

Katie Hofmann died five weeks later, and the extended and scattered Hofmann family collapsed inwardly toward its core, Mark among them. The memorial service was held at the Adventist church in Gardiner on a Friday afternoon, and

Herbert Hofmann, Henry and Katie's son, now an ordained pastor, conducted the service and gave the eulogy, beginning with a portion of Proverbs 31:

> ***A capable wife is far more precious than jewels...***
>
> *Strength and dignity are her clothing;*
>
> *And she laughs at the time to come.*
>
> *She opens her mouth with wisdom,*
>
> *And the teaching of kindness is on her tongue*
>
> *She looks well to the ways of her household,*
>
> *And does not eat the bread of idleness.*
>
> *Her children rise up and call her happy;*
>
> *Her husband, too, and he praises her:*
>
> *"Many women have done well and much good,*
>
> *But you have surpassed them all."*

He continued, his voice strong: "Mother struggled against adversity all her life, adversity of a scale beyond our comprehension here today, and she prevailed through her kindness, perseverance, love, and her faith and reverence for God. She was the embodiment of God's grace in her later years, which should give us—all of us—hope, courage, and strength. Thank God for Mother!" There followed a resounding "Amen" from the assembled family and friends.

Then he began a prayer: "O God of grace and glory, we remember before you this day our beloved mother Katie. We thank you for giving her to us—her family and friends—to know and to love on our earthly pilgrimage. In your boundless compassion, console us who mourn. Give us faith to see in death the gate of eternal life, so that in quiet confidence, we may continue our course on earth, until we are reunited with those who have gone before us, through Jesus Christ our Lord. Amen."

A familiar hymn followed, concluding the service.

When his row was given its cue by the usher, Mark filed to the rear of the church and began greeting, shaking hands, and embracing family members in the vestibule. By the time he reached the outer door of the church, he was separated from his mother and father and his brothers, John and Mike, and found himself walking beside his Uncle Bill and Aunt Ida into the parking lot under a September sun with partly cloudy skies.

After greeting them warmly, Mark said: "It is really nice of you to come up from Montrose for Grandma's service. Are you going to the interment? The procession will start here. The cemetery is only ten minutes away."

"Might as well. We came up for the whole show," Uncle Bill responded. "We heard you moved back east to Washington."

"Yeah, we did, and we are still getting settled."

"It takes a while," his Aunt Ida offered. "Sure was a nice service for your grandma."

"Yeah, Herb did a good job," Uncle Bill agreed. "He tends to go on and on if he doesn't watch himself. But he couldn't screw up this one. Your grandmother was one hell of a woman. Everyone liked and admired her. Hell, your ole man called her a saint on many occasions. She held the Hofmann family together through thick and thin, and unfortunately, it was mostly thin."

"Like your mother, Mark," Aunt Ida offered. "She learned it from your grandma. Your grandpa was strong as a bull and hard as nails, but it was your grandma who held everything together. I think your mother has grown in the same way. Your dad is a successful businessman, but it is your mother who provides the strength and stability in your family." Uncle Bill nodded in agreement.

Mark was embarrassed. He didn't want to be disloyal to his father, nor his mother. He didn't know how to respond, even whether he should. Aunt Ida was too quick to express her opinions at times. An awkward silence followed. Then, like on cue, the sun emerged fully from behind a cloud and shone brilliantly on the church parking lot and the surrounding trees of the nearby park.

Mark blurted: "What a splendid day this has turned out to be!" And as he looked about him, "And such a beautiful place! Why did I leave, Uncle Bill? Did I do the right thing?" he asked almost too emotionally.

"Oh, that's easy. You go where the money is, where you can make a living." Then he added, "Here comes your mother and Clarence, Ida."

"You want a ride to the interment?" asked Mark.

"Naw, we will follow in the procession," replied Bill. "We will see you later at the reception at your folk's place. Sure are a lot of people here. Do you think there will be room for everyone?"

"Sure. Mom and Dad have done it before. Remember all those Thanksgivings and Christmases we had together?"

"Hi, Grandma, Clarence. It is really nice of you to come to Grandma Hofmann's memorial service," Mark greeted them warmly, as did Ida and Bill.

"Wouldn't miss it. She was a fine lady," responded Clara. Clarence nodded in affirmation, smiling like he always did.

"How is your new house at Lake Luna?" asked Mark.

"Good. But it's not new anymore. I don't think you have been there since you helped frame it up with the rest of the family ten years ago after the state bought the chicken ranch for the freeway right-of-way. It's a small house, and not much to look at. But it suits our needs. Doesn't it, Clarence? Come on up if you get a chance while you are home, and we will show you around. We have a house, garage, garden, and some fruit trees, and we buy our eggs, milk, and meat at the grocery store just like everyone else now."

"That would be nice, Grandma, but I have to get back to my job in Washington, and to Wendy and the boys."

"So you are working now?" his grandma teased. "Not going to school. Never knew anybody to go to school as much as you. Let me see your hands." She grabbed Mark's hands unexpectedly and examined them. "Soft as a baby's butt! I can't imagine a grown man having hands like these. Lookey here, Clarence. Look at these hands." Everyone laughed except Mark, who pulled his hands away with obvious embarrassment.

Mark's grandmothers were different from each other. Grandma Dubois had behaviors like the complex characters of many western writers as noted by Wallace Stegner, including individualism, determination, recklessness, endurance, toughness, and resistance to control. She was born in the West and lived there all of her life. Where Grandma Hofmann had overcome the adversity of her life through work, kindness, love, faith, and reverence for God, Grandma Dubois overcame hers through work, determination, endurance, and grit. Reverence for God was shown mostly when it suited her. She was loud—partly because she couldn't hear due to the meningitis she contracted in her thirties—and frequently profane. But she persevered, and accordingly was deserving of respect, affection too, as much as one could muster. Mark reminded himself that he only had two grandmothers, and now one of them was dead. Grandma Dubois was what was left.

"Grandma, surely you and Clarence are coming to Mom and Dad's house after the interment. I will see you there, and you can bring me up to date."

"Yeah, Mom, you and Clarence come with us," said Ida. "The procession is about to form."

"I look forward to seeing you later, Grandma, Clarence," said Mark.

"Sure. You know Henry and Katie Hofmann's tombstone is less than a hundred feet from Tom's and mine. But I am still a long way from being there by a damn sight; isn't that a fact, Clarence?"

"That's a fact," responded Clarence, smiling.

11. Inflation, Rising Interest Rates and Recession

April 1973–March 1982

When Mike Dubois, Sonny and Lise's youngest son, came to work at the lumberyard after graduating from college and a subsequent year-long respite with his wife "ski bumming," most of the employees were confident he would work hard—since all of the Duboises did—that he was smart—maybe as smart as Sonny and Eddie—and that he would quickly learn whatever he needed to know. Employees who had worked with Mike during summers when he was home from college also knew he could cause a stir: he was fearless when it came to doing what he thought was right. Mike was a man of principle, which caused more timid employees to keep their distance. Most of them gave no indication they felt strongly about anything they did, much less anything having to do with principle or their lumberyard jobs with Sonny Dubois.

Mike didn't arrive at a particularly good time. A modest national recession began at the end of 1969 and lasted almost a year—a little longer in the Puget Sound region, with employment plummeting in 1971. Employment at the big Boeing plant near Gardiner was cut to less than a fifth of what it had been a few years earlier. The net result was an out-migration from the Puget Sound region of about 53,000 people, the size of a small city. When Mike started at the lumberyard—of which there were now two—in 1973, the economy was beginning to recover. Housing starts had bottomed out a year earlier and were now slowly increasing.

Sonny's expansion plans survived the recession intact, and the two lumberyards were operating profitably. Eddie was taking on more and more of the management responsibilities at the Tualco yard, which was focused on serving building contractors and which was decidedly the larger of the two. Day-to-day management of the Gardiner yard was done by a trusted, long-time employee, with local "remodelers and do-ityourselfers" being its focus. Sonny spent his time rationalizing and coordinating the two operations.

Mike had quickly shown himself to be very capable in the building supply business, which impressed Sonny, causing him to assign Mike projects of various kinds, mostly involved with improving delivery scheduling and inventory control between the two yards. His work was good and was quickly approved for implementation by Sonny. Unfortunately, Mike was often put in the unenviable position of changing the way the two yard managers operated, with very little authority and virtually no credentials. Tensions inevitably arose, usually resolved by Sonny, at times heavy-handedly, making Mike's position difficult.

While driving back to the Tualco yard from the Gardiner yard, Mike said as if thinking aloud, "If the city widens the street in front of the Gardiner yard, which they want to do sooner or later, parking for the public would have to be shifted from the front of the store to its north side, which would change the way lumber is warehoused as well as the physical size of the lumber inventory. It would also require a 90-degree reorientation of the store in terms of its main entrance, merchandising, displays, and service counters." He concluded, "I don't see how the parking problem can ever be fixed, Dad."

"Yeah," said Sonny, "which is why we have got to fight the city in widening the street every inch of the way. We were outside the city limits when the street was a four-lane highway. Now it wants to make it a six-lane street with a two-way turning lane. If the city gave me a permit to construct the building with parking in the front, how can it now widen the street and take away street parking for the building?"

"I suppose they could argue that the permit was given over twenty years ago, and the volume of traffic has substantially increased. So why not sell the yard and build a new one?" Mike asked.

"It would cost too much, and we would lose the location and all the business it brings," Sonny replied.

"It is going to cost a lot of money either way, Dad. And if the street is widened, the location will be worth less, at least as a lumberyard, because it will be too small."

"Find something better, then," Sonny responded impatiently. "And give me some options with numbers so they can be properly evaluated. You have been working for me for less than two years, and you want to sell property on which I have made a good living for thirty years, with no more than speculation on your part."

"You mean it? I mean, finding something better?" Mike responded, ignoring the rest of what Sonny had said.

"Hell, yes."

Two weeks later, after consulting with several commercial real estate agents and talking to a few property owners in the heavy commercial area near the middle of the town, Mike took Sonny for a ride with two notebooks in hand. A short distance later, he pulled over to the side of a main east-west street in Gardiner.

"Dad, Atwood Structural Wood Products is shutting down, and this building and two acres are available for lease. The owner contacted me and said, 'I hear your father and you are looking for property to put in a lumberyard. If so, I have some property that might be of interest.' You can see paved surface streets are on two sides of the property, an alley is on the third, and a railroad right-of-way is on the fourth. I have some estimates on the range of rents he might want—they are in the notebook—but rent is clearly negotiable. I do know he will insist on a long-term lease, at least seven years. He intends to get out of the glulam timber business and develop the rest of the property for public storage units, I think. He wants all the capital he can put his hands on for that construction."

"What about my property?"

"Commercial real estate guys say they can easily sell or lease your property to car dealers who want to move their dealerships from downtown to the south end of Gardiner. Some of them have already moved in that direction, as you know. The real estate guys say you should get almost enough from leasing your land and building, assuming a few improvements of the existing plant, to cover your lease and building renovation costs for this property. It won't be a wash, but reasonably close. I have omitted a lot of details, but they are in your notebook. You have some serious negotiating to do on this property if you want to pursue it. But I think it's a viable opportunity. That's it in a nutshell. What do you think?"

"I didn't think this property would ever be available. Wow! I like it. Let's walk it. Making glulams can be a pretty messy business, and I want to see how much cleanup would be involved, how much renovation we would have to do."

The time was right for Mike's plan. The old Gardiner yard became a Datsun dealership, and the new Gardiner yard—with its 8,500-square-foot concrete-block building and lots of off-street parking—became fully operational in a matter of months.

Sonny was elated, and not to anyone's surprise, Sonny said when it opened for business, "You're the yard manager, Mike. The Tualco yard is yours, Eddie. Now let's work together and make some money."

***

John Dubois had worked for several engineering consulting firms since graduating from college in civil engineering. The work was interesting, which he thoroughly enjoyed. It was finding the work that was challenging, which he didn't like because it was either feast or famine, too much or too little. He was glad his father had asked him to come up for a company meeting after work. It was a good change of pace. Engineering meetings tended to be overburdened with detail. Meetings of his father's company were stimulating if nothing else. His father painted with a wide brush, so everyone could follow. Sonny's company had operated for two years at the two new locations and was doing very well from all John had heard. It would be interesting to see some numbers.

The meeting began a half hour after closing. Sonny brought in pizza and beer, which everyone liked. After the bookkeeper summarized the financial statements she had prepared and distributed, each yard manager, Eddie and Mike, did a SWOT analysis—Strengths, Weaknesses, Opportunities, and Threats—a modest analytical procedure Mike had read about in a business book that he bought in an airport terminal while on a vacation. Sonny liked the procedure because it was simple, and it got everybody talking about things that mattered.

Three things came out of the meeting. First, the two yards combined had over three times the sales of the single yard seven years earlier. John calculated that 1977 sales were actually 3.2 times 1970 business sales indicating the expansion was an unqualified success. Second, while Sonny had wanted to put in a building components plant, specifically a truss plant, at the Tualco yard for several years now, no one else did—particularly Eddie, who dug in his heels at the very mention of it. Why build a new plant at a location where everything is running smoothly and already on the verge of being cramped for space, was Eddie's reasoning. Third, three home builders, good customers, were doing a lot of work east of the mountains. Home construction in Wenatchee was strong, and there was even more building of second homes around Lake Chelan. Eddie captured John's attention when he said a truck and trailer load of building material went over the pass from the Tualco yard to either Wenatchee or Chelan four times a week.

The meeting broke up at about 8:00 p.m., and people went their separate ways. Sonny asked John if he had time for a drink as he was walking toward his car.

"Sure. Where?" John answered.

"Bart's, by the downtown I-5 on-ramp."

"Be there in ten minutes."

They arrived at Bart's almost simultaneously, and after they ordered, Sonny came right to the point.

"You seemed pretty impressed with the growth of the business during the meeting. You were taking notes and using your calculator."

"I am, Dad. The new yards have worked out well. Eddie and Mike have done a good job."

"You told me you were interested in coming into the lumber business with me when we were hunting last fall. Well, I think the time is ripe to put in a yard with a structural components plant—starting with a truss plant—either in Wenatchee or Chelan. The housing market is growing there and will probably grow even more rapidly, assuming everything remains the same. So I am asking, would you be interested in coming into the business and running a yard and a building components plant in either Wenatchee or Chelan?"

"You're asking whether I would be willing to leave the consulting engineering business and go to work for you, running a new yard in Wenatchee? Hell yes!" John responded. "But tell me what you have in mind in more detail, including how I would fit in with Mike and Eddie. I am sure you know that's critical."

"Yes it is, and I will outline that in a moment. But sleep on what I am proposing, and if you still like it in the morning, maybe we can meet tomorrow afternoon and go over it again to make sure we have a clear understanding. I also want us to go over to Wenatchee and Chelan and look at property within the next week or two."

"Great. I am excited, Dad. Now outline it for me, all of it."

***

Six months later, property in Wenatchee had been purchased and construction of a building was halfway through, funded by a bank loan. John gave his engineering consulting firm notice, and he rented a small apartment to live in during the transition period. His wife would join him after their house in Martinsburg was sold and she had given notice to her employer.

Not everyone was happy with Sonny's Wenatchee venture. It seemed impulsive to Lise, and Sonny couldn't give her a compelling rationale for building a new yard. Mike was concerned about how the venture affected the company's overall capital position, which he saw as being seriously undercapitalized. Eddie did not like the venture because the company had undergone a major expansion three years earlier, and the two yards still had inventory control problems. Sonny's only support for the move came from John, which was not to be dismissed lightly, for he had bet his engineering career on the move.

The Wenatchee yard opened for business in early 1979, unknowingly and unfortunately at the beginning of one of the most volatile periods in the history of US monetary policy. A few months later, in August 1979, Paul Volcker was confirmed as chairman of the Federal Reserve Board. He pledged during his confirmation hearing to make fighting inflation his top priority. Inflation was a chronic problem during the 1970s in the United States, especially when combined with the slow economic growth afflicting the economy, a situation sometimes called "stagflation." The Federal Reserve Board wanted to bring inflation under control.

Volcker announced during a press conference in October 1979 that the Fed would focus on managing the volume of bank reserves within the system rather than the day-to-day level of the federal funds rate, which would be allowed to "float." As a result of the new focus, the federal funds rate reached a record high of 17 percent in March 1980. A small recession developed and the federal funds rate was reduced by 8 percentage points. The economy rebounded shortly thereafter, and the Fed quickly moved the federal funds rate back up to 19 percent in early 1981. A recession began in July 1981, which took the unemployment rate from 7 to nearly 10 percent at its deepest in November 1982. The Fed reduced the federal funds rate by 5 percentage points in response. Slowly, grudgingly, inflation was brought under control, but at significant cost to many.

The size and volatility of these changes in the federal funds rate had a devastating impact on interest-sensitive businesses like farming, residential home construction, and retail automobile sales, which had to borrow from banks to operate and which normally paid the "prime rate," an interest rate set by adding a small fixed number of percentage points— say 2.0 points—to the federal funds rate. The prime rate was adjusted at the same time and in concert with changes in the funds rate.

***

Sonny was seated across from the banker, a normally happy, innocuous fellow whom he liked, whom he had dealt with for several years, and who was attempting to explain, painfully, why he, Sonny, would have to pay 22 percent interest to renew a business loan. He had to have the loan, but, Jesus, 22 percent? He had never earned that kind of return in the thirty years he had been in business. How in the hell could he ever pay off the loan at that rate? Nine months earlier he had paid 19 percent, which he thought at the time was the height of craziness.

"I read the Federal Reserve Board is considering lowering the federal funds rate and that interest rates will be coming down soon, which they damn well should since we are in a recession," blurted Sonny.

"The Federal Reserve Board is committed to wringing inflation out of the economy," the banker responded. "It is not community banks that have raised interest rates. It is the Federal Reserve. When a business loan is renewed, we simply apply the current funds rate plus two points for our prime customers."

"Or so," groused Sonny.

A cold rain was falling outside, cold even for the middle of the spring. But Sonny was sweating. So was the banker, for he had advised Sonny to borrow short when Sonny had some options and when the prime rate was 12 percent.

Sonny remembered his words: "Hell, Sonny, interest rates are at an all-time high. They have got to come down. Borrow on our current loan with you, and we can renew it when rates are lower."

From Sonny's perspective, his whole life was on the banker's desk, every kind of financial statement imaginable, business and personal. He hated being beholden to the son of a bitch, to any son of a bitch for that matter. For a moment, Sonny felt the urge to reach down, lift, and dump the whole damn table on top of him. He could do it. He was still in his prime. Felt like it anyway. But then he would have to go through the miserable process of getting a new banker. *Shit!* he thought. *God dammit!*

The banker paused, sensing Sonny's mind was elsewhere. Sonny quickly came around with the banker's silence and cleared his throat.

"I got all that. So, Larry, are you going to renew it or aren't you. The loan is collateralized. You have my accounts receivable and my personal guarantee."

"I hate to be so cautious, Sonny, but your business is way undercapitalized. I know you don't agree, but that is the reason why you are here. You also know your accounts receivable are aging, and home construction is down and will probably continue to decline because of high interest rates. So your sales for the coming year are likely to be down. Your net profit margin trend is down. And it is also apparent the building supply business is changing. Small lumber yards are going the way of mom-and-pop grocery stores because of the entry of large-inventory, high-volume chain stores..."

Sonny's mind flashed back to a night meeting in December 1979 with his yard managers, his sons John and Mike, and his brother Eddie. Mike had urged Sonny to hold the meeting because of articles in the *Wall Street Journal* on the Federal Reserve Board trying to control inflation.

"Interest rates are sharply rising, and local housing starts are down," reported Mike as if none of them were aware. "At the same time," he continued, "sales at all three yards are flat, accounts receivable are aging, and cash flow is a problem. We are moving toward a very serious 'undercapitalized' position."

Sonny always hated the term, and interrupted: "Jesus, Mike, do you need to use a big word when it only means not having enough money internally to operate so you have to borrow from the bank?" He rushed on, his tongue loosened by having drank several bottles of beer, which usually attended company night meetings: "It's simple, you guys. Thank you, Mike. You each got a yard in a good location. Increase your sales to contractors and other large customers who pay their bills, who keep their accounts current." John nodded in response and smiled. Eddie was impassive, and Mike slowly shook his head.

Sonny looked at him and said, "What's your problem, Mike? Why are you shaking your head?"

"We are already trying to do what you are telling us to do, Dad, and it isn't working because the additional contractors to whom we might readily sell are those in financial trouble or on the verge of it. Maybe there are things we should be doing differently. Maybe we need a new strategy more in tune with what is going on?"

Sonny remembered being exasperated, stammering, and finally blurting: "Like fucking what?" The meeting degenerated after that.

"Right," interrupted Sonny, returning to the reality of the moment, "Which is why I am borrowing money from you, Larry, so I can build stores more competitive in today's building materials market, including the manufacture of structural building components like trusses, so we can increase our cash sales and get away from small, independent, five-house-a-year contractors."

"Maybe the time isn't right, with interest rates the way they are, Sonny?"

"Could be, but we really won't know until we try, will we?" Sonny responded with sarcasm dripping from the "we's" like melted, rancid butter.

"I must tell you, Sonny, the bank wouldn't be renewing this loan if it weren't for you and your successful business experience," the banker responded.

"Well, thank you. Thirty years in business is worth something. I am surprised. So the loan is going to be renewed."

"Yes, and we will need Lise to come in and cosign the property agreement."

"Are you serious? She has already done that."

"Yes. But we are going to have to be able to look beyond the assets of the business in the event of a possible foreclosure, and this is a community property state. The personal property is as much hers as yours. You know all that. So we want her signature on the current agreement alongside yours."

Sonny reconsidered everything for a long moment. He knew it would be a hard sell with Lise. She did not like the way he had expanded his business into Wenatchee. Too much "seat of the pants," she would say.

"What time should I bring her in tomorrow?"

"Would 10:30 a.m. be suitable?"

"Sure. Anything else?"

"No. See you then."

When Sonny got into his Mercedes and inserted the key into the ignition, he was in a swirl of emotions: anger for the hoops the bank had put him through to renew the loan, fear for the uncertainty his business would have to face with a souring economy, guilt for not having been more circumspect and conservative in his decision-making, and apprehension for having to face Lise to ask her to cosign the property agreement once again. She had been vocal in her opposition to many of his business decisions of the past few years.

More often than not, she would say "I cannot understand and you cannot convincingly explain what you are doing in Wenatchee." Sonny would then become enraged, yell, and curse. So would she. He could not intimidate her, and now everything she had predicted was coming to pass.

Who in the hell is Paul Volcker anyway! One of those damn Ivy League economists! Probably never did a lick of work where he got his hands dirty.

Sonny backed out of the parking stall and waited for a few minutes before proceeding to the bank parking lot exit, deciding whether to go for a cup of coffee. He certainly did not want to go back to his office. By the time he got out onto the street and moving with the traffic, he had changed his mind two more times. He decided, finally, about six blocks and two traffic lights away from the bank, to go down to the Elks and have a double scotch straight up.

This is going to be at least as difficult as my meeting with Larry, he thought to himself.

When Sonny opened the doorway into the kitchen, it was nearly three o'clock in the afternoon, and Lise was washing the dishes.

"You're home early," she said.

"Yeah."

"How did the meeting with the bank go?"

"Okay, I got the loan renewed."

"Good."

"But you are going to have to cosign the personal property agreement again. The bank wants to be able to look beyond the assets of the business."

Lise hesitated: "And if I don't?"

"And if you don't, the loan won't be renewed."

As she dried her hands with the dish towel, she asked: "Then what?"

"The yards would not have enough money to operate. They would not have enough money to pay their creditors. They would have to shut their doors," Sonny responded quietly and as close to tolerantly as he was able.

"And so you are saying creditors have extended you as much credit as they are willing, and you have no other place to go."

"Yes, kind of, and I am sorry"

"Don't give me the 'I'm sorry' shit, Sonny. We have discussed this, and the last time I told you I wanted business and our personal finances kept separate, and you agreed, Sonny. You agreed!" she said, her teeth clenched.

"Yeah, and I separated them. But the bank wants an updated property agreement with current signatures."

"So the bank is seeing an additional amount of risk with its loan to you, more than normal. Why?"

"Don't you read the papers, for chrissake?" roared Sonny. "There is a recession going on! It is March 1982. Unemployment is above 8 percent. Interest rates are at unprecedented highs, have been for months, and housing starts have dropped like rocks off a cliff. There is no way I could have foreseen this. Whatever I agreed to was made under different circumstances, Lise. To be honest, I would not have done the things I have, made the decisions I have, if I had known the crap that would happened over the past two years. But it has happened. Extraordinary events and circumstances, which no one anticipated, have proven me wrong."

"Sonny, I told you you were taking too many risks, expanding the way you were, always betting on the come, based on things you wanted, not what made good sense," she raged. "You wanted to be the big shot, a godfather, building yards for everyone. It didn't make any damn sense to me. We had enough. Now everything is in jeopardy."

"Dammit, you are exaggerating like usual. 'Everything' is not in jeopardy," he retorted.

The kitchen became silent. The only sound was when the refrigerator came on.

After several minutes, Lise asked, "What time are we supposed to be at the bank tomorrow?"

"10:30."

"We will have to take two cars. I have an appointment with the hairdresser at 11:00."

"I'm going back to my office," Sonny said.

"Are you sober? You have obviously been drinking."

"Give me a break, Lise. I only had one drink." And Sonny left.

***

Lise arrived at the bank precisely at 10:30. She and Sonny went in together and were quickly led to a small conference room off the lobby.

Larry asked, "Do you know why we are here, Lise?"

"Yes. I have done it before many times."

"Any questions?"

"No. Give me the documents, and I will sign."

Larry passed them to her, and she scanned them quickly. He asked again if she had any questions.

"No. I told you: I've done this before." And she signed. "Now, if there is nothing further, I have to get to my hairdresser appointment. See you tonight, Sonny."

12. Talking Sense

September 1982

Sonny sat down at his desk, which was a mess, partly the result of the accumulation of correspondence, trade journals, and newspapers during his recent two-week holiday in Hawaii, partly the result of him not clearing his desk of earlier correspondence, trade journals, newspapers, used and new truck parts, and samples of various building products prior to his departure. He cleared a spot by pitching all the old newspapers in the wastepaper basket, gathering the correspondence and trade journals and stacking them crisscross on top of earlier stacks, and putting the truck parts and building product samples on the floor behind him among the others. Then he opened the manila file folder with the monthly financial statement and began reading.

It was not good. Sonny rose from his desk, went down to the lunch room, and got a fresh cup of coffee. He returned to his desk and reread the financial statement, quietly sipping his coffee as he did. When he was through, he called the bookkeeper on the telephone.

"Is this statement accurate in terms of where we are today? Is there anything significant missing?"

"No," the bookkeeper answered. "Would you like me to go over it with you?"

"No. It is pretty straightforward."

Sonny clicked the receiver and called Mike, who answered immediately.

"Hi, Dad. Welcome back."

"Yeah, thank you. I've read over the monthly financial statement and want to know if it is accurate. Are there any major changes or omissions you know of?"

"No, it was a slower month then it should have been," Mike responded. "Housing starts in the area are coming around, but nowhere near what they should be. Accounts receivable are aging because contractors are still not paying their bills like they should."

"I thought you were going to lean on them while I was gone and turn things around?"

"Hey, Dad," Mike flared. "It's not for lack of effort. I have been trying. So has John and Eddie and everyone else. We may not always have been pulling in the same direction, but everyone has been working. None of us have been off on a vacation."

"Hey, I started this business, and I am entitled to a vacation any damn time I want," Sonny retorted.

"Suit yourself, Dad, but everyone here has been working to get us out of the financial mess we're in." He hesitated, "Like I said, John, Eddie, and I might be faulted for not always pulling in the same direction, but not for lack of effort."

"Good. Talk to you later," and Sonny hung up, rose from his desk, and watched a fork truck operator set a large load of long roof trusses onto a semi. He had seen the process done many times. But he was distracted by the particular deftness of the fork truck operator, who obviously knew what he was doing. When the fork truck pulled away from the load, Sonny returned to his desk and dialed his brother-in-law Bill at his rock quarry in Montrose, Washington, two and a half hours away. When Bill picked up the phone, Sonny greeted him warmly.

"Hi, Bill. How are you doing?

"Pretty damn good for an old guy. How the hell are you, Sonny? Heard you were over in Hawaii?"

"Good. Lise and I got back yesterday afternoon. Say, how about me coming down to Montrose and taking you to breakfast tomorrow morning? I haven't seen you for a while, and I need to talk to someone with some sense."

"Sure, I don't think I have anything major going on tomorrow. Are you coming alone?"

"Yeah. I got some problems and would like to talk them through with you, with someone who has some business sense."

"Well, I don't know how serious your problems are, but you are too damn old to get up at five, drive for almost three hours, and talk straight about business over breakfast at a truck stop. That's all there is here, you know. How about you coming directly to the office here at the quarry, say sometime between nine and ten, we can talk for a while, then go to lunch? I have a coffee maker, cups, and lots of privacy. The office is plain and simple as you know, so we won't be distracted by anything except maybe noise, of which we have lot because we're awfully busy at the moment."

"Good. Let's do that then."

"Okay. See you tomorrow."

Sonny was up well before six the next day and on the road a half hour later, without Lise stirring from her sleep. He hadn't told her he was going to Montrose. He didn't want to. The trip would only be made more complicated by her asking too many questions.

Two hours later, he turned south toward Montrose on a secondary state road. The graveled entrance to the quarry, cut into the side of a small mountain, appeared twenty minutes later. Behind a berm, intended to screen the insult to the landscape that quarries generally are, was an organized collection of crushers, conveyers, screening equipment, and hoppers, among cone-shaped stockpiles of crushed rock of various sizes. They were tended by an excavator, a couple of front-end loaders, and several dump trucks and pup trailers.

Sonny parked his Mercedes beside a well-used construction job-site trailer with a small wooden sign that read "Office" attached to the exterior. The noise generated by all the equipment almost overwhelmed him as soon as he opened the car door. He quickly walked to the office door and opened it. Inside, as the door shut with a thump, the din was immediately quieted to a tolerable level.

A middle-aged man wearing wire-rimmed glasses and a light blue short-sleeved collared shirt looked up from a desk behind the counter and asked expectantly: "You're probably Sonny looking for Bill?"

"Yeah."

"Down the hall on the left," he said, nodding in that direction.

The amount of grit and gravel on the worn tile floor surprised Sonny as he walked toward the other end of the office trailer. *Wonder how often they sweep around here,* he asked himself. The door to Bill's office opened before Sonny reached it.

"C'mon in, Sonny. Good to see you." They shook hands vigorously, each genuinely happy to see the other, not only brothers-in-law, but old friends.

"Take a seat, and I will get some fresh water and make some coffee." He grabbed the carafe and went back down the hall to a water cooler by the counter.

Sonny sat and looked around Bill's office, extraordinary for its simplicity. The walls were finished with cheap quarter-inch luan mahogany paneling. The floors were twelve-by-twelve-inch vinyl floor tiles, with about the same amount of grit and gravel on them as was in the hallway and in front of the counter. Two small sliding-glass aluminum windows—no curtains—were on the exterior walls. Office furnishings were sparse and utilitarian: one grey Steelcase desk, a swivel chair with armrests, a file cabinet, a small Steelcase office table, and two chairs also with armrests. The coffee maker was on a small stand with a gray metal wastepaper basket beside it. Two framed photographs hung on the wall: one of Bill standing beside a Kenworth dump truck and pup trailer and another of him smiling in front of a large primary rock crusher.

Bill burst back into his office with the carafe almost filled with water, talking as he came through the door.

"Goddamn, it's really good to see you, Sonny," and began pouring water into the coffee maker. "So how is Lise? Everything okay?"

"She is fine. We will get to the other in a minute. How is Ida Mae?" Sonny usually teasingly referred to his sister by her full given name, which she didn't like at this stage of her life.

"Fine. Ornery as hell, but nothing new there." Bill sat down after he had scooped the coffee into the filter, inserted it into the coffee maker, and shut the lid.

"So what do you want to talk about, Sonny?"

"Well, like I told you, I borrowed a big chunk of money from the bank when we expanded a couple of years back, and then the housing market went sour. It is slowly coming back, but sales are still not what they need to be to get the loan down to where it should be, where it was before we expanded. The problem is made worse by several contractors—some of our best customers—not paying their bills on time like they should. So the aging of our accounts receivable has increased. Yesterday, when I looked at the numbers in the monthly financial statement for August, it is pretty clear I won't have the money to pay the interest to renew the loan. We will have to default unless I can work something out."

"When is your loan up for renewal?" Bill asked.

"End of September," Sonny quickly responded.

"How much you need?

"$100,000."

"That's an awfully round number. Can't you be more specific, say to the nearest thousand? It seems to me when people borrow more money than they actually need, they tend to waste some of it. If they borrow too little, they don't have enough to do what they intend to do."

"$96,000 then," Sonny replied over the clatter of conveyor belts, shaking of screens, roars and whines of engines, the metallic banging of rock against steel, and the incessant beeping of heavy vehicles backing up.

"I might be able to help you, Sonny, like I told you last spring. Do you have some financial statements with you, so I can put some numbers with your situation?"

"Yeah, I brought some," Sonny responded as he unzipped his vinyl portfolio bag and handed the documents across the table.

"Give me a few minutes to look them over," Bill said as he briefly hefted the two-inch stack of documents in his hand. "Go outside and look around if you like, or stay here and enjoy the coffee, but I need about twenty minutes of no talking." Bill went to his desk without another word and soon he was immersed in the financial plight of Sonny's business, oblivious to both the noise and Sonny's presence. Sonny watched him read each page, occasionally taking notes on a pad and frequently making calculations with a small handheld calculator on his desk.

Almost at the twentieth minute, Bill looked up and said: "Yeah, I can help you Sonny. I would want some collateral though, like your beach place. I don't want Ida fretting and stewing over an unsecured loan to her brother."

"That's agreeable," Sonny quickly affirmed.

"Good."

"You look like you know what you are doing, reading over those financial statements, Bill."

"I had a lot of training in it when I was logging with Pappas. The costs are so damn enormous with all the heavy equipment, and they can slip out of control in a minute, like when a logging road sloughs off down a mountainside. I spent the first seven years with Pappas afraid of going broke, tossing and turning at night. When we got involved in national forest timber sales, everything became even more complicated, risky and uncertain. Millions of dollars were involved. A bad sale could break us. So I sucked 'em up and went to our accountant and begged for mercy and his smarts. After a while—a lot of nights and Sunday afternoons—I got a better handle on our finances, particularly our per-unit operating costs and ratios, and could relate them to our income statements. Cash flow is a big issue in logging, like in construction, so I learned about that, too. The upshot was I learned how to analyze financial statements, at least for my purposes, and became much better in bidding on timber sales and cutting contracts. Ole Man Pappas relied on me..." Bill stopped. "I am rambling. I am sure you know I don't have any money available to loan you at the moment, and I don't have a blank note for you to sign. It will take time to put this together with my accountant. You will have to come back down, say next Friday or the first of the following week. I will have to call you on the specific day."

"Maybe we got the cart before the horse," Sonny interrupted. "The reason I came down here is to get some financial advice from someone who knows what he is talking about. So maybe we can put a loan on the back burner for a moment. How bad is my situation as you see it?"

"Very serious, Sonny. For you to pay your note down to where you want it, your sales have to be much higher than they are. Even to pay the interest due to renew the loan, sales should be about 20 to 25 percent higher than they are. The economy probably is not going to allow that in the next year or so. I expect you have already cut your costs as much as you are able to and still be in business. So there is not much you can do there and operate as you have. Your accounts receivable have aged, but even if they hadn't, you would still be in a bad way. That's the way I see it, anyhow."

"So how am I going to get out of the situation I am in?" Sonny asked.

"Well, you might start by asking yourself how you got into it. You are a bright guy, Sonny. You are going to have to figure it out. Nobody else is going to be able to figure it out as well as you can. I'll listen to you, if you like."

"Right now?"

"Sure. Go ahead. I got time. Isn't this what you came down here for?"

"Well, I know I expanded at the wrong time. Hindsight tells me that. And I borrowed money to do it. In the meantime, interest rates went crazy and the housing market went south."

"Why did you expand, Sonny?" Bill asked.

"Well, John wanted to come into the business, and I wanted him in it, too. So I thought I would open a lumberyard with a structural building components plant for him to develop and run. The components plant part never got off the ground because the local economy went sideways. So that lumberyard today is a medium-sized yard in a pretty good location. Mike wanted to make the Gardiner yard bigger because it actually has the best location of the three and the capacity to do a lot more retail business. Eddie's yard in Tualco was going steady, but he wanted to make some improvements to take advantage of the yard space he had to make loading and unloading trucks more efficient. Eddie's yard has become basically a wholesale operation, and all the deliveries for both Tualco and Gardiner are put up there. All three of them wanted to put in a computer system for accounting and inventory control. They were sold on computer technology being the coming thing and wanted to be ahead of the competition. So, each of them had good ideas, and to make everyone happy, I decided to go with all of them. I didn't want any conflict, didn't want to support one of them and not the other two, to keep peace in the family. I had to borrow the money because I couldn't finance the expansion internally with the capital on hand. My thinking was to expand so everyone had a fair piece of the action, and when everything was up and operating smoothly, I would be ready to retire, and they could buy me out."

"That's it?" Bill asked thoughtfully.

"Pretty much."

"So you expanded to give your guys jobs or businesses, more or less. Is that about right?"

"Yeah. It's one way of looking at it. I wanted them to be in business with me. So? What the hell is wrong with that?" asked Sonny.

"Well, it is understandable, maybe even admirable, but I am not sure it makes a lot of sense. Having family members in a business complicates things. You remember, I hired my brother Frank when I was with Pappas, trying to help him out. It didn't work, lasted less than two years. In the end, I was happy to pay his bar bill to get him out of town. Pappas handled family members pretty well, but that was because of ole Nick. It would have been a mess without him. None of my sons ever talked about coming into business with me, much less working for me.

It was probably too limiting for them, as I look back on it. They all seemed to want to get the hell out of Montrose."

"I am not sure I understand," Sonny retorted.

"The main reason for expanding a business is to do more business, to make more money. It isn't to meet a family obligation or to be 'fair.' A business and a family are separate things. When they are mixed, decisions become more complicated."

"I wanted to do something for John and Mike and Eddie. I don't want to be remembered like Pop."

"Aw shit, Sonny, your dad was dealt a bad hand from the beginning. Leave him the hell out of it. He is dead, and he did about as well as he could with what he had—about like my dad, only your dad was a helluva lot nicer guy. And he got you to a place where you could be lucky. Hell, if he hadn't, you could be working a ranch on a hillside in southern Idaho, trying to find water."

They paused for a moment because of the whine and din of a front-end loader operating outside near the office, loading a dump truck and pup trailer.

"So what do you suggest, Bill?" Sonny asked.

"Before we get to that, why did you keep borrowing from the bank?"

"That's easy. Once I started borrowing for the expansion for the Wenatchee yard, interest rates started rising because of the Federal Reserve. Of course, housing starts and sales of building materials went the opposite direction. There was no way I could pay down the loan. All I could do was pay the interest and hope the bank would agree to renew it. Wait for a better day to come, which hasn't arrived yet. That's why I am in the bind I'm in. What do you think I should do?"

"I could be wrong. Maybe your sales will turn around. So a loan from me gives you some time and a little flexibility. If your sales don't significantly increase and your business doesn't generate better income statements than those you showed me, then I think you should sell it, wholly or in parts that make economic sense. Have a plan, hire a professional, and market it."

"Jesus, Bill, what about John, Mike, and Eddie? They have put a lot of time and effort into my business."

"They're smart guys and have useful skills. Two of them have gone to college, and one's an engineer. They know there is risk with any business. Sure they'll be pissed, but they'll adjust. The reason you are here and we are talking is because you have a bank loan coming due, which has to be renewed. As I read those financial statements, it would take a damn miracle to turn things around before next summer. My advice is to sell your business, Sonny. I didn't really know how rough a situation you were in until I saw those statements. Interest payments are just eating away at everything you have accumulated. I can help you some because, as I told you, I'm getting out of the crushed rock business and retiring."

"I know," said Sonny.

"There is more to it than that," Bill countered gravely. "My bladder cancer has spread, which makes it likely I can only do this once. Ida and I have talked about it. So I am consolidating my assets, getting them into more liquid forms, and considering buying an annuity or two for Ida May for when I am gone. I have had my day, Sonny."

"Jesus, Bill! I am sorry to hear that."

"Well, bad things will happen to all of us, only a matter of time." Bill's thoughts wandered for a long moment. Then his eyes fixed on Sonny. "Time is very important here. The longer your business goes losing money for whatever reason, the less valuable it is. My loaning you money just gives you a little time and flexibility."

Sonny sat back in his chair and reflected. The noise around the office trailer abated for a moment.

"When should I come back down?" he said quietly.

"Let's plan on next Friday. That should give my accountant enough time to get the money and paperwork together. If it doesn't, I will call you with another time. Bring the deed to your beach place with you. And if you would like, you could bring Lise along."

"Naw, that would be kind of awkward."

"Whatever you like. So its $96,000 at 7 percent and one year to pay."

"Yeah."

"Your beach place as collateral."

"I got that," responded Sonny."

"Okay, let's go for lunch. The truck-stop special at lunch is usually a chicken-fried steak of some kind."

They left in separate vehicles, Bill in his blue Ford 150 pickup, Sonny in his white Mercedes. Sonny was impressed by the number of people Bill greeted and shook hands with at the truck-stop café as they entered. Even after they sat down in a booth, people would stop by and say hello. They didn't linger. Everyone seemed to know Bill was busy, knew he was frugal and usually took a lunch bucket to work. Unusual was Bill having lunch at the café with somebody from out of town, not that there were many other choices available.

They ordered the special—chicken-fried steak, two eggs, and hash browns—and ate it without elaboration—except for ketchup—or any extended discussion. When the check came, Sonny tried to pick it up, but Bill insisted each of them pay for his own meal, which was the same amount. Afterward, they went out across the gravel parking lot to their respective vehicles and their different ways, shaking hands as they left each other. Long-time friends and brothers-in-law; men who had begun their adult lives in the Depression with very little in terms of education and capital, but who had learned what they could do for a living that other people would want and would pay for, who had worked hard, and who had the courage to recognize and seize the precious few opportunities that had come their way.

Sonny decided to drive the freeway back to Gardiner, thinking he would make better time than on the shorter state-road network north of Montrose. Traffic would be slowed at this time of day with all the road construction going on there. Having made his decision on the route back to Gardiner, his thoughts turned to his conversation with Bill.

John, Mike, and Eddie will be pissed when I sell the business, a big problem. On the other hand, if the business goes tits up, the problem will be bigger, much bigger. The boys and everyone else will be pissed, and I will be looked upon as a damn loser like Pop. I may have to live with that, but the chances are less if I get out now. I have got to move with decisiveness. Indecision will cost me... I gave the boys an opportunity to have a successful business. Unfortunately, what is the phrase, "circumstances beyond my control" just messed everything up. I should never have borrowed short like the bank advised me to. Dammit! Interest rates go sky high. Housing construction crashes. Contractors can't pay their damn bills. Damn banks, soon as they make a loan, their only concern is getting their money back. They're like Churchill said about the Germans, either at your feet or at your throat. Screw 'em! All of 'em... Lise will be happy if the business is sold and everyone is paid off. She will have some stability after the chaos of the past three or four years. There will be enough for us to live on, retire on, by any accounting. Hell, we will have more – many times more – than we ever would have had if we'd stayed up at Wallace... I could get a real estate license and sell commercial real estate. Sure as hell could outsell that bunch of lazies and losers in Gardiner. They don't know what the hell good customer service is. Yet they are making money today, right now. Dammit. And they don't have to carry any inventory... I have to piss already. Too much coffee. Better do it now before I get on the freeway.

Sonny watched for a place to pull off and found an entrance to a small clear cut on the side of a hill, about twenty acres. He got out of the car, climbed over the gate that closed off the logging access road, and walked back into the clear cut, looking at the hand-planted Douglas fir seedlings while he went. They seemed to be thriving. He stood on a low stump while he peed and looked down on the Cowlitz River, beautiful in the afternoon sunlight.

A man in grey-green waders was fishing a nice stretch of four-foot deep, fast-moving, flat water, and Sonny walked a few yards for a better vantage point. The man stepped, cast, and let his streamer swing. On the fifth cast, the line went taut and the man had a fish on, a nice one, probably a steelhead. The water sparkled as it came off the fish when it jumped. A steelhead surely. Back in the water, the fish made a long, strong run, the fisherman keeping a taut line. Four more runs, two more jumps, and the fisherman artfully got the fish into slower water and carefully brought it in. He netted the fish, put his rod down on the rocks, and removed the fly while the fish was in the net in the water. After a minute or so, he slowly released the fish from the net and watched it swim away.

"Well done!" Sonny said aloud and alone, the fisherman being too far away to hear.

Sonny walked down to his Mercedes to begin again his drive back to Gardiner.

About six miles down the road, he exclaimed aloud to the windshield: "I'm going to bring my fly rod and waders with me when I come down here Friday. I am going to catch a big ole steelhead!" He laughed aloud.

As he turned onto the on-ramp of the freeway, he wondered what he was going to do with the check and paperwork next Friday while he was fishing. *I could put it under the floor mat,* he thought. *No, too risky. Better lock it in the trunk. Damn, if I don't get moving, I am going to get stuck in Seattle rush-hour traffic.* He pushed the Mercedes up to 75.

Sonny went to his office, slipping in through the side door. It was 4:30. He dialed the bookkeeper and asked if there were any checks for him to sign.

"I have eight that need signing, as well as some other things you should see," she answered. "By the way, you had several calls today, including one from Larry at the bank. He wanted to talk to you today. Better call him."

She was in Sonny's office a few minutes later with invoices, unsigned checks, phone message slips, and some correspondence. An invoice was attached to each check, and she noted the ones that were past due. Sonny signed them without looking up and passed them quickly back to her. After he was through, he asked if any big accounts receivable checks had come in by mail.

"A few," she said. "Not enough to make much of a difference. I will deposit them on the way home. Here are some letters you should see, and your phone messages. You had better call Larry. I have to go." She was off and out the door.

Sonny dialed Larry, whose receptionist put Sonny through as if the call had been anticipated for hours.

"Hello, Sonny." Larry was on the phone.

"I got a message you called, and as you know, I always return my calls," Sonny said with an awkward attempt at humor.

"Thanks for calling back, Sonny. We need to talk about your loan, and not over the phone. When can you come to my office early next week?"

"Sounds serious, Larry."

"Meetings about loans are always serious, Sonny." The friendly chuckle that usually punctuated Larry's telephone conversations was noticeably absent.

"What about Monday at 10:30 a.m.?"

"That will be fine, Sonny. See you then. Enjoy your weekend." The phone clicked and Sonny heard the dial tone.

"Hmm," Sonny said aloud. "That was different."

He was home at 6:00, his usual time, and when he walked through the kitchen door, Lise, who had been standing at the sink washing dishes, erupted, "Where have you been? Everybody has been trying to reach you, including Larry at the bank. Mike and Eddie had no idea where you were. I have been worried sick."

"Thought I told you last night," he retorted.

"Dammit, that's not true, Sonny, and you know it."

"I called Larry," he said.

"Where have you been, Sonny? Answer me."

"I ahh, I ahh," he stammered, "I went down to Montrose to see Bill about business.

"And?"

"About a loan actually, because I am going to have one helluva time paying the interest on the loan at the bank at the end of the month when it is up for renewal. Money is just not coming in like it should."

"So what did Bill say?" Lise asked as she turned off two burners on the electric stove and walked toward the kitchen table, where Sonny was sitting.

"He is going to give me a loan. I'll sign the note and pick up the money probably next Friday..." Sonny's thoughts wandered, then he began slowly, "He also recommended I sell the business before interest payments eat up all the equity we have."

Lise sat down at the table and faced Sonny, seated in his usual place.

"I am listening, Sonny. What else did he say?"

"His bladder cancer is back, and he is selling his business."

"Ooh, I am sorry to hear that. I wondered why we haven't heard from Ida and him. What else?" she asked.

"He said setting up yards for John, Mike, and Eddie was not a good idea because, in his experience, combining business and family makes things too complicated. I suppose that was his main thought."

"I told you that a long time ago. You didn't listen to me."

"So I was wrong, Lise," Sonny said, shaking his head with obvious contrition.

A long moment of silence followed, and Lise's eyes brimmed with tears. She got up, took some tissues from a box of Scotties, and dabbed her eyes several times.

"About half," she responded in almost a whisper, her chin quivering. "Your intentions were always good. They are one of the reasons I have always loved you. You wanted to help John and Mike, Eddie too, like any good father would." Lise's voice became stronger. "But the banks have got you in a squeeze like they have a lot of small businesses. Maybe it is for a good purpose, to wring inflation out of the economy. But you got caught, Sonny, and I don't think you have much of a choice. Bill is right. You have got to cut your losses and get out from under the debt. Sell the business, pay off everyone, make it right with the boys, and we will start over with what we have left."

"It will be more than you think, Lise."

"Enough for us to retire on, I hope."

"Who the hell wants to retire? I'm thinking of going into commercial real estate. Bud Fischer says it is the easiest money he ever made."

"Have you talked to the boys and Eddie since we have been back? Do they know what is going on?"

"I talked to Mike yesterday."

"Answer the question, Sonny. Have you talked to Mike, John, and Eddie since you have been back? Do they know what is going on? The answer is either yes or no."

"I was in Montrose today."

"Yes or no, Sonny? Don't be so damn evasive."

"You are pushing me. Ahh, what the hell. The answer is no."

"Sonny, they are your yard managers. They are actually part owners of the business, since they're stockholders. Shouldn't they know what you are doing?" she reasoned.

"No one ever tells me anything."

"That doesn't make any sense. It is another one your 'non-answers.' So I will answer the question for you. Nobody knew where you were today or what you were doing. If communication in a business is important when times are good, might it be even more important when times are bad, Sonny?" Lise blew her nose and nasally continued. "Please call John, Mike, and Eddie in the morning and tell them what you are doing and why. You might even ask them for their thoughts.

Now the stove is turned off, and the Elks is having a seafood buffet tonight. I'm hungry. Let's go."

"Sure. Why not? It'll be a lot better than anything I might get around here tonight."

"True, and for good reason," she asserted.

They were silent for most of the two-mile drive from their home to the Elks Club. Sonny was thinking about what had happened that day as well as Lise's plea for a conversation with John, Mike, and Eddie.

As they neared the Elks Club, Sonny blurted: "You are right, I will call the boys tomorrow. I will do it through a conference call. That way I can lay everything out and only have to do it once."

"Good," she responded. "But you know, of course, there will probably be many, many meetings and telephone calls with them before the business is sold."

Sonny ignored her. Then, as he turned into the parking lot, he teased, "I think I'll take my fly rod and waders down to Montrose next Friday. Fish the Cowlitz for summer run steelhead for a few hours."

"I'm going to assume you are not serious so the rest of the evening is not ruined," she said, her voice rising with agitation. "You will not be going fishing anytime soon, Sonny. You know that. It is going to be all business until the yards are sold, everyone is paid off, and we know where we stand. You can fish winter run steelhead on the Suquamish, should you be so lucky to have everything done before the end of the winter. You can do it all, like usual, Sonny, but not all at the same time, not anymore."

The room in which the seafood buffet was held was the cavernous Elks main meeting room and auditorium, made necessary because of the large number of people who attended the buffet. Five large stainless steel serving counters were the epicurean focus. A salad bar was on the first. Scalloped potatoes, a rice pilaf, and green beans with bacon were on the second. A third serving counter had trays of baked salmon, Pacific cod, and halibut. The fourth had trays of deep-fat-fried shrimp and oysters, and steamed clams. The last counter—always at the end of the serving line and Lise's favorite—had large bowls of Dungeness crab on ice, split in half and cracked. The Elks Club had learned complaints on the preparation of its seafood could be compensated for by providing large quantities. So while the salmon may have been overcooked, the shrimp and oysters tasteless from deep-fat frying, and the clams tough and rubbery from prolonged steaming—as they all were occasionally—the answer to complaints by the wait staff was, "Can't you can find something else you like? By the way, double martinis are half price."

Sonny and Lise joined some friends they unexpectedly found, seated at one of the twenty-four round tables with two empty chairs, side-by-side. Sonny ordered a double martini with three olives and a gin and tonic for Lise from a waiter after giving her his member number. They went through the serving line, and then settled into the camaraderie of the table and the banality of drinking and eating, putting aside the turmoil and uncertainty afflicting them but thirty minutes before. That could wait until tomorrow.

She watched him, confident, enthusiastic, maybe becoming a little intoxicated, relishing the conviviality. Already he had ordered a second martini. For the first time in months, Lise understood what he was going to do and was confident that everyone—the boys and Eddie—would be taken care of. She would see to that.

After the initial courtesies, the conversation turned to the economy and interest rates, since two of the men at the table in addition to Sonny were small businessmen. One—a car dealer—lamented how bad the economy was.

"High interest rates are killing me," he asserted.

Not unexpectedly, at least to Lise, Sonny charged in with his usual optimism: "Sure, they are way too high, but they are going to come down. Things will turn around soon. You've just got to hang in there." Sonny took a drink of his martini and began to eat the second of its three olives.

"How the hell do you keep such a positive attitude, Sonny?" the car dealer asked.

"I remember how bad things were in the Depression, when there were no jobs, nobody was working, and the woods and mills up and down the Suquamish Valley were closed."

Lise got up to get more crab. She knew Sonny was performing, putting on the thin veneer of past business successes, relieving himself for the moment of the reality of his current financial fragility. *I wish he would eat some food,* she thought.

When she returned to the table, the car dealer asked, "How does Sonny keep so positive and upbeat, Lise?"

She twisted the legs off a crab and began removing the meat, adding it to the mound of crabmeat already on the plate in front of her.

"He loves to operate on the edge, seeing risk as if it were a personal challenge. He believes perseverance and hard work will usually prevail."

"So what happens when they don't?" the car dealer continued.

"He's lucky. Someone bails him out."

"Like whom?" the car dealer asked.

"My folks when we were first married and later getting started in business," she quickly responded. Sonny scowled. She was talking too much.

"A generous brother-in-law, for another," she added. Sonny sighed, grateful for the fortuitous help Bill had promised him earlier in the day. He lifted his glass toward Lise in acknowledgement and took another sip of his martini.

"Sure, I've been lucky, and I've had some help, but enough of that," he said. "How's the crab, Lise?"

"Good. Bigger and heavier than usual." She turned to the rest of the table. 'Sonny can't eat crab. He's allergic to it." Then to Sonny, "Better start eating your salmon, Sonny. Get something in your stomach. You've had a long day."

On the way home, Lise said, "You only had two martinis tonight. I am proud of you."

"You noticed? Yeah, I am at a different stage of my drinking life. Drink two and coast. You piss off fewer people, and you are sharper the next day."

"Are you being a smart ass again?"

"No, not really. Tomorrow morning is going to be hard, and I want to make sense to the boys."

***

Selling the business took longer than expected, almost a year and a half, significantly eroding its value. A principal reason was the dramatic changes occurring in the building supply business. Large inventory, high-volume national chains were entering local markets in urban areas, and they tended to build their own physical plants, not buy existing stores and yards, which were seen as too small.

Sonny became unnerved by the lack of interest from potential buyers of his business, which frequently caused him to behave in both problematic and unpredictable ways. His decision-making was often impulsive, even panicky, and he was frustratingly evasive and erratic in his communications. Mike, John, and Eddie grew resentful and often angry at Sonny as a result, and the heroic dimensions they attributed to him because of his extraordinary experiences and past successes eroded. They appreciated that Sonny was under great stress. But so were they. And the measuring stick of success and failure at the moment was pretty much the same for each of them.

Mike, John, and Eddie were competent and resilient; they each quit when it was timely, and engaged in some other business activity suited to their respective interests and skills—businesses that were growing, where they could be lucky. The word in the Gardiner business community was "they landed on their feet," which gave Sonny some comfort in the decision to sell his business. He understood it meant Mike, John, and Eddie were seen as being capable and knowing what they were doing, and by god they had to have learned something working for him.

Several years passed and soon the family was gathering together at the beach for summer holidays. While it was never quite the same between father and sons because of wounds from the sale of the business, the grandchildren never knew the difference. The wounds had healed into scars, not disfigurements. Eddie never came to the beach after the decision to sell. He usually had too many other things going on, and he never really liked eating crab or fishing for salmon. After his divorce, when he had free time from the real estate business in which he had invested, he would go back to Idaho, fly fish for trout, and hunt elk. He bought a cabin in the woods east of Horseshoe Bend and, later, married his high school sweetheart, also divorced.

Lise thought Sonny and she had enough to retire on after selling the business—more than she had ever expected, anyway.

Sonny didn't, and so he got his real estate license and began selling commercial real estate. The economy had finally come around and was growing.

A year after he got his license, he told her while finishing a late afternoon meal of barbecued salmon at the beach cabin: "I didn't realize how easy selling real estate was, how much money you could make with so little investment. And hell, you don't have all the personnel problems."

"Well and good," she quietly responded, "but shouldn't you understand by now that many of your personnel problems of the past were of your own making?"

"What in the hell do you mean?" he snorted.

"You were never easy to deal with because you were usually too full of yourself. Most people understood it after a while. Actually, I found your self-centeredness to be part of your charm. Made you quite predictable," she laughed teasingly.

"Jesus, Lise. What a hell of a thing to say!"

"Relax, Sonny. You're still touchy because the last few years have been really hard; hard on you, hard on all of us. Sure you made some mistakes, but there were also major things going on in the economy that impacted you, things beyond your control. You are still a remarkably good businessman. Most important, you have lived up to the opportunities that availed themselves and made the most of your capabilities in seeking a better life for us. I love your spirit and have no doubt you will be successful in selling commercial real estate. Now forget all your insecurities and do what you are inclined to do. The rest will take care of itself."

It was high slack tide, and the Sound was quiet. Several hours of daylight were left.

After looking about, Lise said impulsively, "Let's go into town tonight. I have a hair appointment at 9:30, and I haven't been to an Assistance League meeting in ages. I also have some business at the bank. So pull up the crab traps and bring in the boat. I will put the food away and do the dishes. It will be good to spend a few days at home in town."

"Sounds good to me," Sonny responded. "I have to be in town tomorrow morning anyway to meet with a client."

The client was a member of the same Kiwanis Club that Sonny had long been a member of, and he said he wanted more liquidity in his balance sheet because he was going to retire. Sonny thought he may have been sick because he was paler and thinner than he usually was. The client gave Sonny a listing for a 38,000 square foot warehouse worth $3.5 million. Sonny told him that seemed to be a fair price in the current market and it would take about three to four months to sell. He actually sold the property five days later and received a full five percent commission.

"Better to be lucky than good," Sonny told Lise laughingly.

"Sure," Lise smiled as she spoke, "But if you are going to depend on luck from now on, you might want to see what you can do to improve its timing."

Sonny's grin turned rueful, and after a moment, he sighed, "As if."

"As if what?" Lise asked curiously.

"As if I could do that. If I could, I'd probably still be in the lumber business."

Hearing the wistfulness in his voice, Lise said: "Sonny, I'm very happy where we are. You should be, too. Now let's move on."

Acknowledgements

The encouragement I received from family and friends in writing this book is remarkable. That from my wife, Kathleen, who listened to my reading of virtually every word in the manuscript, is extraordinary. I could not have completed this work if it were not for her.

My sons, Paul and Matt, kept me true to the tale. My brothers, Dale and Curt, were helpful with their encouragement and suggestions. My dear aunt, Jeanette Edgerton, and uncle, Bob LeMaster, told me many stories and anecdotes I have incorporated in the manuscript. I hope I have not done them any harm. It was unintentional if I did. My cousin, Dick Barker, kept me going with some good ideas when I was stymied.

Alan Fleishman, Larry O'Donnell, Ellen Price, Bill and Janice Rucker, and Len Hudson gave useful commentary and advice.

Two Master's theses were informative in writing the chapter titled "War." The first is: Louis A. DiMarco, Major, "The U.S. Army's Mechanized Cavalry Doctrine in World War II," Master's thesis, U.S Army Command and General Staff College, Fort Leavenworth, Kansas, 1995. The second is: William Stuart Nance, "Patton's Iron Cavalry: The Impact of the Mechanized Cavalry on the U.S. Third Army," Master's thesis, University of North Texas, Denton, Texas, 2011. The battle at Schmitten, Germany was real and fairly well documented. Nevertheless, the tactics used in getting out of the town are of my own imagination, based on my father's account, topography, and Schmitten's road network as well as on tactical knowledge gathered from my experience as a U.S. Army armor officer and scout platoon leader.

Of course, all mistakes contained in the manuscript are mine alone.

About the Author

Dennis LeMaster was born and raised in western Washington State. After receiving his baccalaureate degree in economics, he served as an U.S. Army armor officer in a tank battalion in Germany and later as a special agent in the Federal Bureau of Investigation. After receiving a Ph.D. in economics at Washington State University, he worked as director of resource policy for the Society of American Foresters, the national association representing the forestry profession, and staff consultant on forestry for the Committee on Agriculture, U.S. House of Representatives. He rejoined the faculty of Washington State University in the fall of 1978 and became professor and chair of the Department of Forestry and Range Management. In 1988, he became professor and head of the Department of Forestry and Natural Resources, Purdue University. He retired in 2004.

While Dennis has over 100 publications of various kinds in natural resource science and public policy, *For a Better Life* is his first effort in writing fiction. He found it more difficult than he thought it would be.